Clo
S

Close Quarters

Clare Curzon

G.K. Hall & Co. • Chivers Press
Thorndike, Maine USA   Bath, England

This Large Print edition is published by G.K. Hall & Co., USA
and by Chivers Press, England.

Published in 1997 in the U.S. by arrangement with
St. Martin's Press, Inc.

Published in 1997 in the U.K. by arrangement with
Little, Brown & Co. (UK) Ltd.

U.S. Softcover   0-7838-8214-9   (Paperback Collection Edition)
U.K. Hardcover   0-7540-3056-3   (Chivers Large Print)

The text of this Large Print edition is unabridged.
Other aspects of the book may vary from the original edition.

Set in 16 pt. Plantin.

Printed in the United States on permanent paper.

British Library Cataloguing in Publication Data available

Library of Congress Cataloging in Publication Data

Curzon, Clare.
        Close quarters / Clare Curzon.
            p.   cm.
        ISBN 0-7838-8214-9 (lg. print : sc : alk. paper)
        1. Large type books. I. Title.
    [PR6053.U79C56   1997b]
    823'.914—dc21
                                                         97-15222

Close Quarters

One

When the last train from London arrived at Mardham Halt doors slid open and seven alighted, one couple together, the others from separate compartments. Behind them the automatic doors slid shut again. No one spoke, tucking chins into upturned collars, shoulders hunched against the shock of autumn's first frost, ghostly breaths hanging on in the air, visible reminders that summer was finally gone.

Hollow footfalls on frost-sparkling flagstones, a thudding tramp across the wooden footbridge. Three threw used tickets into the bin at the unattended exit; the others had passes. Out in the yard they separated. The couple and one other went left towards the deserted car park. Another turned right, up the approach road to the village.

Three went separately ahead, took the six steps and the steep path that led to the south side of Mardham. They were a girl and two indeterminate men, one with an our-man-in-Moscow fur hat, the other pulling a woollen ski cap from his pocket.

The girl was bareheaded. Her long hair, spread over her shoulders, reflected gold from the lamp at the top of the steps. Beyond its brief light the path rose between bare trees into darkness.

Young and fit, she took the slope fast, drawing ahead, losing all sounds beyond her own footfalls and deep breathing. Twelve minutes, she promised herself, before welcome warmth and her landlady's greeting. A hot drink, a few words about the success of the evening, then cosily to bed. Tomorrow, up early for college, unless by some miracle the car was back from being serviced.

Her throat felt rough with the coarse taste of fog as her legs pumped athletically. She didn't mind cold but disliked the dark, wasn't a natural night creature.

Crossing Lower Church Road, she faced a choice of School Lane or the path between backs of long rows of Victorian villas. The old fences were tall and solid, overhung by spiky limbs of untrimmed fruit trees. Bare of foliage, on branches silvered with frost, a few unwanted apples still dangled, gold in the light from a lamp at the path's entrance, shining like Christmas baubles.

The path being shorter, she took it, turning left, downhill now. Yesterday's wind had brought heavy drifts of leaves that crackled drily under her shoes; aromatic, without any taint yet of decay. She scuffed through them, briefly recalling childhood scampers; lost speed; reached the bend in the path shaped like a dog's hind leg. And the lamp at the far end wasn't on.

She halted, dismayed at the solid dark ahead,

and heard the first shuffling echoes of her own footsteps. She looked back and saw, looming black against the distant tunnelled light, an immense shadow, static a moment, then advancing again in an ungainly loping.

Fear gripped her. She began to run, driving forward into the dark, desperately clutching her flute case and the file of sheet music against her chest, heart pounding, sobbing breath sliced from her open mouth by the ice-cold of the night. The muffled thud of her own shoes covered any sounds from behind. She could not tell if the distance between was shortening. She dared not turn and look. Such a huge, lumbering figure.

For a terrifying instant she thought she had half recognized his outline . . .

Mrs George was dozing in the old leather chair pushed into a corner of the kitchen's big bay window. Behind her the curtains were closed and the chair turned to face the doorway. Gayle had once tried persuading the old lady not to sit up. At home no one did. But Mrs George preferred it to lying awake in bed and fretting.

Since this was her only quirk and she never asked direct questions, Gayle had found it easier to accept the gesture. There was no need to keep her comings and goings secret.

Tonight, once she'd reached the porch light and her key found the lock, winded and scared she had to find a new calm, forcing a few deep breaths to ease the searing obstruction in her throat. Indoors, as she opened her arms the sheet music burst from its covers, showering the floor. She bent double, waiting for her heart to steady and slow. It would take longer to laugh off her fears and fancies.

But she hadn't imagined it. Someone had actually been padding after her. Until she'd outrun him.

Mrs George called out to her from the kitchen. Gayle straightened, called back, 'It's only me,' and started to retrieve her belongings. She wouldn't mention the incident: no need to disturb the old lady.

They had established a rite of passage to bed, and she performed it for them both, warming milk for their drinks while she gave an account of the evening's rehearsal.

Mrs George relayed the news that the garage hadn't returned the car. An old Triumph: they didn't stock the right replacement hose for the cooling system.

Did it matter so much now the weather had broken? Gayle asked, vague about car maintenance. Mrs George relayed the mechanic's caution that the new part was vital, since the heater came off the same system. They'd need another day to hunt up the replacement.

Warming her hands on the steaming mug, the girl nodded. She would catch a bus to college tomorrow, because begging a lift had drawbacks. It could mean repaying in kind later; possibly to a student less punctual than herself. This year they were mostly deadbeats who lodged out this way.

At least she needn't use the station until next week's rehearsal, and by then surely the car would be fixed. So there'd be no more running through the dark on her return. She'd have only the hundred yards from platform to car park.

They went up to bed on the stroke of one and divided at the top of the stairs, Gayle towards her bedroom overlooking the road. Mrs George, in the house's rear, rewound her ancient alarm clock and went to check that a window was slightly open.

She stood a moment in the dark, holding back one curtain to look out at the hard frost-twinkle of stars against country-black sky. And then she caught the faint voice from the water meadows beyond the back gardens. Urgently pleading, but quiet so as not to disturb anyone but the single person it was meant for.

'Harry! Harry, love, where are you? Come home, love. It's late and it's getting so cold.'

Poor Mrs Snelling. She shouldn't risk a chill in her frail condition. The man was a terrible burden to her, but what else could she do? He was her son and she loved him.

It was too late for the morning papers, but the item was picked up by radio and breakfast television: in Mardham, a quiet Buckinghamshire village, murder had unaccountably struck. A vicious crime; the woman's body — unidentified as yet — mutilated after savage rape. Thames Valley Police were combing the woods and lanes for clues, the inhabitants were shattered. What kind of unnatural monster had surfaced among these ordinary country folk and commuting business people?

Gayle, snatching a quick coffee before running for the bus, listened with growing dread, last night's brief terror renewed. She saw again the huge shadow under the passage light, heard a phantom echo of the padding footfalls that she'd managed to escape.

Cheated of one victim, had her stalker gone on to find another? And brutally killed her?

She could never again walk home in the dark. That poor unknown girl; a hideous end, she thought. It could have been me.

An image of herself, sprawled lifeless in that dark passageway, flashed on her closed eyelids. She saw her sheet music pathetically scattered over the frosted ground.

The dark shape had long gone but there were others gathering, staring, touching, intimately examining. She shuddered.

She knew she must report the incident to the police. They would be following up any suspicious events of last night. And it *had* happened. Not just her imagination, though they wouldn't know that, might think she was the hysterical type. Maybe they'd not believe her, would think she simply wanted to be the centre of attention.

At best they could leave her sitting about during

pressure of more urgent matters. And it was her finals year. Every lecture missed was extra work to make up, and she found it hard enough already. It couldn't matter if she left telling them until evening.

But she knew that for an empty excuse. What paralysed her was fear: the superstition that talking of it could make it come back, one way or the other. In the mind or in the flesh.

Black fingers of skeletal trees clawed upwards through the milky denseness that shrouded the river's slow flow towards the Thames. On the higher banks the stiff, glassy stretches abruptly met fresh, beaded green where early sun emerging from mist had begun the thaw.

There were darker patches of flattened turf marking a confusion of footmarks, although some attempt had been made to avoid the direct approach to where the body lay. Over a group of whins a plastic tent had been erected, but the steep bank was awkward for so many experts to get access.

Police had taped off some hundred yards of river-bank from the bridge carrying Mill Lane, turning back several workmen accustomed to trudge that way to the brickworks or quarry. And now three schoolchildren cycling in towards Mardham from outlying farms, their breaths streaming like scarves, were being hastily diverted to the parallel Buckman's Shoot and escorted past the line of police cars.

Two unmarked saloons had just parked together at the rear. In the open doorway of the last, a red Saab, a strongly built man with crisp blond hair sat pulling on farm boots over hefty woollen socks.

The local reporter behind the police cones nudged his neighbour as he recognized Detective-Inspector Angus Mott. 'Serious Crime's number one on the job,' he said shortly. 'The other's his sergeant, a joker called Beaumont. The girl with them has a Polish name, but they call her Z.'

The more modest Ford parked ahead was having all its tyres methodically kicked by the sergeant, while a pretty plain-clothes policewoman waited alongside, hands in the pockets of her sheepskin jacket, a bright silk scarf twisted into a turban hiding her hair.

'So how far have they got?' the blond man demanded of his sergeant.

'Doc Goodwin's seen the body, done the necessary and departed. Pathologist's on his way. SOCO's nearly finished. They're holding back bagging face and hands until Littlejohn's seen everything.'

'Any ID yet?'

'Nothing on her clothes that we could see. Handbag seems to be missing.'

'And nobody's recognized her so far,' the girl said quietly.

'Right.' Mott stretched to his full six feet two, eased the door shut and zapped the central locking. 'Let's go, then.'

At the break in the thicket which marked the narrow track down to the river-bank he turned back to scowl at the collection of official vehicles.

'Useless to expect any tyre marks to survive that scrum.'

'The local man thinks the more likely bet would be near Mill Lane bridge. There's a lay-by there where the fishermen park. One of the SOCO blokes is up there looking for traces now. If any car was used, that is.'

'Fishing, you say — is much done here?'

'Weekends mainly. Dads and kids stuff. Chuck-backs. They might not care to eat anything they did catch.'

Mott grunted and ducked from a shower of loosened frost, one sleeve of his leather coat rasping back overgrown hawthorn. They scrambled in single file along the bank and came on the spotlit area. 'A bit quick with the tent,' he grumbled, stooping to enter. Admittedly it was best to preserve the murder scene, but within its confines their warm breaths could play havoc with air temperature readings.

'Too much to hope Goodwin hinted at time of death,' Mott said gloomily and looked back for confirmation.

'I spoke by phone to Littlejohn. He's on his way. Seemed hopeful for a PM later today,' Beaumont consoled.

'Who found her, and when?'

'About twenty to seven. A night-watchman,

knocking off from the building site down Buckman's Shoot. Lives in the last cottage on Pottersfield, a turning just beyond the bridge. Our local man says it's a reasonable route for him to take on foot.'

'You'll need to see him next. I'll wait for Littlejohn. Take Z and the constable along. What's he called?'

'A Rupert Crick found the body. The local beat man's called Bond, PC J. Bond.'

Mott stopped in his tracks. 'Not James, by any mischance?'

'Jeffrey, Guv. It's OK. No need to encase Z.'

The DI stood back and gave a wry glance at the woman detective. 'You'd better take a look, Zyczynski. Not nice, I'm afraid.' He made way for her to pass in.

Mott's words were inadequate description. The body lay with the face exposed. Frost, webbing the features like fine silver net, failed to hide the hideous distortion. A single glance confirmed it as a case of strangulation. The hair was long and blonde with darker roots. The woman had been a natural brunette.

Z knelt on the cold grass and with a single finger parted the hair at the neck to look closer, but could see no mark of a ligature. Yet there were several fine red cutting marks as if from fingernails, more pronounced on the body's right side. So strangulation had been manual, probably from behind, probably by a right-handed person. Perhaps she had never seen her attacker.

The face was terrible, blue and distorted, eyes bulging, the open mouth filled with out-thrust, discoloured tongue. The left cheekbone and eye socket had been bloodily smashed in by something heavier than a fist.

Clothes? — tight red leather mini-skirt; dyed rabbit-fur jacket. She could have been a tom. Black tights, wide runs showing white flesh from ankle to thigh. One high-heeled black shoe, twisted half off. The other apparently missing.

Tights? Z frowned, running a hand up one hip, inside the skirt, to the elasticated waist. Underneath she could feel the firm outline of briefs.

But the radio had said the woman was raped. What rapist would struggle in the dark and cold, after frenzied coitus, after murder, to put her close-fitting clothes back on her dead weight, and exactly in the order that they should have been? As smoothly as though the woman had dressed herself.

So had death come to her later: perhaps during a quarrel over payment? Or had she not had sex at all? Where had that report of rape originated? The early radio news item had certainly mentioned murder with rape. Murder was true, but who could be sure about the other at this point?

Doc Goodwin was too experienced to have interfered with the clothing. Once he'd confirmed death he would have left everything for the pathologist to examine *in situ*. But perhaps the man who found her had moved her. Z wished she had arrived earlier, before the body had been handled

17

at all. So much could be told by the way that it lay.

She got to her feet, rubbed her chilled knees, backed out of the confined space and rejoined the other two detectives. 'Do we know who leaked the news to the media?' she asked. 'Its speed must qualify for the *Guinness Book of Records*.'

Mott gave some thought to positioning the Incident Caravan. According to the map the stone bridge some fifty yards distant was the central one of three that carried Mill Lane, a slow bend, across the tightly winding river and the railway line to the north. The lane itself was hypotenuse to the roughly triangular village, its right angle contained between the main Chesham Road and the east-west railway line. From here, the murder site, the built-up area lay mainly to the north and west, separated from it by a spinney, the gravelled Buckman's Shoot and water meadows.

Just beyond the bridge on its nearside was the lay-by with a telephone kiosk which Beaumont had mentioned. This would prove useful for posting a notice to passing motorists requesting information. And almost opposite was a narrow turning known as Pottersfield, with a grass verge at its opening wide enough to take the Mobile Incident Room.

'The villagers will be questioned house-to-house,' Mott conceded, 'but the caravan placed at that point should pull in any regular motorists as possible witnesses of a vehicle parked at the relevant time — whenever that was. It's unlikely many pedestrians passed after dark because there's no street lighting and few cottages in that direction.'

The village lay just inside Amersham Police Area. The uniform Superintendent would even now be ordering visits throughout the neighbourhood to find witnesses, and for searches on all approaches to that point of the river-bank.

'This Crick, who found her,' Mott asked, 'where's he now?'

It appeared that having phoned the local man he had waited by the call box by the bridge for PC Bond who went with him to view the body before radioing in for support. Crick had then insisted on going home for his breakfast, claiming he was half-way to rigor himself and his wife would be getting anxious.

'So tackle him on his own ground,' Mott ordered.

PC Bond escorted Beaumont and the WDC on foot. They found Crick in a terraced cottage in Pottersfield, his flannelette shirt unbuttoned on a muscled chest of black hair as he sat with a mug of tea by the kitchen range. He wore a matching piratical beard and the rest of him was black too, except for his excellent square teeth and the whites of wildly rolling eyes as he recounted the discovery.

'Jeez,' he said, 'Jeez, all that on an empty stomach. That ain't the best way to vomit, I'm telling you.'

'What time would this be?'

'Six-forty? Somethun like that. Still quite dark, see?'

'So what caught your eye?'

'Ain't nothun wrong with my night sight, man. Got eyes like a jungle cat. Makes me the tops as night-watchman. Don't need no flashing torches to warn folks I'm on to them. Jest as well, because there's them round here wouldn't think twice about helpun themselves to a load of hoggin or a barrow of bricks.

'Well, I spied this liddle bitta pale stuff under a bush, see? Thought it mighta bin someone's shirt or knickers. Amazin' what you'll sometimes find along the river-bank.'

He grimaced. 'Then I saw. Bitta white leg showing through her stockuns. So I went real close and took a good look. Wish now I hadden. Made me puke, man, what'd bin done to her.'

'Stockings,' Z said thoughtfully.

'Yeah, dark ones. Black mebbe. With big holes in, so the skin showed through.'

'She wore tights,' Z said quietly to Beaumont, but the man picked it up. 'Tights, stockuns, what's the difference? I sure didden go poking to find out. I jes bobtailed outa there, and when I saw the phone box I rang Jeff Bond. Wouldn'ta said who I was if I'd known you all'd keep me so long from me kip. Look, can I getta bed now? I gotta see the dentist this afternoon.'

'Where and when?'

'Four forty-five, in the village.'

'So drop in at the Incident Caravan on your way back. We'll need a written statement. But yes, you can knock off for now.'

The man rose, picking a bomber jacket off the back of a chair, ready to go upstairs. He stood at a hefty six feet tall, his head threatening to collide with the low beams of the cottage ceiling.

'Apart from your wife,' Z put in, 'how many other people have you told about the body?'

'Ain't seen no one, have I? Jes' phoned the site office while I was waitun for the PC at the box. Told them I jes' might get held up this evenun if the police were longwinded.'

'What exactly did you say?' Beaumont was on to this like a shot.

'That I'd found a body on my way home. A woman, and it looked like she'd been strangled.'

'Nothing more? No extra details?'

'That's the lot, man. It was Morgan took the message, in the office. Got a bit eager, wanted more, and it sicked me off him.'

Beaumont was staring at the man with total lack of expression. It could be disconcerting, as Z well knew.

'You're sure that was all you said?'

'God's truth, man.'

'Right,' the DS acknowledged. 'And thanks. You did the right thing phoning in at once.'

'Some wouldn't,' Crick said laconically. 'Only, being black, I allus gotta act whiter than white.' He snorted at his own joke, ducked his head under the cross-beam of the doorway, and they

21

heard his slippers scuffing up the wooden stairs.

'You can believe everything he says. He's a good, honest man,' said the Caribbean woman who had stayed silent after showing them in. She started clearing his crockery from the table with an air of determination. 'It surely did upset him.'

Beaumont stared at her, balancing on his heels. 'I know you. You're a nurse at Amersham hospital.'

She beamed at the recognition, then her smile slid away. 'Was. Until I put my back out, lifting a patient. I'll be lucky if I get my old job back, but I keep on hoping. Is there anything else you gennelmen need?'

'Just your husband's clothes. The ones he was wearing when he came home.'

'God Almighty!' the woman said fervently, nearly dropping the dishes. 'You don't think it was him done that awful thing?'

'Routine,' Beaumont assured her. 'Until we're quite certain he was elsewhere at the time it happened.'

She stared at him, baffled, then turning stiffly with one hand pressed into the small of her back, she followed her man upstairs. Beaumont nodded to Bond who brought up the rear to see fair play.

After mounting protests and murmured reassurances which came clearly through the floorboards to those waiting below, PC Bond returned alone carrying a bright blue plastic sack printed with the words PROPERTY OF THE PATIENT.

'Rupert and Madeleine Crick,' he announced

22

as though ticking their names off a roster. 'Where next, then?'

'Wherever they make tea hot and strong,' Beaumont commanded. 'That's where you can drop Z and me off. Then chase up this Morgan feller out at the building site. Get his version of everything Crick told him. He must be the one who contacted the media. Probably knows someone in it. It was a lightning job to get it on the breakfast news. And I need substantiated times for Crick arriving at work last night and leaving this morning. It could be he rang through with the intention of Morgan fitting that up.'

Z hid a smile at the self-satisfaction on Beaumont's Pinocchio features. Yes, he was heading for Brownie points already. But she hadn't been dozing herself. 'Did you get a look at their bookshelves, Skip?' she asked as they walked back towards the cars.

'I get a feeling you're going to tell me you did.'

'Well, apart from a collection of true-crime paperbacks and a couple of well-thumbed nursing manuals, there were a number of new and expensive-looking textbooks. I think our Rupert Crick's a bit of a dark horse: studying civil engineering in the quiet of his night-watches, perhaps working to put himself through college.'

Two

'Olive George,' the white-haired woman had told the young constable who came knocking at her door. 'I'm a widow. And there's nothing I can tell you about last night, I'm afraid, since I never went out and nobody called. That goes for my student lodger too. She was in London rehearsing with the Youth Orchestra.'

He seemed satisfied, thanked her and moved away down the four stone steps to the gravel driveway. She stood on under the portico, watching until he was out of sight.

The house was quite unlike the other five in Orchard Close, being three times as large and a good deal older; rather grand in its way, with the name Polders carved into one of the lion-capped stone pillars at the entrance to the curving drive. The whole of the almost-circular Close could once have been part of this house's grounds, the four newer buildings to its left being an expensive sixties development of the type advertised as executive, whatever that might mean.

It sounded, the constable thought, too much like work, whereas these were places that begged you to put your feet up. In great comfort, even luxury. In one of them he'd got as far as the kitchen and been dazzled by the computerized display.

Number one, though — on Polders' right — was different, an immediately post-war fill-in, cheaper-looking and divided into upper- and ground-floor maisonettes.

He guessed that Polders itself would be comfortably old-fashioned if a little shabby. In the square hall he'd glimpsed solid, carved furniture, oil paintings in heavy gilt frames and a polished brass gong like a miniature of the one that introduced old Rank movies.

The elderly woman hadn't known about the killing, having rather overslept, she said. So he'd broken it to her and of course it knocked her back, the idea of murder almost on her doorstep. Not that she'd squawked, like the scrawny middle-aged blonde at the previous house he'd visited, no. 4 with the gadgety kitchen. Made of sterner stuff, some of these old dolls, whether raised on upper-class privilege or not. No, she'd just given her name for the check list and said she was sorry she couldn't help.

Beyond Polders (which rightly was no. 2) lay their final house to visit. He and Michaels had tackled the numbers in descending order, ending with those whose backs were nearest the riverbank where the body had been found. He waited for his partner to finish at no. 3 and then, since no. 1 was divided in two, he offered to split it with him.

A varnished whitewood board at the foot of

external stairs to the upper floor bore the hand-painted words '1B, Ibbott, A.', but Ibbott, A. was apparently not at home. The constable promptly returned to ground level and his partner.

The woman who had opened the door there would be in her middle fifties, thin and dumpy with an anxious frown and washed-out blue eyes. More of a town than a country face, it struck him. She was dressed for outdoors and carried a string bag with a parcel in it.

'Oh dear,' she said on seeing the two uniformed men. 'That awful murder!'

Her name, according to the street list, was Snelling. She confirmed this, adding '*May* Snelling. There's just my son and I live here. We can't help you, I'm afraid. We spent all evening watching telly. Neither of us goes out much if we can help it.'

'He'd be at work now, would he? Can you tell me when he'd be back?'

'He — doesn't work. He's not up to it, you see. Too delicate.'

'I'm sorry.' Certainly there was no call to disturb an invalid. Complaints from the public about harassment were too easy to pick up.

'That's the lot then,' the first constable said with satisfaction. 'There's a mobile canteen down the lane past the caravan. I could do with a thaw-out.' He sounded deliberately casual, as though being directed on to a CID case was no big deal. In fact it was his first experience of anything more serious than illegal parking and domestic affray.

He was already rehearsing what he'd say when he got home and claimed he'd been on a murder case. *The* murder case. His old mum would imagine he was heading straight for Chief Constable on the strength of it.

All day, as the river mist dispersed and the sun shed a cheerful brilliance over the village, bringing little warmth because of a slicing east wind, the questioning continued, doggedly, perceptively, dismissively, according to the individual inquiring. The results were all fed back and collated as of equal value and correctness, to be manually noted until analysed for inclusion into the computer programme.

Superintendent Mike Yeadings was familiar enough with the way things went at the start of a manhunt. Either his team would be on to the killer at once, or there would be endless days, weeks, sometimes even months, of seeming stalemate while the information was painstakingly sifted and checked, specimens collected and sent for scientific analysis. Eventually, luck permitting, tentative conclusions drawn and a clear direction recognized.

The Mardham Village death threatened to become just such a slow and demanding inquiry since the victim was anonymous, there was no immediate material clue to follow up and no witness had so far come forward offering information: all symptomatic of a waiting game. Accordingly the Superintendent decided against cancelling his personal arrangements that night for a long-overdue jaunt to London with Nan; particularly in view of the cost of good seats at Covent Garden. But sad experience and team loyalty made him leave a phone number for them, and his card with seat placement at the theatre's front desk.

DI Mott, still at Amersham Area, took the 9 P.M. call from the ACC Operations, overrode an initial decision to plead ignorance of the Boss's whereabouts, then gritted his teeth before passing on the message. The Superintendent would be far from gruntled, deprived of the finale of *Die Meistersinger* for a lightning dash to Kidlington Headquarters.

Mott arrived on the job next morning to find Beaumont and Z already swamped by the rising tide of statements. 'It's doubtful if the Boss can make it this early,' he told them. 'He was called to Kidlington last night from some musical do at Covent Garden.'

Z made a lemon-sucking grimace.

'Dis-*concert*-ing,' Beaumont decided, after a moment's po-faced silence.

The other two accepted this without comment. Puns were a fact of life when Beaumont was on form.

'Z,' Mott said, 'after you left last night I had another phone call I want you to check on first thing. A young woman claims she was followed home from the station close on midnight, possibly about the time of the murder. I've insisted she stays put this morning until you've questioned her. She's a student at Bucks College, Newlands Park, and — Saturday or not — she's chafing at the bit about getting there this morning.'

'Right, Guv.'

'Take along the uniform man who's already done her street.' He dived into a sheaf of papers. 'Got her address here somewhere. Yes; Polders, Orchard Close.'

'Have you got his report?'

'It's not yet cross-referenced. Beaumont, can you find it among that lot?'

The DS burrowed and came up with a list. 'Negative on the only two residents, Mrs Olive George, widow, and Gayle Dawson, student. That's all it gives. So watch it, Z. The girl may have had wiser second thoughts. Or she may simply have dreamed up a story later to snatch a moment of fame.'

'Um,' Zyczynski agreed. She wished the sergeant wouldn't sometimes assume she hadn't eyes, ears or commonsense. 'What about the PM, Guv?'

'On ice. Littlejohn couldn't fit it in yesterday. Busy with a multiple crash on the M25. We're waiting for a call this morning. I'll try to cover that myself, but ring in after you've seen the girl, in case something unforeseen arises. I may need you to stand in.'

Z nodded, hastily copying from the sheet Beaumont had offered. 'Right, Guv. On my way.'

The allocations sergeant had just tasked PC Worrall to join a second fingertip search of the river-bank, and called him back as he was leaving the building. He joined Z in the car park and accepted the passenger seat beside her. His delight at being selected for special duty fast faded as she explained the circumstances.

'What did this Miss Dawson actually tell you yesterday?' the WDC demanded.

'She — wasn't there. She'd gone early to college or whatever.'

'But her name's not listed for a second visit. Why not?'

'Her landlady explained. She was away, in London.'

'Overnight? Did you query that?'

'Well, no. She said — the old lady said — she couldn't have seen anything last night because she was in London playing in some orchestra. Isn't that enough?'

'Not if she had to come back late, and thinks she was followed home by someone after she'd left the station.'

'Gawd,' said the constable, blanching.

Z darted him a swift glance and decided not to lay it on too thick for the moment. The Boss would certainly want to pick up on the gaffe later. 'Of course,' she allowed, 'there's a possibility she's not telling the truth: for some reason lying about coming home at all. Or even imagining someone was stalking her since she's heard about the murder. Some teenagers can be very suggestible. We'll have a few words with Miss Dawson and make up our own minds.'

PC Worrall had been right about one thing. Polders was both old-fashioned and comfortable. As Mrs George led them through the hall, past several open doors and into a bright conservatory warmed by a wood-burning stove, he made a further assessment on furniture and furnishings: definitely pricey, if slightly worn; *Antiques Roadshow* stuff. So the old doll could have taken on a lodger for company, rather than to help out her purse.

'Gayle,' the old lady said, 'this is Detective-Constable Zyczynski and the young man who called yesterday.' She made a creditable effort at pronouncing the surname.

The girl student, seated at a small table in warm sunlight, appeared to be taking notes from a heavy volume with its pages open on a set of graphs. She was blonde and pretty, with a heart-shaped face and a warm smile. 'Hello,' she greeted them, rising. 'Am I in trouble because I didn't get in touch at once?'

'You phoned the murder line number last night. Is that right?' Z accepted the chair she offered.

'As soon as I got back from college.'

'Could you have done so earlier?'

She grimaced. 'I heard about the murder over breakfast yesterday. But I didn't want to miss out on lectures. And I've felt guilty about it ever since.'

'Is it your finals year?'

'Yes. That's the rub. I'm reading Business Studies.'

'I'm told it's better to panic early and get it over. Are you heading for a first?'

'No, I'm not that brilliant. My only hope is to scrape through on hard work.'

'I see. That's probably worth more in the long run. Now can you tell me in your own words what happened on Thursday night?'

'It was just into Friday morning actually. I was on the last train down from Marylebone. There weren't many of us got off at the Halt. I was the first up the railway footpath. I think there were just two men behind me, but I was walking fast and lost them quite quickly. It was when I was coming through the path between the gardens of Greenway and School lane that I realized I was being followed. There's a forty-five degree bend half-way. I reached it and saw the way ahead was dark. Then I looked back and saw this huge figure under the light at the beginning. When he saw me looking he suddenly bounded forward and started — running in my direction.'

'Running? You didn't seem quite sure of that.'

'Running, yes.' She had almost said 'shambling' but it was too emotive, too pointed. 'So I just sprinted. I was a bit out of breath already, but it's amazing what you can do when you're scared.'

'Did you look back again, when you'd reached the road?'

'No. I wanted to get safely inside the driveway before he could guess where I'd gone.'

' "He." You're sure it was a man.'

'Of course. What else? I mean, he was really big.'

Z placed a photocopied enlargement of the map on the table. 'Would this be the route you took?' she asked, indicating it with a pencil.

'That's right.'

'And the time then, as exactly as you can make it?'

'The train was two minutes late in, at 12.32 A.M. And I looked at my watch when I entered the house. It was 12.43. I'd managed to knock half a minute off my record.' For the first time she managed a faint smile.

'Right. You seem quite clear about that. I'd like to try an experiment with you, if you would. Tonight, as soon as it's dark we'll go over the same route. I'll have someone standing under that light when you look back. You can tell me if he looks the same or different.'

'Does that mean you've got someone in mind already?'

'I wish it did. But let's try it, shall we?'

'If you think it'll help.' She looked shyly at the policewoman. 'Is it possible — I mean, do you really think . . .'

'That this was the same man who killed the other woman? At this point that would be guessing.'

We'll know more when Littlejohn's completed

the post-mortem, she thought to herself. At least he should be able to suggest a rough time for when it happened.

'Do you often come home late?' she asked. 'Because if you do, it might be a good idea to have someone you know meet you off the train. How about a boyfriend? We're advising all women in the locality not to walk the streets alone after dark at present.'

Gayle explained about rehearsals in London and the current state of her car. 'Next week I'll have only a hundred yards to cover to the car park, and someone else always comes off the last train. You can bet I'll not take any chances.'

Z made a note of the main particulars. The girl was no teenager but already twenty-one. And her head seemed screwed on the right way round. No obvious reason to disbelieve what she had claimed.

'So,' said Z severely as she walked with PC Worrall to her car, 'where did you go wrong there?'

'Believed what the old doll said: that the girl was up in London.'

'But she never said "overnight". If people go places, they can come back. You gave up too soon on the questions. How many other houses did you visit where you got only half the story?'

Worrall was sweating uncomfortably under his helmet. The question had no sure answer. 'I think I'd got it right up to there. It was the next to last place I visited. Maybe I was getting tired.'

'A girl running for what she believed was her life. And you missed it. "Maybe getting tired" — or were you bored? Police work isn't all brilliant deduction. It's mainly dogged plod and listening to what exactly people are saying — or withholding.'

From the car Z contacted Control at Amersham. Mott had just left for the post-mortem and her report on Gayle Dawson's statement was passed on to the collator.

She turned back to the young constable. 'Now, do we need to re-interview anyone else round here?'

Furious with her but mortified, he thought a moment. 'I did the even numbers, starting at 6. I saw both the Wichalls. They'd seen nothing unusual. At no. 4 only the woman was in. There's a husband and two adult children yet to be questioned: the Fields. I put them on the list for a second visit in the evening. Polders would have been no. 2. Actually it wasn't the last house in the Close that I went to. When we reached no. 1 it was a pair of flats, and I offered to do the top one. There was nobody in.'

'You mean nobody answered the door.'

'That's right. I marked it down for a second visit.'

'Just one occupant, according to the list. So let's check now. Saturday may find this A. Ibbott at home.'

They approached the house and went up the external stairs. A sound of loud music came from within. 'This one's yours,' Z told the constable. He took a deep breath, determined to grill whoever lived here.

'Mr A. Ibbott?' he demanded aggressively of the man who opened the door. He was a weakly-looking individual with a deeply lined face and haunted eyes. His grubby striped shirt was collarless and unbuttoned, half tucked in his jeans.

If Z had unnerved PC Worrall, the constable now had his turn to produce this effect with interest. All colour left the man's face and he stepped back unsteadily as if about to collapse. 'Oh no,' he said faintly. 'No. I know nothing about it.'

'Can we come in, Mr Ibbott?' Z asked, following him closely. The man moved back, his eyes on the constable. They stood crowded together in a small room that had been made over into a kitchen. 'Through here?' and Z squeezed past to lead the way.

Ibbott seemed to have lost the power of speech. Worrall looked towards Z, uncertain whether he should proceed. She nodded. 'Let's all sit down, shall we?'

'Your name *is* Ibbott?' the constable began. 'Speak up, sir. We can't hear you.'

'I said yes.'

'What's the A stand for?'

'Albert. Albert Ibbott.'

Worrall continued, gaining confidence as routine asserted itself, but still marvelling that he should be the one leading the initial questioning of the Mardham killer. Never in his wildest dreams . . .

The man was a postman. He lived alone, a widower. He'd been a wood turner, but had given up some years back. There was so little demand, and a man had to live. So he'd applied to be a postman, did that for four years and after a bad bout of bronchitis recently had asked for a transfer to sorting duties. What he'd really like was a counter job but just now he was still recuperating . . .

He seemed to shrink into himself the more his life story came out. Z couldn't see him as the 'huge figure' Gayle Dawson had glimpsed in the lamplight. But fear could cause distortions. She must keep an open mind.

Worrall was asking now about Ibbott's moves on Thursday night: had he gone out, was he alone, could anyone vouch for him?

Ibbott was petrified, tried to speak and was overcome by an appalling stutter. Worrall looked triumphantly at Z, unable to believe in his own luck.

She leaned forward, shaking her head at the constable. 'Mr Ibbott, if you really can't remember, is there anything that is likely to remind you? Some television programme, the radio, someone phoning? Do you keep a diary?'

'No,' he whispered. 'No. I just can't remember.'

Z stood up. 'Do you mind if we take a look around?'

'No! I mean, yes, I d-do mind. You c-c-can't do that!' But he made no attempt to get up and prevent her. When he heard her move into the bedroom he hid his head in his arms and wept. Worrall half rose from his chair, unwilling to leave the man but tensed for any sound from the further room.

Z knew at the moment of opening the door; the smell was so strong. She had guessed when she got a whiff of it off the man. The light was dim, shining in through thin curtains still dragged across at this hour of the morning. The bed was unmade, stinking of vomit and urine. A single crack of light entering where the curtains failed to meet shone back from dark green glass on the rumpled pillow. As she stepped forward her foot struck another bottle which rolled under the bed.

If this was the way Ibbott spent all his evenings, she could well believe he couldn't remember how Thursday ended. But then, again, there could have been some specific horrendous experience that set him off on last night's drinking jag. He had to be worth looking at again.

They rejoined Beaumont at the caravan and while Z reported on her morning, PC Worrall was dispatched to collect sandwiches from the mobile canteen.

'He slobbed the job,' Beaumont said gloomily. 'How many more of the house-to-house men have put in a half-effort?'

'The old-stagers are all right,' Z comforted. 'It's a question of experience. Worrall's new to it, was a bit overwhelmed by the idea, so he never got stuck fully in.'

The DS grinned at the serious young face. Sometimes Z looked all of sixteen, losing a decade. 'There speaks the hardened old-timer. What's the matter with kids today, eh?'

'Has Angus got anything from the post-mortem?' she asked, stiffly on her dignity.

'There's nothing through yet. I suppose we'd better follow up your drunk at his workplace. Ibbott, you said? Postman, and he's off-duty on Saturday morning? On shifts maybe. We'll not get anything from his bosses before Monday.'

'A little jockey of a man, and Gayle's follower was described as huge. I'm walking the same route with her tonight, and I need someone equally small to stand in. It could be a trick of the lamplight, magnifying the figure into a long shadow.'

'Small and inadequate? But that's the type the psychological profilers look for.'

'But the murder wasn't a sex crime. Despite what the media claimed, the woman wasn't raped. I'm pretty sure of that.'

'So the killer's impotent too? Makes your man more likely, doesn't it? There has to be some reason that he hits the bottle. It could be to forget his hopelessness. But when he's tanked up the old beast comes out and he strangles.'

'You're talking as if this killer makes a habit of

it. We've only the one case. Statistically it's more likely a killing for personal reasons, by someone who knew the woman and bore some grudge against her; no connection with Gayle Dawson's stalker.'

Beaumont grunted. 'It's only speculation until we've got an ID on the corpse. When we circulate photographs of her reconstructed face there's a chance someone will recognize her. If she's not a local, she had to get here somehow. She could have done a round of the pubs, to pick up a man. Or been brought here by one in a car. Probably not driving her own, though, because there's been no report of an abandoned vehicle.'

'She had only one shoe,' Z remembered. 'High-heeled, not really new, but it didn't have scuffs from car pedals. Has the other turned up yet?'

'No. Maybe in the river. We've got divers along the banks right now, trying to find the instrument she was battered with. They'll be dredging up all manner of irrelevant rubbish.'

PC Warrall arrived at the door with their package of sandwiches and two sealed polystyrene beakers. He stood waiting with a hangdog expression, expecting some slanging from the DS after Z's inevitable exposure of his ineptness.

'Thanks,' Z said shortly. 'You'd better rejoin your shift.'

'His sergeant will give him hell after Mott's made a report. Still, only one of many bollockings before this inquiry's done. God, I hate this waiting phase. What next for you, Z?'

'I'm wondering about Rupert Crick. Did PC Bond mention whether he was carrying anything when they first met?'

'Not to my knowledge. What had you in mind?'

'His studies, assuming that the books I saw in his home meant he was seriously into something. Wouldn't the night watch be an ideal time to get to grips with things? So was he carrying books to and from the site office? Or would he keep some there?'

Beaumont's wry face clearly was meant to imply she was fiddling while Thames Valley burned.

'I know it's a small detail, but I'd like to know all there is about one of the few characters involved to date. He travelled along the river-bank on his way to work and on his return. He might even have gone there in between. There was no one to check on him, because he was left in charge at the site all night, alone.'

'*Quis ipsos custodes custodiet?,*' Beaumont quoted smugly. 'I cribbed that from some upmarket novel my wife was reading.'

'Spot on,' Z encouraged. 'So where's the statement from the site manager which PC Bond collected yesterday?'

'Probably on disk by now, but he won't have been asking about textbooks.'

They went through to consult the bank of VDUs in the inner compartment. Morgan, they found, had confirmed the hours Crick claimed he had spent on the site. According to the time-sheet and Morgan's own testimony, the watchman had left at 6.18 A.M. on Friday morning. The signed office log had recorded regular inspection tours of the site timed roughly on the hour throughout the period of duty.

'A bit too good to be true,' Beaumont considered. 'There's nothing to prove he actually did what he claims to have done.'

'Unless there are security buttons to push at various points on his rounds.'

'So one of us had better question Morgan again and see what the system is.'

Z gave a hollow laugh. 'I know which one of us you mean. Right; I'll do that now, and ask him about Crick's study habits at the same time.'

According to the map the site could be reached by car only on a roundabout route, although the river-bank walk was almost a direct crow's-flight after the first kink past the bridge. Buckman's Shoot — originally Chute — ran in the right direction but had a steep gravel dip beyond where they had parked the previous morning, then deteriorated into a rutted track which would do the car's suspension no good. Z made a U-turn off the grass verge, crossed by the bridge, then headed north along Mill Lane, passing the entry to Orchard Close again, looking for a second right turn.

It was almost half a mile farther on, concealed beyond a plantation of conifers, a proper metalled roadway for taking heavy goods vehicles and meeting the far end of Buckman's Shoot at a right-angle within sight again of the river.

The development site was vast, threatening eventually to take Mardham out of the village category and into that of a London dormitory zone. A billboard at the entry displayed a plan of the final project in three colours denoting stages of development, and including shops and a community centre. It implied enormous resources behind the concept, and Z wondered how much local opposition had been incurred in getting it officially approved. Was this the real reason behind such stringent precautions in guarding the site?

It being Saturday, none of the earth-moving plant was in operation, but by the little group of hutments three hatchbacks were parked. Two men leaning against one to talk over a spread sheet of diagrams looked up as Z pulled alongside.

'Would I find Mr Morgan here?' she asked.

'Inside.' The tweedy man puffed out smoke and waved his pipe stem in the direction of the nearest mobile office. They both looked curiously after her as she went up its steps and knocked.

Morgan, as the name promised, was Welsh. He was also in a filthy temper and glared at her from reddened eyes.

'WDC Zyczynski, Thames Valley Police,' she told him. 'Could I have a word?'

'Not again!' he protested, retreating reluctantly for her to enter. 'What is it this time?'

Let him talk his paddy off, she told herself. 'Have you anything to add to your earlier statement, Mr Morgan?'

'Yes, I bloody have,' he shouted. 'How can I get any work done with you lot never leaving me alone?'

I've missed something, Z thought. 'Regarding the statement you made to PC Bond yesterday morning concerning the hours worked by Rupert Crick, night-watchman . . .' she began.

'Oh yes? And what about the one made to your Inspector Mott only half an hour ago?'

With an effort she managed to suppress any change of expression. 'That is being processed, sir,' she said with an inspired burst of bureaucracy. 'It's another small matter I'd like you to set me right on, if you would.'

He relented at her tone. 'Well, have a seat. I'll see what I can do, but I really can't spare the time.'

'I understand Mr Crick's something of a student,' she ventured.

'He is.'

'Does he study here?'

'No reason why he shouldn't, is there? Better that than sleep, like some lazy buggers.'

'True. I just wondered if he kept his books here.'

'In the little safe.' The man pointed to a corner of the office. 'Keeps his writing things and instruments there, and usually a couple of books or so. Has his own key to it.'

'Have you a key?'

44

'Course I have; it's my office.'

'I'd like to look inside.'

Morgan stared at her. His eyes said clearly that she was an interfering cow and had no place in his scheme of things.

'This is a murder case I'm investigating,' she reminded him firmly.

He hummed, chin down, selecting a key from a heavy ring on a chain from his belt. Inserting it, he watched her with a malicious smile. When the safe door swung back he stood aside.

Three textbooks, a loose-leaf file and a plastic box of geometry instruments were stacked to one side on the only shelf. On the other end were a tea caddy, a mug, a spoon, a screwtop glass jar with sugar in it and a jar of powdered milk.

'Satisfied?' Morgan crowed. 'Now can I get on with more important matters?'

Three

Five hundred yards short of the Mill Lane bridge on her return route Z's pager buzzed. She drew into the verge to read its message: *Caravan immediately Mott.* Even allowing for the miniaturized screen, it was ominously terse. Now how had she stepped out of line?

Mott's face, as she entered the caravan, was thunderous. Normally sunny, he had clearly suffered some reverse. With her arrival all four of the team were now present, the Boss presiding at the table.

'Take a seat, constable,' he invited. Now she was distinctly uneasy. Superintendent Yeadings had never since their first meeting addressed her by her lowly rank.

'Sir?'

He didn't appear annoyed, more ironic. His face had taken on its Welsh operatic baritone look. 'You probably heard I was untimely summoned to a higher authority?' he enquired with mock ceremony.

Called out of some Wagner at Covent Garden last night, she remembered. Now he was being humorous about it. Was that to hide some fresh calamity?

'There's good news and bad,' he went on unoriginally. 'The bad is that we are to lose DI Mott. Only temporarily, I trust. There is a sudden greater need in Ascot.'

With priority over their own murder inquiry? Had some horsey royal been assassinated?

'Detective-Superintendent Willows of Windsor and Maidenhead Area has been injured in an RTA,' Yeadings explained, 'and is undergoing surgery there. There is some anxiety about his condition.

'It happens at a particularly bad moment for their CID, faced with a series of unexplained cases of chemical food poisoning among stable-lads. The latest threatens to be fatal. Since the best possible substitute is required, the ACC is sending Inspector Mott to lead the Area team. With the rank of acting-superintendent.

'Here the good news is that we shall not be left comfortless. A stand-in has been found.' Yeadings scanned the room with a sardonic eye. 'From Banbury Area.'

Z heard Beaumont s breath expelled in horrified disbelief.

'From Bicester, in fact. We shall be welcoming Detective-Inspector Jenner, whom some of you have already met.'

Oh no, not that insufferable coffin-faced misery! Z prayed inwardly. But it was a *fait accompli*. Jenner was already on his way.

'I made the point,' Yeadings continued, well aware of the reaction his news had evoked, but not by an eagle-eyed flicker permitting any comment to escape his audience, 'that although seconded to us on a previous case[*], his relative unfamiliarity with the area should be backed up by stronger support from the home team. As a result —' His eyebrows rose in pleasurable anticipation of the effect he would cause — 'WDC Rosemary Zyczynski is made up to full sergeant as from today. A rank she was due to receive some time ago in uniform branch and obliged to forgo on transferring to CID. Congratulations, Z.' There was a murmur of warm applause from the other two.

'Cunning old codger,' Beaumont marvelled afterwards, when he had Rosemary on her own. 'There's none can beat the Boss at horse-trading with the brass!'

'I'm not sure I care to be ranked as a marketable mare!' But Z was glad Beaumont showed no obvious resentment at her level-pegging him. The humorist was still touchy about seeming rooted at present level, and could be hard to work with when reminded of it. She intended being careful to acknowledge his seniority through length of service.

'But Jenner!' Beaumont repeated, swinging back into despair. 'It'll double the slog, with his nit-picking over our methods, antagonizing the locals and going off at half-cock with impossible suspects. This is going to be Balaclava, Z, with our OC as Enemy No. 1!'

[*] *Cat's Cradle*

It struck her as a bad beginning. Jenner was prejudiced enough without provoking the same devil in others. 'One thing's certain,' she said comfortably, 'the Boss won't waste this excuse to dive into the thick of things. Can you see him sitting it out at his desk?'

'There's that,' Beaumont allowed. 'But Jenner — shit! Let's get everything sorted before he blasts in.'

Mott knew that the Ascot opportunity could prove a fillip to his career, but he was irritated that it should occur when he was already becoming involved in a murder case on home ground. Particularly so since he had been the investigating officer present at the post-mortem, and had now to pass on verbally such findings as Littlejohn had chosen to make known while working on the body.

'Nothing much we hadn't gathered,' he told the Boss. 'She was in her mid-forties and probably died somewhere between 10 P.M. and 2 A.M.'

'Write it down for Jenner,' Yeadings instructed, 'and I'll see it goes into the computer.'

At no. 4 Orchard Close in Mardham Village, the Field family were at lunch. 'Where will you all be this afternoon?' Phyllida Field demanded over dessert. 'The police are coming back to question everyone.' She managed to make a threat of it.

The twins eyed each other. 'Around,' said

Colin coolly. 'Out somewhere, anywhere,' said Rachel simultaneously. They both tittered at the lack of accord.

Their father ran a hand backward through his thinning hair and said petulantly, 'Can't you deal with them, Phyl? I really do need to get over to see Battersby.'

'I've already bloody dealt,' she said viciously. 'They won't take hearsay. Not as though, as a mere wife and mother, I'd have any idea of where you all were at whatever time it is they want to know about.'

'Thursday night, wasn't it? I attended the Lodge. Nothing difficult to remember about that, I should think. Tell them when they come. I have no intention of hanging around on the off-chance.'

Donald Field pushed back his chair, rucking the Persian rug over the parquet and consciously losing some dignity in the process of disentangling it. His nineteen-year-old offspring watched with cool mockery, his wife balefully. Field made his escape. He had gained the hall when the front door-bell shrilled. Visible through the glass panels, he had no option but to open up.

A man and a woman stood there. Well, really a girl, he supposed; undeniably pretty, her cheeks shining pink from the cold wind, her hair a close mass of warm brown curls. Big brown eyes and a slim figure.

'Sergeants Beaumont and Zyczynski, Thames Valley CID,' said the man, and in unison they flashed warrant cards at him. Field gave a tight-lipped sigh, slid his cuff back to dart a glance at his wrist-watch and shrugged. 'You'd better come in, then.'

He ushered them into an elegant but untidy sitting-room where television entertained a semi-circle of empty chairs. He turned down the manic voice of a woman presenter battling against a background of racing cars screaming at full throt-tle.

'Do sit down. I'll fetch the others.'

The cars continued streaking, cornering, screeching and throwing up sparks.

Beaumont twitched an open newspaper off the settee and deftly booted it out of sight. Then he shrugged his car coat off to the floor and sat down expectantly.

Z — *DS* Zyczynski now, and determined that the interview should prove worthy of her new rank — surveyed the room before settling with her back to the light.

'All yours, Z,' Beaumont offered. 'Do a Jenner on them.'

As the family straggled in and distributed themselves among the chairs, she rose again to face them, reaching to switch off the distracting images, and began.

Nothing particularly strange or promising in what they told her, she decided. Donald Field, mid-forties, possibly a few years younger than his scrawny wife, and partner in an Amersham legal practice, had been at a Lodge meeting there. That

51

could easily be verified. He'd returned home late; nearer 2 A.M. than 1.30, he supposed; and his son interrupted to claim it was 1.43 precisely when he'd heard the garage doors go up.

'You heard the car too?' Z pressed him.

'God, no. You don't think he drives a tin can, do you? Besides, the drive's on an incline. He always coasts in when he's late.'

There was a hint of malice there, as if . . . But no, she hadn't enough yet to base suppositions on. 'And you?' she enquired of the son.

Like his twin, he had a perfect egg-shaped head with classical if deliberately blanked-out features and fine light brown hair worn close to the temples; his severely short, hers around her shoulders dressed forward almost to hide her face.

'Well, obviously I was here or I wouldn't have heard him.' He was taunting her, his voice exaggeratedly public school.

'I'd like your name first, and a little about you.'

With sudden animation he leapt to his feet, rigid as a tin soldier, hands down the seams of his corduroys, shouting manically at a point above her head. '*Sir!* Field, Colin, aged nineteen and seven-twelfths, *sir!* Student accountant, *sir!*'

His father wasn't amused. His mother hissed disapproval. The sister folded up her long, fine, trousered legs, clasped them under her chin and hid her mirth between her knees.

'Bit of a humorist too?' Z asked calmly.

'Life's so dreary otherwise.' He smiled winningly at her, conceding she wasn't too bad, for a woman.

'We had a quite appalling coq au vin on the dot of seven-fifteen so that everything would be cleared away by eight for Mother to watch *The Bill*. Ritual soap of the evening. By half-past the Roach was busy at barre practice so I sought a bar of my own, called in on Jasper at no. 6 and we slouched off together. I came back after a couple of lagers, and left him to get legless. He was on one of his utterly boring monologue jags and he's not of the wittiest at the best of times. Have you met him?'

'We have that pleasure to come.'

'Graduated in Media Studies at Southampton Uni and he's playing around making videos. That's his personal line: visual impact. Like I said, his audio's less than riveting.'

' "*As* I said"; not "like I said," ' his father corrected irritably in an undertone. No one appeared to notice the interruption.

'You arrived home at what time?'

'Er, somewhere round ten. Didn't actually clock in. But there was a rather fetching lady on TV groping a map to show off her isobars.'

'The weather forecast: more like 10.30,' his mother said.

'Maybe. What next? Had a bit of a barney with Phyllida.' He nodded towards his mother. 'Tried to phone the new doll at Polders but she was out. Couldn't get any change out of the Roach here because she'd got her head in some squishy love story —'

'It was the *Roman de la Rose*,' defensively from the girl.

'So I took a shower, cut my toe-nails. I've got a quite grotesque one on my left foot if you'd like to —'

'Did you leave the house again that night? Or see anyone from the windows?'

'No to both, I'm afraid. I've bored you, haven't I?'

'Thank you Field, Colin, nineteen and seven-twelfths, student accountant,' said Z on a monotone. 'Miss Field?'

The girl referred to as the Roach unfolded gracefully. She placed her ankles neatly together on the floor and folded her hands in her lap. Her spine was ramrod straight. She shook her hair back, taking herself seriously.

'My name is Rachel. Colin and I are twins, though fortunately not identical. I do ballet.'

As if in proof she lifted one languid arm before her, drifted it sideways at shoulder level with the fingers delicately extended and looked soulfully along its length. Her hand dropped back lifelessly in her lap.

'I didn't go out after my barre practice Thursday evening. I liquidized some lemons and nectarines in the kitchen to make a fruit drink and took it up to my bedroom. I have a mini-fridge there. Then I read in bed until I fell asleep, woke up about two and switched the light off. That's all. And I didn't see anyone from the windows, because of course the curtains were closed. And anyway, my room's at the back.'

She had answered factually, but with a measure of self-display and something like disdain for the two detectives.

'If no one else lives in this house,' Z said, 'that's the lot then. Thank you.' It wouldn't sadden her if she never came across the Field family again.

Out in the cooler air, Beaumont chortled. 'Amusing, that. Barre and bar. Do we suppose it's family compensation because Dad only solicits and didn't qualify for practice at his own bar?'

Z allowed him his brief pleasure. She turned back the pages of her notebook to check. 'At no. 3 we still haven't found Dr Goodwin and wife at home. Or her brother, Malcolm Barrow. Maybe they've all gone off for the weekend. In which case they should be back sometime tomorrow, ready for Monday's surgery.'

She looked up to meet Beaumont's drolly amused eyes. 'What are you grinning about?'

'The good doc being questioned on his whereabouts at the time of the murder. Too ironic if we'd made him confirm death on his own victim!'

In a crackle of static, Beaumont's car radio was trying to contact him. He unlocked and reached in for the handset, growled into it.

'Report to DI Jenner at the mobile Incident

Room,' came the message from Control.

'I'm involved in a questioning. ETA in thirty minutes,' he said doggedly and pressed the button for Off.

'We'll fit in one more house,' he told Z. 'The next along has been visited: Eustace Potts and his housekeeper Ena Judd. Then comes no. 6, at the end: Francis Wichall and son. Come on, we'll check with young Jasper on Colin Field's story.'

It was the father who opened the door to them, wiping his mouth with a paper napkin. 'Late lunch,' he explained apologetically. 'I saw you working this way. Come in.'

They were shown into a masculine version of the Fields' sitting-room. The green leather suite, worn and stained in places, showed circular depressions where the two were accustomed to settle. There was a clashing of crockery in the background and a male figure went bouncing past the open doorway with a loaded tray. 'Be right with you. Just need a leak first,' he shouted happily back.

Z had no difficulty grasping the image the son projected: bright-eyed and bushy-tailed, life of the party stuff. Unlike the more ironic and sartorially elegant Colin Field, he presented himself to them in the perennial teenager's uniform of jeans and trainers. His open-fronted pink cotton shirt trailed its tail half in and half out out at the waist rear. Beneath it a black T-shirt proclaimed BUGGRIT in large white capitals.

His face was radiant; sand-coloured curly

lashes framed wide-spaced blue eyes of unbelievable innocence. His hair was a mass of uncombed golden curls with darker roots, his designer stubble almost ginger.

'Hi!' he greeted them fondly on his return, hands spread palm-outwards as in an Al Jolson chorus. Even on the spot he seemed to be bouncing, rocking from one spongy sole to the other, a golden golliwog.

'Jasper Wichall?' Z enquired politely.

The father snorted. 'His name is James. I don't know where the Jasper business started.'

'This tendency I have to tie my wimmin to railway lines,' said the young man, beaming. 'Melodrama villain stuff.'

'Shall we all sit down?' Z suggested. 'Mr Wichall, we're checking whether anything unusual was noticed on the night of Thursday/Friday. And it helps if we know in further detail where everyone was at the time. Let's start with your name, age and occupation.'

He was Francis Wichall, 49, widower, a civil servant employed at the DSS. His main concern was in identifying and investigating illegal claimants for benefit. On Thursday he had got home at about 11 P.M., having dined out with a friend at the Crown in Old Amersham.

'Your friend's name?' Z pursued, sure that Jenner would later be sniffing for such details.

'Er, a lady friend. Married, actually, so is it absolutely vital that I — ?'

'Unless the information impinges directly on

the murder, I can assure you of our discretion.'

Reluctantly Wichall mentioned a name known to both detectives. 'She's, er, a Probation Officer,' he said wretchedly.

A strong-minded woman of unquestionable virtue. With a solid marriage. Wichall must have been dining out on a fantasy if he thought there was room for doubting her wifely virtue. And home by 11 P.M.!

Perhaps he too was keeping up an image, and for his son's benefit: the sexually active older generation.

'Did you go out again later?' He hadn't done.

'See or hear anything unusual from indoors?' Apparently not. He had started to watch a film on TV, fallen asleep over it and finally got to bed about 1.15 A.M.

'Were you in by then?' Z swung round on the younger man and launched the question out of the blue.

'God knows. A bit hazy about details, I'm afraid.'

'So perhaps we can go through the evening and help you remember? You are James Wichall, known to contemporaries as Jasper. And your age?'

The young man looked regretfully towards his father. 'Twenty-two,' he admitted.

But rising sixteen, in Z's opinion. He had stuck at that stage of development; would probably stay little changed into middle-age.

'And on Thursday evening?'

'Was gonna pig out with a mate, but he'd had his meal early so we went to the Barley Mow for a jar or two.'

'Your mate being?'

'Colin from no. 4. We have a project in mind, but it didn't get off the ground that night.'

'Are you going to tell us about it?'

'Sure, why not? I did my degree in Media Studies, and I'm into making videos. Colin's sister dances and he's a closet choreographer.'

'A what?' Beaumont exploded.

'They're twins,' Jasper explained, 'and their mother always lumped them together. Right from age four Rachel had dancing lessons. So Colin had to do the same. Saved petrol and time if they were dumped off together. He did it for about four years until he rebelled, but he still had to go along, as spectator. So he got to know the ropes, as you might say. In fact he got quite keen on the stagecraft angle, later started making model theatres, designing tableaux and costumes. That's what he'd have liked to go into, but his old man had other ideas. But *serious*, man.'

'So he's studying to become an accountant, while hankering after the theatre?'

'That's how it is. He had hopes his mother would finance him because she's the one with money and she's a bit arty-crafty herself. But for once she backed the old man. So Colin's only hope is to make a hobby of it. Trouble is he hasn't any patience with the technical angles and he

59

doesn't like being told.'

Which went some way to explain young Field's reference to Jasper having been on 'one of his boring monologue jags' when they went out drinking together.

'Let's get back to Thursday night. You were at the Barley Mow.'

'Old Col was in a funny mood. He'd had the brush-off from some chick. Well, the new one who's lodging at Polders actually.'

'Gayle Dawson?' Z remembered now, Colin had said he'd rung her and got no answer. Because, of course, she'd been at her rehearsal in London; but the boy wouldn't have known that. If Mrs George had been in she would have answered the phone. Someone would have to ask her what message he'd been given: whether she'd suggested the time Gayle's train was due back at Mardham Halt.

'So, being a tad cantankerous, Col didn't stay long. Pushed off. Left me playing darts with some blokes from the quarry.'

'Until?'

'Closing time plus sup-up. Left about 11.20 P.M. Took a pillion ride on some bloke's bike to Pottersfield and we sat around making music of a sort for an hour or two. Then I guess I must have legged it home. Woke up here, anyway. With a sore head.'

Possibly 'making music' had covered smoking pot and downing a few more jars. His father wasn't looking any too pleased at the recital.

'You still can't remember what time it was then?'

'Not the flimsiest notion.'

'Which way did you come home?'

'From Pottersfield? On the hoof there's only one way. Over the bridge, and along Mill Lane.'

'Nowhere near the river? Nor the passageway from Lower Church Road?'

'I shouldn't think so. Both right off route. My boots haveta remember the way home if I don't.'

'You don't drive?'

'Had a car. Bent it. Can't afford another yet.'

'I see. And nothing happened on the way back that sticks in your mind?'

He did the Al Jolson hands thing again and shrugged, pulling down the corners of his mouth. His father cleared his throat as though he might venture some remark, but then thought better of it.

And that, Z thought, was that. They had computer fodder to bear back to Jenner, but not with any recognizable value as yet.

She considered young Wichall. Since the questioning had swung round to Thursday night she sensed a change in him. Despite his determined merriness, his hands were nervous. His eyes flicked at her and away. He was not as at ease as he wished to appear; had rushed to fill with words the gaps that might give her time for thought.

Borrow a technique of the Boss's, Z told herself: his devastating silences. Make the young man run out of patter, stumble to a halt, reveal himself.

She waited.

But it wasn't working. She lacked Yeadings' gravitas. Jasper's flow of words continued. Once he recognized her mind was on hold, he saw it as retreat. His darted glances were prolonged. Beyond his compulsive self-admiration he began to assess her as a person. As female. She felt his gaze become assertive, probing her, speculating. She knew she had lost the advantage.

He was not the sort of man she cared to have take such intimate interest in her. Was this an intuitive warning that he was dangerous? A possible for the killer? With his vagueness over the time of his return he could well have been Gayle Dawson's stalker, only a little off the route he'd quoted.

'Right.' Her voice was firm, with more confidence than she felt. 'Back to something you said earlier. Colin Field was "in a funny mood" and "cantankerous". You supposed this was because he'd had the brush-off from some girl. Then you suggested it was "the girl at Polders". Did he mention her by name?'

'Sure. He'd tried to get her to come out with us, but Mrs George said she'd gone to London and wouldn't be back till late.'

'So not exactly a brush-off. More a disappointment.'

The old lady could even have said 'by the last train', and young Field might have been on the lookout for her. He'd left the pub well before her return. But in that case why not wait openly at the station and offer to walk her home? Was he shy of approaching girls directly?

'So Colin Field is interested in Gayle Dawson. That's not surprising: she's a very attractive young woman. But closer to your age, surely?'

'We're both interested in her.' His eyes mocked her now; his tone almost jeering. 'You've got it wrong. Not for her body. Not yet anyway, unless she insists. Gayle's musical.'

Z took a moment to grasp the significance of this, and by then Jasper was openly scornful. 'She — *plays* — the — *flute!*' he said, making it obvious by emphasis. 'Well enough to be in an amateur orchestra.'

Of course: Rachel danced, Colin was a 'closet choreographer', and Jasper was into making videos. They needed Gayle to supply music. An amateur group project, so they weren't prepared to pay for recorded musical backing! After her original suspicions of their motivation, it seemed gloriously innocent that the young people of Orchard Close were into the arts.

There was nothing more to ask. Z felt slightly abashed. They stood on the doorstep and Beaumont demanded, 'That's the lot then, apart from Doc Goodwin's household? Everyone else in Orchard Close has been seen personally now?'

Z looked down the list. 'Except Mrs Snelling's son at no. 1, and apparently he's an invalid.'

There came a choking laugh from behind them

as Jasper lingered over closing the door. 'You mean Harry? He's no invalid. He's kept under wraps because he's a dangerous nutter!'

Four

Superintendent Yeadings was at the caravan again to effect the hand-over. 'You've all met before,' he said briskly. 'No need for me to give you my blessing. You have my number in case there's anything to query.' He nodded, seeming casual, turned up his coat collar and let himself out into the slicing wind.

There were three old codgers opposite, leaning on the bridge's parapet with a dejected whippet at their feet, perhaps driven from home by house-proud wives who reminded them that women could never retire. The Superintendent wandered across to join their mesmerized staring into pewter-grey water which, faster in mid-stream, dragged at its edges, combed into scummy off-white bubbles by straining green reeds.

He secured the flapping edges of his charcoal-grey overcoat, slowly patted his pockets, took out the empty pipe that he no longer smoked, and started absently scraping at its innards with a blade of his penknife, elbows planted on the gritty coping stones a few paces from the other men.

His gaze strayed upriver towards where the body had been found. There the trees grew quite close to the water's edge. Backed by a sombre band of conifers, some still held their leaves, a vivid palette of autumn colours caught by the lowering sun. And there were subtler, dead-bracken tones, just as beautiful to his mind, reminding him of tawny background foliage in old tapestries.

Jarring the idyllic scene, the murder site's loops of plastic tape restlessly twisted and untwisted on their bollards, white marking the outer exclusion zone, black and yellow closer in. Under an ash tree a deeper shadow stirring stiffly was the dark uniform of the man on duty, stamping his feet against the invasive cold. But yesterday's drama was over, the experts departed.

The old men on the bridge continued to stare at the lack of action as if it took all their minds' energy to take in what had occurred. They seemed to need no words for communication.

The silence building round Yeadings as outsider had no dampening effect on him. He knew better than most that a vacuum required to be filled, so settled into it like a well-worn armchair. Sooner or later one of the old codgers would be moved to speak. If he waited he just might learn something.

Within the caravan Jenner squared his thin shoulders. He was every bit as bleak and bloodless as Z remembered him. The long, inquisitorial nose, slightly askew in his mournful face, was made more unlovely by the remnants of a cold. Its end was red, with scaly soreness extending into the groove that led down to his tight, single-line mouth. She should feel sorry for him, stranded among reluctant underlings at such a disadvantage; but she reserved her sympathy for the team he'd been inflicted on.

'WDC Zyczynski, sir,' she declared herself, in case he needed reminding. Then remembered she was DS now; but it would seem pointedly boastful to make the correction.

Beaumont wasn't slow to put things right. 'Promoted to Detective-Sergeant as from today,' he said emphatically.

'Er, yes. I was told. It's policy, of course.' The last part was added as if to himself.

It's nice, Z wryly told herself, to be regarded as the token female; but nothing new.

'I've been familiarizing myself with the village layout,' Jenner said, nodding towards the sheet maps open across the table. 'It *is* a village, I suppose. Or do the locals consider it a town?'

'A bit in between,' Beaumont offered. 'Like a lot of small places round here, it's growing. Outsiders coming in all the time. Handy for commuting to London. Three churches, two pubs, a tea shoppe and a railway station that one in every three trains deigns to stop at. No nick, but there's a local bobby by the name of Bond, lives here and works out of Amersham.'

'Right.' Jenner stopped to blow his nose, started to trumpet, winced, then dabbed pathetically at his sore upper lip. 'Let's have a report on your morning, then.'

'Following our briefing by Superintendent Yeadings, we continued the questioning of residents in Orchard Close,' Beaumont informed him. 'And we missed out on lunch.' He conveniently forgot the sandwiches snatched some three hours earlier.

A beady eye confronted him over the damp handkerchief. 'In a serious crime investigation, sergeant, you must expect to make some personal sacrifices. A sense of proportion, above all.'

'Like observing Health and Safety at Work, sir.'

Ooh-ooh; Z turned away. Beaumont was making a stand. The repeated 'sir' should have mitigated the hostility, but it was too obviously an avoidance of the familiar 'Guv'. And that doubly barbed reference to health: not kind, in view of the Inspector's infectious state.

Jenner's overriding of the objection was on auto-pilot. Their peckish condition was lost on him as he had lunched adequately with the Superintendent at the Feathers. He was, furthermore, accustomed to begrudged co-operation.

'Why Orchard Close in particular? From the large-scale map it looks like a development of upper-income properties. Big houses. There are plenty of other streets where no one has yet been questioned. Uniform branch should be able to fill in any gaps.'

'Its situation is vital to the case,' Beaumont gave as his opinion. 'At the rear all six houses give on to a thin, downhill strip of woodland and then the water meadows. Crossing them obliquely you meet Buckman's Shoot, a gravel lane that runs almost parallel to the river, separated from it by a band of trees and undergrowth. Any lights used at the point where the woman's body was found could have shown through to residents in their upstairs rooms at the rear of the Close.'

Not by a flicker did he betray that he had spontaneously invented the theory.

'And there was the testimony of Gayle Dawson to follow up,' Z put in before Jenner could disagree. Certainly no. 1 and Polders might have a direct line on the murder site, but there were trees in between, and all other houses in the crescent would be blocked off by the bulk of those first two. Significantly, at none of them had Beaumont gone upstairs to check the visual angle.

'Gayle Dawson,' Jenner repeated, searching unhopefully among the papers in his hand. 'Refresh my memory.'

Z did so, aware that the stalker incident was news to him.

'I suppose I'd better see the young woman. You say she didn't report this until the evening afterwards?'

Before he should write the girl off as hyperimaginative or an attention-seeker, Z put in, 'So I've arranged to walk the same route with her tonight and check the details.'

Jenner considered this. 'Yes, do that. I'll leave it to you then. We don't want to be cluttered up with irrelevancies. There's always that problem with a murder case, sightings of vampires and little green men from all directions.'

'Nutters,' Beaumont breathed, and his eyes met Z's as both wondered uneasily what the new man would have made of Jasper Wichall's offering about the unseen son Mrs Snelling kept 'under wraps'.

Apart from the absent Dr Goodwin, his wife and brother-in-law, this Harry was the only resident of the Close so far not interviewed.

The inspector was scowling now at a VDU screen where the earliest statements were entered. 'This man Crick who claims to have found the body . . .'

Again Beaumont and Z exchanged apprehensive glances. There was one other kind of suspect Jenner was known to handle badly, apart from the mentally handicapped. Sooner or later he would have to be warned of what to expect, before they came face to face.

Beaumont put on his most wooden expression — lost on Jenner who had again hidden his face in his handkerchief. 'Crick gave a clear enough account, sir. A night-watchman from a building site along the river. And — er, he's black.'

Jenner looked up, his eyes pinholes. The baleful look he treated the two sergeants to implied that they'd deliberately set this up to annoy him.

'Crick's time of arrival at work Thursday night was verified by the site manager who spoke to him before leaving,' Z claimed. 'Crick is studying for qualifications in Civil Engineering and fits in some of his academic work during duty as night-watchman. He also makes hourly rounds of the building site and checks back electronically to the site hut. The manager explained the system to me. If he doesn't insert his card in the locked units at various points within a given time, an alarm rings at the manager's home.'

She waited for Jenner to object that anyone could have clocked in for Crick using his card, but the Inspector let the point stand.

There was no reason why she should be especially protective of the man, except that Jenner was automatically suspicious. She must watch it, otherwise she'd find herself opposing the DI on some quite rational supposition, out of habit.

'Sir,' she said, to move him off the subject, 'did DI Mott get anything useful from the post-mortem?'

'Dr Littlejohn's preliminary written report will be available tomorrow. Meanwhile DI Mott's notes indicate that he favours provisional time of death as between 10 P.M. and 2 A.M. It took a matter of seconds, since the hyoid bone was fractured, the blow to the face being delivered after death. Also — interesting point, this — the killing was carried out elsewhere and the body taken to the river-bank before onset of rigor.'

'Rigor wasn't complete when I touched her,' Z murmured. 'That would be at 7.15 A.M.'

'Moving the body makes the timing more difficult to pinpoint,' Beaumont grunted, 'because of temperature changes. Littlejohn must have found lividity in areas not in contact with the ground. There certainly was no appearance of a struggle having taken place in the vicinity.'

Jenner was reading from the notes again. 'Petechiae present in scalp.' He turned to the two sergeants. 'Minor haemorrhages,' he explained unnecessarily. 'Frequently indicative of death from asphyxia, so she was choking before the hyoid ruptured.'

Beaumont stared back owl-eyed, as if these were wise words from the oracle, and news undreamt of.

'There were also faint traces of some lubricant found on the front of the neck and probably coming from the attacker's fingers, too smeared to leave clear dabs. Dr Littlejohn queried lip salve, although the woman herself wore heavy lipstick of a purplish red. Analysis may later tell us what the substance actually was. As indicated by bruising and nail marks, the strangulation was manual, executed from the rear.

'What we don't know,' he complained, 'was who the wretched woman was. Nobody has yet reported a recent missing person who answers to her description.'

'There's *Crimewatch UK* on BBC 1 next Tuesday,' Z suggested, 'in case we haven't a name by then. Could I script a piece for their portrait gallery?'

'You intend sitting still for three days, waiting for it to fall in your laps?' Jenner accused them, almost apoplectic. 'No. Get out there and start asking questions.'

Z opened her mouth to protest that the photos of the dead woman weren't yet to hand, but Beaumont stood gently on her foot and rolled his eyes towards the door. Well, he was right, she accepted: pointless to waste energy on countering everything their new DI said.

Outside, buffeted by the easterly wind which had failed to go down with the sun, she hugged her sheepskin closer.

'I'm sure the woman's not local,' she told Beaumont. 'Her clothes were wrong. She looked like a town tom dressed to go off with a client.'

'You're probably right. But she wasn't invisible. Either the woman, or the person who dumped her, or the transport they came in must have been seen by someone. I'd agree that it looks like a village where everyone fills their hot water bottle at 10.15 on weekdays, but we know there were some people abroad that night and into the early hours. Until the photos are ready, let's have another go at them.'

'What about Harry Snelling? If we can clear him now, Jenner may not have to meet him.'

Beaumont hesitated. 'Why didn't we ask young Wichall exactly what he meant by "a nutter"?'

'He was being clever, showing off. I didn't want him thinking he'd set me on a special line of inquiry. There's a deal of mischief in that young man. I'd rather find out for myself what Harry Snelling's nuttiness amounts to.'

'Fine. So let's do it now. No. 1 Orchard Close,

ground-floor. One of what Jenner referred to as upper-income properties. He probably thinks we go there to wallow in whisky and cigars.'

The DI's concept was questionable, he saw, on reaching no. 1A. It was unlike the other houses in being smaller; none of the windows appeared double glazed and the blistered woodwork was in need of repainting. Z, having visited upstairs with PC Worrall, watched him register the difference. Beaumont pressed the bell and stood back.

Their approach must have been observed because the door was opened immediately by a great bear of a man who stood looking at Z with a sad smile, huge hands hanging at his sides. She was put in mind of a young gorilla, but a mildly affable one dressed in freshly laundered white shirt and chinos. From somewhere inside the flat came little cries of distress, the flushing of a lavatory cistern and a slammed door.

A middle-aged woman came running forward, reaching for the man who filled the door frame. 'Harry, what is it? There's no need for you to . . .'

He still said nothing.

His mother peered through at them, a little above elbow level to her son. 'We don't need anything, thank you,' she said anxiously. 'Would you latch the gate again as you go out?'

'We aren't selling anything,' Z assured her. 'We'd just like to come in and talk to you. Sergeants Beaumont and Zyczynski of Thames Valley CID.' They both offered their cards for

74

inspection. This lady needed calming: it was no case for flashing badges and leaning on anyone.

'But the police have been here already. I told them —'

'We're still short of information,' Beaumont said, 'so we're making a second call. People often remember something later when they've had time to think.'

She hesitated, Harry still blocking their way. Then Z smiled at her. 'We'll try not to be a nuisance. But we do need everybody's help on this.'

'Well, since you're not in uniform . . .' The woman gave way reluctantly, patting her son's elbow, and at the touch he started plodding backwards down the narrow passage to a doorway on the left.

'You go and put your video on, love,' his mother told him. 'It won't disturb us.'

'We need to speak to you both,' Beaumont said firmly. 'Shall we all sit down?'

They seemed to have penetrated her last defences. Mrs Snelling's resistance gave way.

'I don't suppose we could have some tea?' Beaumont asked, still standing. 'It's bitterly cold outside. I'll come and help, if you like.'

Leaving Harry to the nice young policewoman. You could see Mrs Snelling thinking that. Z sank into an easy chair, smiled and picked up a video from the floor to read its label. '*Postman Pat*? Lovely. My nephew's got that one.'

'And his black and white cat,' said the young

giant: the first time he had spoken. His voice was deep, the delivery slow. He seated himself on a monstrous bean-bag cushion and his haunches were swallowed in its depths. Again he gave his sad smile. Reassured, Mrs Snelling edged out to the kitchen.

'Mardham's a beautiful village,' Z began. 'I think I should like living here. It's got some lovely walks. The woods. And the river. Do you like walking?'

He stared at her. Either it was too hard a question or she'd been too sudden. She waited.

'Animals,' Harry said after a moment. 'I like animals.'

Promising, Z thought. Woodland animals, riverside animals, even fish. Eventually she could get him round to the subject of owls and nighttime sorties. If only Beaumont delayed the tea-making to give her a chance.

Mrs Snelling came back looking flushed, but it was with pleasure from Beaumont's kind attentions. He had been telling her of his wife's recent venture: home-cooking for a partner who kept a café/wine bar and did party catering. He bore in the tray with tea for three and a pint tankard of apple juice for Harry. While Mrs Snelling cleared a space to put it he picked up Z's nod. Right. Since she alone knew how far she'd got, he'd leave the rest to her.

'Have you lived here long?' she asked casually when she'd been served with tea and a slice of lemon cake.

'No. No, we haven't really. About eight months.' Mrs Snelling was looking haunted again.

'It's a lovely part of the country. Do you have pleasant neighbours?'

The answer came reluctantly. 'Mrs George next door is very kind. I don't really know the others. There doesn't seem to be a lot of socializing at this end of the Close. Polders is the only house we share a fence with.'

'Of course. And Mrs George has a student lodger now for company: Gayle Dawson. Have you met her?'

Mrs Snelling set down the teapot carefully. It was a heavy silver one, which Z guessed was Georgian, and there were matching milk jug and sugar basin on a silver tray. Yet everything else in the room was utilitarian, modern and inexpensive.

'I've seen her coming and going. And heard her music.'

'Music,' Harry said, gazing absently at one of his enormous slippers.

'Harry used to play when we had a piano,' his mother said. It sounded apologetic, which struck both sergeants as curious. Beaumont looked at the huge hands and wondered how he could fit them to the keyboard. Perhaps he had been much younger then.

Z appeared to have given up on the questions and they took their leave soon after, thanking Mrs Snelling and seen to the door by her, with Harry looming in the background. He seemed loth to let them go.

'Well?' Beaumont demanded as they regained the pavement.

'It seems he goes walkabout at night. When there aren't any noisy people about, he said.'

'He could be Gayle Dawson's enormous shadow. How about the strangling?'

'Under the circumstances we met him in,' Z said cautiously, 'he was gentle enough. I couldn't even guess until we know what his trouble is.'

Beaumont sighed. 'His mother told me he's a depressive, has to take medication. Which is why he can't really live on his own. He forgets to take it.'

'I'm rather out of my depth on this. Do you know anything about it?'

'Depressives, no. Except that they're meant to be more danger to themselves than to anyone else.'

'He's fond of animals. And — you won't believe this — he said he has a farm in the back garden. It can't be much more than a cabbage patch.'

'So what do you think — rabbits? Or hens? Or was he just fantasizing?'

'Whichever, he believes it himself. Beaumont, I'm famished. That cake helped, but it only made an opening for a real meal. Can't we drop into the Barley Mow for an early supper?'

'And keep our ears open for mention of the mystery corpse. Why not?'

The blackboard menu was still on display outside. 'Pub Grub all Day'; which seemed promising. Beaumont held the door for Z and they went in to buzzing warmth. And the sight of a familiar pair of shoulders hunched over the bar counter. The Boss was engaged in a jocular argy-bargy with a little group of locals who were well on the way to having drunk enough. Unwilling to cramp his style the two sergeants chose a window table and Beaumont ogled the barmaid over.

With two servings of hotpot and coffee, they settled to admire the senior detective's information-gathering technique. Whatever the subject, he'd been playing Devil's Advocate and was now sitting back enjoying the result. A wizened little jockey of a fellow was stabbing the air with a forefinger and insisting, 'Let me tell you —'

And the Boss was letting him tell him.

By the meal's end the group at the bar was breaking up, a sleepy whippet being noisily cajoled out from under a table to join them at the door. One of the trio was a man Z had already met that morning: Albert Ibbott from the flat above the Snellings'. She wondered if he had cleaned up his bedroom after last night's drinking before he came out to restore the required alcohol level in his blood.

The Boss climbed down from his stool, spread some money on the bar counter and came across. 'Saw you both in the mirror. I trust you've left enough in that coffee pot for me.'

'I'll get a refill,' Beaumont promised, rising, pot in hand. Yeadings slid on to the padded bench beside Z. 'A profitable day for all?'

'We went back to Orchard Close.' And she explained what they had learned about the Snellings. 'The man's mother says he's a depressive. He told me he likes animals. And despite her denials he does get out at night.'

Yeadings stared at his clasped hands. With a Down's Syndrome daughter he was sympathetic to anyone mentally disabled. But also, as a policeman, well aware of the inherent dangers.

'It must all go into the computer,' he warned her.

He remembered Jenner's handling of a simple lad in the earlier case they'd shared, and he'd picked up her reluctance to let the DI know of Snelling's condition.

'Quite a problem house,' she offered. 'The man in the flat above is a drunkard. Albert Ibbott, the little one who was with you just now.'

Yeadings seemed amused. 'What did he tell you about himself?'

Z repeated from memory the man's history as she knew it, and the Boss nodded. 'M'm. The man's a compulsive liar. He's not a widower, Z. His wife left him three months back, mainly because of his drink problem, but also because he couldn't hold a job down. I had a look through minor local cases this morning. He's on bail from Amersham magistrates' court pending further reports, social and medical.'

'On what charge, sir?'

'Interference with Her Majesty's mails. Over a period there's been a lot of post gone missing. A search brought to light an accumulation over almost a year, stowed in Ibbott's locker. He pleaded absence of motive to defraud. Blamed fatigue: he was just too exhausted to deliver along the whole route; put some aside for tomorrow. Which never came. But Nemesis did.'

'So he's unemployed, yet can still afford enough booze to get legless?'

'That's one of life's little conundrums that is being looked into. Despite all warnings, some people still put banknotes in envelopes and post them. He may come up on a second charge over some blank postal orders he cashed locally, once they find who sent them. He's not the brightest of men in his sodden state.' The Boss sounded regretful. 'And apparently he was once a wood turner of some skill.'

During this conversation Beaumont had returned to the table and a few minutes later the barmaid brought fresh coffee. When she was out of earshot he grumbled, 'We're wasting time milling round the natives while we've still no idea who the dead woman was.'

Yeadings grunted disagreement. 'Not wasted time. The more we know of the people here the better we can assess what they are — and what they aren't — capable of when pushed. Strangulation is a highly emotive crime whether it has sexual overtones or not.'

'Going mainly from the way she was dressed, Z believes she was a town tom out for the night with a client,' Beaumont persisted.

81

'Or a semi-pro.' Yeadings nodded. 'Which of course brings us to means of transport. And there I may have picked up something from my late companions of the bar.'

The two sergeants focused full attention on him. He had this teasing habit of keeping the best for last.

'They were all three drinking here on Thursday night and hung on a bit after closing time. The landlord turfed them out at 11.20 P.M. And Zachary Lewin, of the greater pot belly, stayed on even later, in the shrubbery outside. Something he'd eaten, he said. Which you can believe, if he eats ale with a fork. And he saw something.'

This was dragging it out too long. Beaumont's shoes made restless scrapings on the floor. The Boss smiled benignly.

'After the pub lights were all extinguished, a closed van drew into the car park. That's what brought Lewin out of his stupor sufficiently for him to observe a tailboard dropped and a motor cycle rolled out. He thinks there were two men, one in leathers. But at that point he keeled over on his face and passed out again.'

'So we don't know what they were up to.'

'Something unusual; you can bet your annual leave on it.'

11.00 P.M. closing, Z was thinking; and then twenty minutes for 'supping up'. Suppose those two had brought the body here straight after, to dump it. But Gayle's stalking happened almost an hour later.

'You said, "after the pub lights were all extinguished", sir. When would that be?'

'I'll leave you to question the landlord and staff about how long they took clearing up. Even with that known precisely, we must add a period which Lewin was in no state to measure. And for the present, Z, since there are only two pubs in Mardham we won't lean too heavily on the landlord for allowing excessive drinking of alcohol. Just mention it in passing. We'll leave it hanging over him, until our needs are less.'

Five

Wind rattled the ornamental shutters at the window. Out in the Close approach, trees rolled like small ships tossed in a tempest, strobing the yellow lamplight and sending solid shadows racing over tarmac and neat white railings. Leaning a fevered forehead against the pane's welcome coolness, the man watching groaned quietly through clenched teeth, echoing the gale's raging in an eruption of agony.

It was intolerable, became more so each torturous day. This driving need. And the rancour burning away acidly inside, so that there was no escape but one: to remove the source of it all, find a solution, a new peace. No, it couldn't go on. There had to be an end, and soon.

To continue submitting was the madness of despair. To act was the madness of desperation. But beyond that sacrilegious act — what? The achievement of everything he had ever craved? Or disaster? Perhaps no further pain, no more need for desperate measures. But there was risk: you could never be sure.

It was numbing not knowing in advance the results of such irreversible action. The future was an impenetrable void. But no, a void was a physical impossibility. There always had to be *some-*

thing. Black holes yawning to drag you in. Consequences more horrific than the present torment?

But that just couldn't be.

For a freak brief instant the wind dropped; the trees' tossing was stilled. Light shone pure and direct from the street lamp on the corner into the watcher's tormented mind. And in the centre of the aureole the fair-haired student from Polders came jogging lightly into view.

Gayle Dawson, who had been frightened by some man stalking her on the night of the unknown woman's murder. Both blondes, so it was thought the stalker might have failed to catch this girl and gone on to kill the other; a man who preyed on fair-haired women. It hung on in his mind, tantalizing because the connection seemed incomplete. There was some further inference he should draw from this fact.

He shook his head, straining forward against the glass as she passed close under the front garden wall. Strange that so recently frightened, she should feel safe jogging after dark.

But then he saw she wasn't alone. She had outrun her companion, and stood laughing, waiting for him to catch up. Colin, red-faced and out of breath, pulled up at the entry to the Close, waved and limped over, to bend painfully double at the kerb edge, one hand to his ribcage. Unfit, too self-indulgent. He hadn't been seen abroad in that track suit since he left school.

The watcher drew back into the shadowed

room, an outsider, of another generation, discounted. These two had their small, uncomplicated lives, he quite another.

The shadow came over his mind again. There must surely be some way to resolve it, a door ready to be opened, or even by a hairline crack already ajar? Then all it would need was a few steps, the resolute courage to accept the way on offer. It must be possible. It was meant to be. A few more steps forward. To come out of the dark.

On a long sigh the wind came back, the trees' branches heaved, fragmenting the light in their meshes. His house withstood the blast, the window shutters clanging on their iron hooks; the panes shuddering. With unsteady hands he dragged the curtains across, but the gale raged on outside. Within the room familiar uncertainties returned to take him over.

The office surrendered to Superintendent Yeadings at Amersham faced east. He had enjoyed the early morning light, warmed behind the double glazing. But now, at night, the hurly-burly of the wind as it buffeted that angle of the building interrupted the progress of his thought. He was glad to be diverted by the arrival of a man from SOCO with the photographs he'd been waiting for.

They were laid out on the desk for him to study. 'The right profile's good,' he gave as his opinion.

'The left one was a real swine to reconstruct. They had to remove some broken bone and put in a brace to take the resurfacing.'

It could have been a stuccoed wall under discussion. Yeadings looked again at the full face view. No one could truthfully say it was a living likeness, but it was a workmanlike attempt. Whether any acquaintance of the woman would immediately recognize the subject depended heavily on whether the cosmetics used in the reconstruction were of the style she'd worn herself.

A tom, Z had thought. Yes, he could go along with that. She looked the age that Littlejohn had calculated from her bone development: 42–48. What had once been a pertly pretty face was coarsening. In these photos the make-up still hadn't totally hidden that something was wrong with the neck flesh, but a patterned scarf disguised the worst.

'Have Press Office received a set?'

'They've been faxed through to Kidlington and all Areas.'

'Good. I'll keep these. Too late for the Sundays to have held a space, but we should get a splash on Monday's front pages.'

He sat on for a few minutes after the civilian had gone, then rose and reached for his overcoat.

Once he was home he would put on his *Meistersinger* CD fortissimo and, irrespective of whether the kids were already in bed or not, he'd have that final act which he'd been cheated of last night. To think that he'd sat through all the earlier lead-up, in that ball-grinding seat, and then been done out of the very climax he'd gone there for!

Essential village life, based on local birth, marriage, death, and the community structures arising from them, was not to be long thrown out of kilter by the killing of a stranger. If on Sunday morning the tumbling peal of church bells brought more folk out on to the streets than usual it was because of Harvest Festival, not superstitious terror. And the well-wrapped figures scurried with head bent on account of the wind, still from the east, but now with lessened violence.

Having no specific allocation for that morning, Z quitted the mobile Incident Room and joined the general flow of villagers. She told herself it was, if nothing else, an exercise in community policing.

The nearest source of a single-note bell was the Baptist Church in Chapel Meadow on the corner of School Lane. Z joined the movement up the wide steps into a modern foyer buzzing with cheerful chat, was fussed into possession of a service leaflet and ushered into an aisle seat half-way towards the polished rails. Below them were piled loaves of bread, plaited and gold-glazed; small sheaves of corn; maize cobs; vine tendrils; giant tomatoes; pumpkins and smugly plump marrows; all to witness to the richness of the good earth. The air was heavy with the autumn scent of chrysanthemums and the pollen of pink-stippled lilies. Warm subterranean drifts rising from gratings in the aisles marked the heating's dusty awakening from summer disuse.

Swaying collectively in their pews, the congregation sang with gusto the harvest hymns remembered from her schooldays. The best of your life, someone hadn't failed to tell her. And she supposed that they had been good, while her parents still lived: years of unquestioned security, abruptly shattered. After that, aged ten, she had never quite trusted again what tomorrow might bring. Nor fully trusted adults, always conscious that they might desert her, even if they didn't actually choose to get killed. And then there was her aunt's husband; and she'd been too frightened to tell anyone about him, for fear he thought up something even more vicious to do to her. Thank God she was adult now and childhood was done with.

She wasn't familiar with the Baptist form of service. It seemed hearty if somewhat formless, the sermon decidedly lengthy. Without a central altar, the pulpit dominated. Which must have convinced the preacher of his total authority. Even while counting the season's many blessings he went on to thunder against those who were non-productive, counter-productive, anti-social. In sum, Sinners.

Aren't we all? Z agreed, but felt uneasy at being required to throw herself on everlasting mercy and open the innermost recesses of her soul, taking no thought for the morrow. Perhaps police work was unsuited to following the godly path. Probably most professions were. Innocence had a way of getting lost in the complexities

89

of earning a living.

Darting sidelong glances as she rose to sing, she began to recognize faces. Mrs Snelling was there, but not Harry. Did she lock up her depressive son when she went out, or employ a minder? And how did he manage to escape her custody for his night-time walks?

Two rows ahead Z thought she saw a stern-faced Francis Wichall. Again the younger generation was missing. Across the aisle, and nodding to her from under a straw hat decorated with a selection of shiny artificial fruit, was the ex-nurse Madeleine Crick. Beyond her the huge frame of her husband lumbered to his feet for the final hymn and revealed a deep brown, melodious voice that reminded her of Robeson.

A big man. Perhaps another possible as Gayle Dawson's enormous shadow? If so, he had lied about staying all night on duty. And if he lied about that he could also have lied about not being near the river at the time the body was deposited. He just might have got there and back between his hourly card-punching.

And, if the woman had been killed elsewhere, why not at the building-site office? She hadn't been all that big. It wouldn't be beyond the strength of a man like Crick to carry the body in his arms to where it was found. And he'd then know its exact position, ready to be 'discovered' on his way home in near daylight.

But still there was no name for the woman, no background, and therefore no connection at all with anyone in Mardham Village.

Shuffling out in the densely packed queue of friendly gossipers, she was tapped on the shoulder and turned to trace back the bony hand via clerical grey sleeve to the awesome revelation of DI Jenner's grinning dentures. Free of the outer door, she waited for him on the steps. He shouldered his way through to her.

'Miss *Jick*jinsky! I'd no idea you were one of us.'

Z forbore to put him right, smiling noncommittally.

Jenner flapped open a black umbrella and as he waved her under she saw that a slow drizzle had started. The wind had dropped and veered to southerly. It was already noticeably warmer.

'An interesting service,' she offered, obliged by his grabbing hand to walk close.

'Colourful, certainly,' Jenner said and sniffed.

So what was he accustomed to in Bicester? Then she remembered the man had a cold. They made small talk as far as the caravan.

Beaumont was sitting there, the shoulders of his raincoat darkened with damp. He had observed their joint approach through a window and switched on his most wooden expression to hide his amusement at their seeming intimacy.

'It looks,' Z said, on entering and removing her sheepskin to shake it, 'as if I'm the only one who didn't tune into the weather forecast this morning.'

'Sunday; so your mind's on higher things,'

Beaumont commented drily. 'We've got photos of the victim.' He laid a pile of glossy 10 x 8s on the table.

'And a list of recent chummies from Criminal Records. No female stranglings without rape within a thirty-mile radius.'

'He could have been disturbed before the act,' Jenner suggested.

'In which case we'd have a witness, or at least someone to admit being in the vicinity about the time she was dumped.'

'Or else our attacker is impotent. Has some kind of hang-up,' Jenner countered.

Since it was a free-for-all in the guessing stakes, Z made a bid. 'By that token the killer could even have been a woman.'

The two men considered this. 'Motive?' Jenner demanded, jutting his reddened nose in her direction.

'Jealousy? Revenge? A quarrel over a man?' With so little data to hand, the possibilities were limitless.

'I'd go for a quarrel *with* a man. Over payment for services rendered,' Beaumont gave as his opinion.

'Based on her appearance?' Jenner queried.

'That and precedents.'

There was a sharp knock on the van's door. The duty constable unlatched it and PC Bond, the local man, came in streaming wet. 'Just seen Doctor Goodwin's Volvo, with three aboard, drive into the Close,' he reported. 'They haven't been questioned yet, so I wondered . . .'

'I'll see them myself,' the DI said quickly. 'Sergeant *Jick*jinsky, you can come and take notes.'

Assuming that that's what women are for, she told herself. And I do wish he'd pronounce my name right. He's so very nearly there.

Because Jenner was unwilling to wait, they caught the Goodwins at a slight disadvantage. Meredith's brother was still garaging the car after a quick hose down. She was upstairs unpacking her case; the doctor had subsided on a settee in the lounge with what looked like an orange squash in his hand. He got wearily to his feet as his brother-in-law ushered the visitors in. 'Police,' Malcolm announced baldly.

'Oh really? Does that mean there's been some progress?' Goodwin sounded hopeful. 'Malcolm, could you rustle up some tea? We shan't need to call Meredith down.'

The other man moved off, more peeved perhaps to be missing the detectives' news than resentful of use as dogsbody. It looked, Z thought, as though this was his accepted role in the family.

Jenner was not one to answer questions but to ask them, even with someone with an interest in the inquiry. He frowned, instructed Goodwin to take his seat again (on the man's own ground) and explained that he wished to speak to all members of the household.

The doctor gave him a coolly assessing look, then walked to the open door and called up. 'Meredith, would you mind joining us for a moment? Malcolm, you too. Don't bother with the tea.' Then he turned to Z and invited her to sit.

A formal little man who respected old-fashioned courtesies but was brusque with underlings, she registered. One who wouldn't much care for the DI's social ineptitude. He remained standing until his wife had come in and taken her place on the settee.

'You've been away since Friday morning,' Jenner began, when the woman's brother had joined them. 'Otherwise we would have been to see you before. With regard to the murder of an unidentified woman during the night of Thursday/Friday.'

It sounded accusatory. Dr Goodwin's back stiffened. 'No doubt you identified yourself at the door. Perhaps you would do so again for the benefit of my wife and myself.'

Tight-lipped, Jenner complied. Z produced her warrant card and held it out. 'Detective-Sergeant Zyczynski,' she murmured, since the DI hadn't troubled to include her.

'Thank you. Now sit down, Inspector. You do realize that I was the duty police surgeon who confirmed death in the case you mention?'

Jenner hadn't picked that out of the report, and clearly thought it remiss of Z not to have informed him of the fact. 'Is that so, sir? At that point I had not been called in to take over.'

But he'd certainly had access to all the early bumf on the finding; more than one Dr Goodwin in the locality would be unlikely, and his failure of observation wouldn't be lost on the police surgeon.

Jenner proceeded to put the usual questions and was assured that none of the three had been out after ten on Thursday night. Meredith and her brother had played chess together until a little before midnight. Dr Goodwin had retired to bed early, at 8.45 P.M.

'Can anyone vouch for it that you were actually indoors from that point onwards?' Jenner blundered. Z held her breath.

Goodwin's jaw tightened visibly. 'I am afraid you must make do with my word on that since I sleep alone. I was tired, took a sedative and fell asleep reading the *Lancet*. I slept until my wife brought my tea in at 6.30 A.M. on Friday. And shortly after that I was called to the sudden death.' He was clearly offended.

Not that his being a doctor, and by chance required to examine the body, should prevent him being treated like anyone else. In fact, Z cautioned herself, if he'd been the killer he might have chosen a specific time and place for the deed so that he would be the doctor on call, in case scenes-of-crime experts should later find any traces from himself on the body.

She looked hard at him. Thin and drawn, he still looked tired, despite his long sleep and the two days' holiday since. Perhaps more than tired; really ill. A desolated face, she thought, then pulled herself up for being fanciful.

But there were mauve grooves under his eyes

and a sallow tinge to his complexion. Although he could have been no more than fifty the lines of his face, vertically between the brows, and bracketing nostrils and mouth, were deeply etched. A colour photograph on the coffee table, taken some years back which showed him sprawled alongside Meredith on a sandy beach, was hardly recognizable: such a comfortable Toby jug of a man then.

He was more than disconcerted by Jenner's offensiveness. She read him now as being in some considerable pain. So, the sedative he said he'd taken on Thursday night; was it actually something stronger? Was he into morphine? It wasn't unknown for stressed doctors to pick up the habit. She found herself wondering how strong he was. Up to carrying a dead woman from the roadway fifty yards along the river path? She doubted it. So why not take the easier option of weighting the body and dropping it off the bridge?

I'm chasing phantoms, suspecting everyone, she thought. But how else can it be while we've no lead on the woman's identity? It means imagining killers, inventing motives, with nothing to show whether we're on the right lines or hopelessly up the creek. It was frustrating and time-wasting.

Jenner had now moved on to identify and question the brother-in-law, checking that he was quite sure he'd heard nothing, seen nothing from the windows, on Thursday night.

'Just myself reflected in the panes,' the man

said. 'It was pitch black when I went to bed. Windy. A few stars but no moon. Just the lamp at the entrance to the Close.' Which implied his room was at the front of the house.

Malcolm Barrow's face wore the sulky droop of a discontented and unsuccessful man: a spiritless mockery of his sister's calm beauty. He had the same wide-spaced large grey eyes but they were fugitive, the chin weak and the mouth slack. His hair, like hers, was a warm russet, but where hers was thick and long, twisted up in an elegant French pleat, his scalp shone through pink in places like someone twenty years older.

'Are you a medical man too?' Jenner demanded suddenly.

'I —'

'My brother is in advertising,' Meredith said quickly.

'Was,' he corrected bitterly. 'I'm a victim of the recession.'

'Presently unemployed?' Jenner pressed.

Nobody denied this.

'Mrs Goodwin.' Jenner turned to the woman. 'Can you help us? Anything unusual you heard or saw at about the time you went to bed?'

'Nothing, Inspector.' She sounded assured. 'My room is at the back, opposite my husband's, and it looks out east, but the river turns away before that point. I just get a view of the water meadows and trees. Then as Malcolm said, it was pitch dark, until the moon rose towards two o'clock. As for hearing anything, the double glazing doesn't allow much noise in from outside.'

She sat straight, in command of the situation, waiting for him to finish and go. Jenner must have made some slight movement because she picked it up and rose, ready to see them both out. There was no further reason to stay. The DI conceded, pursed his lips and allowed himself to be shown to the door.

As they belted themselves into the car, Jenner behind the wheel, four figures emerged from a gateway ahead and moved as a group towards the exit road from the Close. Even in silhouette, almost identically dressed in bobble caps, windcheaters, stretch pants and boots, it was obvious to Z who each was. Jasper Wichall pranced, arms gesticulating; Rachel Field walked with the slow, self-conscious grace of the ballerina she saw herself as, ankles almost scraping as the rear heel came forward to be set, toe angled outwards, precisely in line before the other. Her brother mooched alongside, hands deep-thrust in trouser pockets. The other girl, the newcomer to Mardham, walked chin high and a little apart, both hands hugging her collar ends.

'Who are these?' Jenner demanded.

Z told him while he put the car in gear and quietly rolled up behind them. As it came almost level, Jasper skipped out into the road and swung round to confront them, crouched to peer under the roof. The car screeched to a halt. At the DI's nod, Z wound down her window.

Jasper bounced round to the nearside and

treated her to an impish wink. In the watery midday light his designer stubble glistened like demerara sugar. 'Fair sleuthess, will you join us? We're piggin' out at the Barley Mow. They do a nice drop of real ale.'

Jenner's audible snort wasn't lost on him. 'Bring the boyfriend too. We're easy.'

Whatever had been Jenner's intention in pulling up by the group he had swiftly changed his mind. Horror came off him in waves, that he should be coupled so with his female assistant. Until this point he had managed to overlook her being a woman. He sat stiffly upright, limbs drawn close.

'Young man, you'd do well not to make yourself a traffic accident statistic.' He put the car in gear again and attempted what he'd probably deem a Le Mans start.

Pathetic, Z decided. But really she should give up resenting the stand-in DI and start protecting him instead. All that wordy business to Jasper! Angus Mott would have capped his nonsense with a crisp, 'Fox-trot Oscar!'

Six

'You couldn't wait to tell that nerd about my job,' Malcolm Barrow accused his sister.

Meredith looked calmly at him across the kitchen counter. 'He would get to know anyway. He's of the sniffing kind who root things out; truffles or turds. And I merely mentioned you were in advertising. It was you added chapter and verse.'

' "Victim of the recession," ' Goodwin quoted from the doorway. 'A nice line in self-pity.' He didn't disguise his displeasure.

Barrow stood between them cracking his knuckles. 'You do a helluva lot to build up a man's self-confidence. So bloody successful, the pair of you. And you can never let me forget I'm living on your charity.'

'You're not obliged to,' his brother-in-law reminded him. 'There is a wide world outside these walls, waiting to discover your skills. Meanwhile —'

Meredith watched her brother's hands spasmodically jerking open and shut, kneading the air because they couldn't get at Stanley's throat. 'That's enough,' she warned quietly. 'Let's stay civilized. There's no call to behave like spoilt children.'

Her husband rocked a moment on his heels, studying her face. A little while back she wouldn't have included him in the rebuke. She would have taken his part; but it seemed he'd lost some of her loyalty along the way. Perhaps even her respect. Over the last months so much distance had opened between the two of them, and yet she did still try to be fair-minded.

Poor Meredith, devoured inside by dragons. Her exterior was like blindfolded Justice over the Old Bailey building, a cold statue holding up her scales to find that he weighed dead-level with that hopeless brother of hers. In her eyes family still counted for a lot; but in Malcolm's case it was sympathy wasted. Didn't she know he would sell her ten times over for the price of a dead cert at Aintree that could fall at the first fence?

He felt a new wave of weariness roll over him and turned away to cover his pain. 'Talking of children,' he said, halting again in the doorway, 'I see James Wichall and the young Fields have roped in Olive George's girl student. I can't imagine it will be much to her advantage. They've just gone off in a gang together.'

Meredith disagreed, but had enough sense not to take a stance on it. It was good for young people to socialize. That was part of Stanley's trouble: that he couldn't. Had never really been young.

'She seems a pleasant girl,' she said mildly. 'I'm glad Olive has someone to share the house with.'

As her husband had made off during his last remark, she went round to Malcolm who was muttering viciously under his breath. She laid an arm on his bent shoulders. 'Just as I'm glad we have you to share ours.'

'I could kill that man,' he breathed through gritted teeth. 'Always so bloody superior. Merry, what on earth possessed you to marry such a slab of deep-frozen cod?'

'Malcolm, please! He's not well. It makes him — sombre. You must try to get along with him.'

'Like you do? That's no answer to my question. Why, Merry?'

'You've no right to ask that. Especially since —'

'Since I made such stinking crap of my own marriage? I should have thought that experience qualified me as some kind of judge.' He tasted bile in his throat but managed only to sound petulant.

'Well, I don't intend you to judge me. Or Stanley. We married — as most people do — for love, and hoping that we'd make a success of life together.'

'Only it didn't turn out that way, did it? God, I've watched you, Merry. Over the last year, turning into the Ice Queen. What's happened to the way you were? How can you go on like that? I remember you as a wild young thing taking every risk that came your way and chasing a whole lot that didn't. Where's all the passion gone?'

He was watching closely and saw the sudden flush before she turned her head away. 'What good is passion?' Her voice was low and harsh. 'Look where it got you, Malcolm. I settled for security and a home and —'

'And a family.'

'You're on forbidden ground, Malcolm. Get off it.'

'Or else you'll turn me out? The only family you're ever likely to have?' He was openly out to wound her now, stung by reminder of his own personal failure.

'I've a steady husband, a lovely home and good friends for neighbours. Plenty of blessings to count.' She spoke tautly as if trying to persuade herself, then turned to him in pleading. 'I don't need anything to change. Except I'd like you to get over your anger and put your bad experiences behind you. You know you're welcome to make your home here with us. But you need to look forward, start making fresh plans for yourself.'

'Find a job. Lay a new woman. Just like that. Only I've no fancy for either. The very idea makes my gorge rise.'

She sighed. 'Well, just give me a break then.' She busied herself checking the contents of her grocery cupboard, then poked her head round the door.

'To change the subject: I was thinking it's time we gave a dinner party.'

'Therapeutic social engineering. Why not? Give yourself a cause to light up for.' He spoke with sardonic indifference, but his mood had shifted. She was dangling an occasion for which he might see fit to display his own personal gifts. 'What had you in mind for the menu?'

'I haven't reached that point. Just thought up a guest list. Stanley mentioned that the new girl at Olive's has already met Rachel and Colin next door. With their parents that would be five. Olive no longer accepts invites to dinner. Stanley and me, seven; with you that's eight, which balances the table. I could see if they're all free tomorrow. What do you think?'

Malcolm narrowed his eyes. 'I'm curious to see how you're pairing us.' He reached into a pocket, produced a stick of gum and began unwrapping it, his eyes still following her.

'No pairing. A mixed group.'

'So long as you don't expect me to make a pass at the new chick, half my age.' He threw the gum in his mouth and began to chew, exaggerating the action because he knew she found it disgusting.

'No. Of course, she's included to divert dear Stanley, while you have your wicked way with Donald Field.'

Meredith had moved back behind the cupboard door, and from the total stillness that followed he knew he'd scored again.

'I don't know what you mean.' It came out in a rush, but a tad too late.

Malcolm Barrow smiled, secure in the knowledge that however threadbare his brother-in-law's welcome wore, he could always rely on Merry not turning him out. His observations had been spot on. She was still the passionate sensation-seeker under her ice-floe surface. She was getting next door what was no longer on offer at home. Small wonder she 'needed nothing to change'.

And now she knew that he'd seen what was going on. He wasn't as blind as his brother-in-law. And he wasn't stupid enough to pass up using the knowledge as pressure on her. If ever that became necessary.

Although television coverage of a crime always brings a host of calls from the public regarding police mug shots, seldom does one genuine claim come in first. This case was an exception, beating the expected string of loony sightings and mistaken identifications.

It was Sunday afternoon when the reconstruct photo of the strangled woman went out with the news headlines. In Shadwell, London E1, Derek Monkhouse had just made his first significant decision of the day by opening his eyes. He had groaned his way to the over-shared bathroom, staggered back, fallen again on his unsavoury bed and reached for the TV's remote control.

The screen lit and he latched on to his new possession. His only one, apart from a handful of grubby garments and his satchel of crayons. His joy, his baby: an obsolescent monochrome portable which he'd received in payment for a bruiser's charcoal portrait.

And there, confronting him on the screen, was the sour bitch who'd stood him up on Thursday.

He was good on faces because faces were what he did, pavement artist until he'd worked himself into the little clique at the bottom of Shaftesbury Avenue; School of Piccadilly Circus. He'd set up a borrowed easel there almost a week back and made enough to live on since, with a room at this artists' squat.

The woman had wanted to be sketched. She'd seen a kiddy portrait he'd just finished — little blonde angel in soft pastels — and she'd fancied the same for herself. Well, thirty years back, maybe.

His sketch had been too truthful, and she wouldn't pay up when it was done. He should have demanded money up front.

So he'd threatened to bounce her around, only their raised voices had scared some of the other artists. Fear of the police sorting them out; some of them non-Brit, illegal immigrants, and God knows where from. So he'd let her go with a promise to pay in kind. Because she was a slag. Only she hadn't come back that night for the screwing, when he was packed up ready to go.

So it seemed she'd tried to cheat the same way on someone tougher. And got herself killed for her pains.

He had a vague idea that the police paid for information. Sort of reward. And maybe the slag had a pimp who needed to even scores and would come up with bread too. Not that any information he had would likely lead to the killer. But he could identify her as 'Sheena' someone. She'd told him that much. Might not be her real name, but she'd be known locally. Sheena who hawked her arse round Soho.

The Thames Valley information number was again flashed on the screen. He seized a loose crayon and scrawled it on the cardboard stand-in for a window-pane. His torn jacket went on over the crumpled clothes he'd slept in, and then he faced the dilemma of letting in cold air or committing the number to memory.

The cardboard should stay until he'd struck rich on the Sheena business. Maybe he'd get some real glass then, or shout for a room that was bigger than this box. For the moment though, no change. He copied the figures on to the back of his left hand, scrabbled under his blanket for his coin bag, and went out to find a phone.

The call to Thames Valley force was recorded at Kidlington and telexed to the mobile Incident Room at Mardham. DI Jenner, snatching a late lunch of bacon, eggs and beans there, fell on the news with his own brand of mean enthusiasm. 'That's all? Just Sheena? A Soho prostitute?' he demanded of the air.

'She'll have a record with the Met,' Beaumont pointed out.

'And how long will they take to latch on to it?'

'No time at all once the Boss gets them moving,' Z consoled.

Jenner sniffed, not entirely on account of his cold. 'It's too much to hope they'll pin this artist fellow down, force a clear connection between him and Mardham.

'Get me through to Superintendent Yeadings,' he instructed the civilian telephonist. 'I want one of you two up in London keeping an eye on things.'

Beaumont locked glances with Z, and she shrugged behind the DI's back. It was all the same to her; nothing was happening at this end, and she wasn't enchanted with partnering Jenner. In any case, if anyone was sent to stand in with the Met, it would be the Boss who'd decide between them.

In the event Mike Yeadings was untraceable. Supposedly at home, he had left no contact number with his wife. Nan was a discreet woman, as the team appreciated. It was no coincidence that, within twenty minutes of being asked for, he cruised up to the caravan, parked and came strolling across, fully conversant with the latest development.

He received Jenner's request blandly, the two sergeants observing with interest his furry eyebrows rising in an expression of utter innocence. 'You feel a presence there is essential?'

'We should have someone on the spot. This artist could well be our man, not the Met's.'

'Mmm. I take your point. Perhaps, as it is so important, you should go there in person. Tomorrow, first thing.'

It took Jenner aback, but only for an instant. He almost managed to hide his pleasure at the prospect of coming the heavy with lesser ranks of the almighty Met. A further opportunity to make his mark.

'Very good, sir. If you think so. I'll advise the appropriate — er, authority.'

'Why do I get the impression,' Beaumont asked of Z while the Boss accompanied Jenner outside, 'that it was no vintage year when that skinny fart made inspector?'

'Language!'

'That cellulite-deprived emission of foul gas . . .'

'Right!' said Yeadings, reappearing abruptly on the scene, 'now let's consider our next move with regard to this Sheena.'

'Find out which of the locals was anywhere near London on the fateful Thursday,' Beaumont offered instantly.

'And subtract the seven whom we know returned on the last train,' Zyczynski added. 'Because none of them was carrying a body and, apart from Gayle Dawson, the only other woman was a Mrs Floyd, accompanied by her husband.'

'Right. They were the pair who picked up their car from the station parking lot.'

Beaumont nodded. 'We've had statements from all seven, and none recognized the dead woman's description. So we visit them again with her photo in case they've missed it on TV.'

The door opened and Jenner reappeared. He carried some papers and Yeadings' car keys which he handed over as if involved in some highly confidential transaction. The other two, familiar with the Boss's devious humour, silently questioned whether the charade was to cover private words shared with the DI outside, or the opportunity he'd made to speak with his two sergeants unheard.

'To work then,' said Jenner briskly. 'I'm still running this end for today. DS Beaumont, I want you to accompany me. DS *Jick*jinsky, you can lend a hand with the Incident Collator at Amersham.'

'I thought *you* were his blue-eyed girl,' Beaumont muttered as he reached into the cupboard for his windcheater.

'For a brief hour of fame. I've young Jasper to thank for this release. Sir doesn't care to be called my boyfriend.' She made a sour face at Beaumont, lifted her own sheepskin down and they went out together to where the DI was waiting by his car.

'You can use your own transport, Miss *Jink*jinsky,' he said coldly.

'Yes, sir.' As she drew away, following the other car, she passed the Boss's bulk filling the van doorway. His head was tilted to one side, his glance quizzical. Rather than be offloaded as a supernumerary, she would consider herself free to follow up Thursday's seven off the last train, with Yeadings' unvoiced approval.

Jenner held several simple equations as working principles. One of them connected prostitutes with disease and hard liquor; another assumed that any brains in the force were exclusively CID's, and mainly his own. It was therefore desirable to make a personal tour of the local licensed premises posing the same questions about the dead woman which had already been asked by uniform branch.

Beaumont, always willing to accept refreshment on official expenses, cheerfully fought his way to the bar through the lingering Sunday evening drinkers. He returned to Jenner's table against the wall balancing on a plastic tray his own pint with chaser and the DI's tomato juice.

Their entry had caused only a short break in the general hubbub, no more than three exits, and a few curious glances. No one approached them voluntarily with help, but what would you expect? Beaumont asked himself, we're foreigners, even if not The Filth as it would be in town. Out here, more on a par with gamekeepers and tax inspectors, for traditional locals and incoming wealth respectively.

'Well, get on with it,' Jenner prompted testily.

The DS wiped a moustache of foam off his upper lip, burped delicately and rose to approach the next table. He laid a copy of the photograph beside a wet ring from somebody's tankard.

'Questions, and more questions,' he said dolefully. 'You can't be half as tired of them as I am.

But the, poor lass is dead, and we have to do something about it.'

'Outsider,' said the spokesman damningly, staring at the dead face, while the others blanked out. 'Never seen her in me life.'

'Foreigner, yes. Sure to be,' Beaumont agreed. 'So must be whoever did it to her. Can't let outsiders get away with murder in a peace-loving little place like this, can we?'

There was a rumble of dubious assent. One man picked up the photograph and shook his head. 'Nothun to do with Mardham folk.'

'Still, she had to get here somehow. There's been mention of a van pulled into the pub yard some time after closing that night. Does that ring any bells?'

A fat chuckle escaped a man opposite. 'Happens sometimes. Coulda bin anythun. Bit of cattle movun, moonlight flit, swoppun labels on past-sell-date goods. There's plenty outside folks get up to that they doan want no one knowun of. They think us respectable folks are all abed by ar parst ten.'

'Cattle moving?' Beaumont picked up. That sounded possible. The van the Boss had mentioned was a large one, or had seemed so to a supine drunk in the shrubbery alongside. 'After dark, though? Rustlers?'

Guffaws all round. 'Naw, 'tain't the wild west here.'

'Well, aren't you going to put me right?'

There was some reluctance, then a little fellow

112

with a monkey-face piped up. 'It's them reggyla-tions. Can't move tested herds over public roads in case they get infected. But need to switch 'em for a fresh feed on other pasture. Done at night, none's the wiser. They're back again before the Ministry man comes round next.'

That sounded like a genuinely local enterprise to Beaumont, in which case he should be looking for a farm truck, and any link with the Soho tom was unlikely. However, it suggested another line of inquiry: the known night pursuits of rural villains. The chill of Thursday/Friday night wouldn't have put off poachers from checking on their traps. And poachers, if anyone, kept their eyes open and their approach quiet. There was just a chance one of them had observed the body being dumped, but kept quiet from fear of inviting prosecution.

'Thanks, fellers,' he said, straightening. And before they could demand liquid reward for their information, 'Sorry you couldn't help me. But, if anything comes to mind . . .' He wagged the photograph in their direction suggestively and moved on to the next table. Which was promptly vacated, with a drift towards the dartboard.

He hoped Jenner would be satisfied with a negative report before he'd destroyed any personal cred he might still have with the regulars of the Barley Mow. To save time later he re-ordered for them both.

As he turned to carry the filled glasses back he was halted by a burst of laughter. In the lounge across the bar from the snug the young glitterati of Mardham made up a group by the window. As he watched, a blonde girl rose and seemed to be saying good-bye. Jasper bobbed up beside her, imprisoned her against the wall between his outstretched arms and leaned in on her with some private exchange.

And the girl wasn't fancying his closeness. The others followed it with their eyes, the Field girl expectantly, her brother with some doubt. Beaumont strained to catch the taunting of a superior drawl foreign to the rural accent still in his ears, but no words came through the general buzz of conversation.

The young man's face was almost touching the girl's and she turned her head away. He pressed closer and kissed the exposed cheek.

With a rapid movement she had dodged under his arms, out of reach, and a cry went up from the table, half jeer, half cheer.

'Fifteen all,' called Rachel Field coolly.

'Thirty-fifteen to Gayle,' her brother corrected.

'Can't win 'em all,' Jasper shrugged it off. 'There'll be other times.'

Without a backward glance Gayle Dawson slid through between the tables and out by the lounge door.

Just kids' stuff, Beaumont told himself. A bit of ragging. But it was interesting that Jasper had to keep at it, forever shoring up his public image, even at risk of souring a possible new friendship.

Or did he think that sort of approach made him inescapably attractive?

Was it credible to see him as the stalker who'd shadowed the girl from the station? He certainly was abroad at the time, supposedly with friends at Pottersfield on the farther side of the Close. His prancing gait could have made a gorilla of him against the light of the single street lamp. Worth bearing in mind.

'Well?' Jenner demanded as he delivered their drinks to the table. 'What did you find out?'

'Nothing,' he admitted. 'Not a sausage.'

'So go on trying. And you'd better ease up on the drinking. There's the Feathers to visit after this. A rather better class of pub.'

Beaumont put on his wooden puppet's face. Pure Pinocchio, as Z called it. He could easily resign himself to another jar or two. There had to be some compensation for stringing along with poison-piss here.

Mercifully Jenner knocked off before the Feathers closed, using the excuse of an early rise tomorrow for his meeting with London's Met. It left Beaumont ample time to catch up on consumption before ringing the Boss at home as directed.

He didn't get the answering machine because the Superintendent was still up and working. Nan took the call and put it through to the study. 'Yeadings,' he answered on a hopeful note.

Beaumont repeated the negative report he'd given Jenner. Then he passed on in detail his

115

observations of the evening. Nothing was too in-significant for the Boss's vacuum-cleaning intel-ligence. He believed in getting to know the people and the scene, living in it and becoming a part, with members of his team taking on the nature of familiar furniture, so that witnesses relaxed and unthinkingly passed on more than they some-times realized they knew.

'Mmm,' he said at the recital's end. 'No plums, but not totally without interest. I'll see you at 9 A.M. tomorrow. That'll give you time to catch up with DS Zyczynski's report. We're hoping for a second sighting of the van from the pub yard, and there's some tittle-tattle on young Jasper's friends out at Pottersfield.'

But still no one locally had recognized the dead woman, bus crews and station staff included.

Seven

Donald Field sat with bowed head, elbows on knees, in his dressing-room lavatory, the only place where he could find any kind of privacy; in an exercise of will to create his own anaesthesia.

The head pain had been coming back, in deep throbs. Black bars on the vision. Stress, the London doctor had said; nothing organic. It was one thing to be told to take it easy, but another to shrug everything off. Where was ease? There were so many crowding emotions, such complications. And no real choice. Just a matter of going on the way he was driven.

In the end . . . But what would the end be? Unbelievable that there could ever be any way out.

He heard his wife's voice sharply calling his name. 'Donald? Donald!' Afraid perhaps that he was opting out. She was determined to go to this damn dinner party, if only for the twisted pleasure of watching the two of them at close quarters, yet divided by the terrible distances of civility, the monstrosity of neighbourly behaviour.

For him this evening would be unrelieved hell, endured in a strait-jacket and black tie. He must force himself to stand off, dehumanize himself, observing himself perform as though he was one of those out-of-body subjects who experience near death. It was too much to ask. He'd little hope of pulling it off. Meredith must have been out of her mind to invite them.

He heard the twins laughing in the garden under his window and fancied there was malice in the sound, at his expense. They had to have guessed by now. They'd witnessed enough of Phyllida's hellcat viciousness and his own powerlessness to fight back. They'd overheard him phoning Meredith, listening in on the extension. You would think they'd show some understanding, but the young were pitiless.

Inheriting their mother's genes? Yet they didn't openly take her side, kept off, appeared to regard both parents with equally sly dislike while milking each of what they regarded as their justly deserved necessities of life.

However wrapped up in their teenage self-discoveries, they were acutely aware of influences that threatened their own enjoyment. They had extended their contempt for him to cover Meredith too. In their eyes his passion for her would be reduced to the level of their own grubby little sexual experiments.

Once so lovable and innocent as small children; when had it all changed? They were aliens now, having passed through the stage of regarding him as hostile authority. They considered themselves equally adult, contemporaries. *Contempt*uaries! He was totally discounted as a person, diminished to an on-site facility used to sustain their lifestyle. And a subject for their black humour.

He steeled himself with a large whisky, then a second. The bile remained, but he had geared his mind to function with less raw feeling by the time all four gathered, left the house together, moved next door. They were greeted by Goodwin as a family. But weren't: each contained and isolated.

Perhaps the children — not children any more, but what else do you call them — offspring? *Away*-spring, perhaps — the two children were nearer being a pair, having youth in common, inexperience and undulled expectations. Above all, a common need to display themselves, to stand for something and rebel. In their free time they tended to drift around together, if only as a united front against the notion of parents; sometimes echoed each other, but were really rivals, private enemies.

Phyllida and he shunned contact. What intimacy there'd once been — hot lusting and the desperate need when young to believe oneself wanted — was long over. Custom had staled their sex together. Not only beauty, but hideousness, lay in the eye of the beholder: in the grating, soul-repudiating sourness of prolonged proximity, with love turned to loathing.

Helping her from her fur wrap — Phyllida still defied those who screamed against wearing dead animals, and the thing's cost reminded others that she counted, if only in hundreds of thousands sterling — helping her from its supple silkiness, he coldly observed the hard body; the salt-cellar hollow below the scraggy neck; sharp shoulders; claw-hands. Above gaunt cheekbones slatey eyes in deep sockets, and the long, harsh platinum hair loose about her shoulders, making her a peroxided parody of a witch from Macbeth.

He watched Phyllida pause at the softly lit hall mirror and smile into her reflection's eyes. She tossed her hair free, let it fall back, pale on the midnight blue of the Versace dress, ran her fingers sensuously through and adjusted its curtain half over one eye, in the style of a long-dead film star.

'Meredith,' she observed, gazing around, 'you've done something different. Had decorators in?' Thinking, this house isn't a patch on ours. She has no taste.

'Nothing's changed,' her neighbour murmured. There was no need to compete. She had the woman's husband.

All Dr Goodwin's life force seemed concentrated behind his eyes. Physically flaccid, almost catatonic, yet he had become hyper-observant. Passively he watched as Meredith's dinner party, immaculately conceived, disintegrated in a rout.

It wasn't only the alcohol which heightened contrasts and exaggerated the excesses. There was other fatal chemistry at work; deadly ingredients. None of us is safe, he thought. We pretend to have control, but it's a deception.

A masque. The anonymous figures begin stiffly

circling, each contained, inhibited. But from somewhere invisible steals in a seductive music that penetrates their apartness, ruptures seals. A formal obeisance, a few courtly advances, set figures, a single less seemly contact; still not beyond the point of no return. But gradually — secretly at first, but oh so dangerously — a quickening excitement, mounting urgency, a sudden wild need to dare further.

Which once I knew, but am no longer involved in, he thought. He felt no bitterness, no envy any more. He found it immeasurably sad that they should be entrapped physically, compelled into this *danse macabre* of deadly sins.

All of them? Principals were Meredith and the man. The others, wholly aware, supported like *corps de ballet* to balance the stage, converging on the dominant pair, then scattering to reveal them tragically alone, balefully spotlit.

For a moment he saw them both as strung puppets, inanimate without this driving force of sex. But inside — he knew, because he still could remember — there would be raw bleeding. Any pain his love for Meredith still permitted him was on her behalf, that she must continue to have feelings. Only himself in creeping coma.

He could still appreciate her beauty; and, with regret, her passion. Tonight she was superb, the tawny hair fiery with life, coiled on top of the tiny, proud head with its striking features; overlarge grey eyes; queenly nose; curved, teasing mouth; kitten chin. A voluptuous body moulded

121

over fine bones. So touchable. Magnificent vitality held in precarious check.

He closed his eyes, then opened them on Field's vulpine gaze, the rapid shuttering that concealed his searing contempt. The man had been drinking even before he came. Did the occasion demand such false courage?

Discount me, he silently commanded his replacement. I am not here. I have more affinity with the dead.

Malcolm Barrow had not yet surrendered to the evening. Resentful of his brother-in-law, wary of his sister's overt disillusion with himself, he started hesitantly, hanging on the outskirts of the earlier conversations, ran the tip of his tongue over dry lips, waiting for the alcohol to talk through. Eventually his charisma would awake and take over. And who would be enchanted? The new girl, Gayle, obviously.

But wasn't there more credit to be gained from winning round the others who already knew him? — who had been enchanted before and then fallen away. All in good time. One would see.

He assessed what was there to work on. Goodwin had withdrawn into the fastness of his shrivelled mind; had abdicated, leaving Field to take over physically as host. And flaunted as consort by Meredith.

There was a flashiness in the way the man opened his hosts' bottles, a contemptuous flicking of the released cork. But smooth — so smooth — as he offered the wine swathed in a starched white napkin. Barrow imagined the muscled, dark-matted chest concealed under the fine, pin-tucked cambric and black worsted. A male scent came off him to match the lusting eyes as they sought his lover's. God, but the man was sex-driven. It was pitiable what demonic slaves women could reduce their prey to.

Sufficient to each other, Meredith and Field were on orbit beyond his charming; Goodwin stoned on his private miseries. There remained the three other women and the boy for intellectual diversion. He continued to observe them.

Phyllida's eyes were half closed under their deep lids, but a dark gleam betrayed how she watched — and mocked — her husband's subjugation, while offering no protective or possessive counter-action. Let him get on with the distasteful business she had long opted out of. With other interests, having whiphands elsewhere, she seemed to ignore the others, unconcerned what her children might pick up of their elders' inclinations.

If young Rachel was, as ever, self-absorbed, in love with her own near-neurosis and her anorexic body, Colin at least was sparkily conscious of all that was afoot. Such intense predatory interest would have seemed precocious in Malcolm's own pre-twenties, but not today. The boy's fascination with sex was both personal and general, sufficiently detached to appreciate, even provoke, the adults' dangerous absorption in each other. Playing hassle was clearly to the boy's taste. A manipulator, Malcolm recognized. Colin was someone to beware of, too similar to one level of himself.

And lastly he came to consider Gayle, the outsider and Meredith's false excuse for launching this blatant statement of her takeover of another woman's husband.

What did Gayle make of this? — blonde, almost Nordic in build, a fresh-faced innocent whom he'd watched for days from behind the curtains as she came and went in the Close, conceiving a desire to become her mentor.

Tonight her simplicity was complicated with make-up and a broad, stiff bow of black organza tying back her shining hair high on her crown, the ends a golden candy floss spread over her shoulders. Her wide-set blue eyes, under dramatically darkened and lengthened brows, were outlined in a way that suggested experience. It forced him to review his plans for her. He must watch more carefully now, paying attention to all she said. Which was little enough. She answered questions, gave the required account of herself, smiled, listened. And secretly recoiled?

Colin Field was speaking. The silkily taunting voice came at him out of a void. Barrow had no idea how that conversation had begun. '. . . but then I'm always attracted to older women.'

He shared his impish, dark gaze equally between Meredith and the girl. Was he goading his father, entering the lists as his rival, or could he have referred to Gayle, surely by no more than two years his senior?

Neither woman betrayed a flicker of reaction. By now they were deep into the territory of *double entendre*.

The music playing softly as background throughout dinner had ended. Barrow made some technical suggestion about looped tapes, and Field was scornful about the inescapable repetition of hotel muzak. Colin, with a puckish 'Permiso?', pushed back his chair and went through the archway to the Goodwins' music centre, laying a hand gently on Meredith's bare shoulder as he passed behind.

He searched through a case of CDs, switched across from the stack of records on the turntable, and the strains of Mozart stole over the candlelit room.

But not *A Little Night Music*. Barrow, no lover of classical scores, recognized *Così fan tutte* and the mischievous intent behind the boy's selection. He glanced sideways at Meredith who this time replied to the taunt with a wicked smile.

Goodwin sat still, eyes closed, not so much refusing credence, but as though he simply breathed in the liquid notes like the bouquet of a fine brandy. Fool! Impossible that he should miss what his wife was up to under his very nose.

Meredith crumpled her napkin. 'Shall we — ?' and rose, Field leaning over to draw her chair away. They all followed suit; the sounds of heavy chairs scraping the parquet scarred the music.

125

There was a drift back through the archway to the dimly lit lounge. Everyone was quite high, subject to the vibrant atmosphere.

Rachel came last after a little, noticeable pause. Her long, clinging skirt, slit to mid-thigh, was a muddy charcoal, anything but balletic, and the matching chiffon tunic she wore above accentuated her sharp frame. Her patchwork make-up — silvered eyelids, lilac triangles under her cheekbones — made a zombie of her. In slow motion, with a long, catwalk undulation, her jutting pelvis picked up the music. Rachel began to dance in a strange, self-administered hypnosis.

A cobra swaying to the reedy music of a pipe, Barrow thought, fascinated despite his cynicism, despite knowing it was merely a dysfunctional's bid for attention. The girl was asexual. He'd personal evidence of that.

The hired maid brought in coffee and, while Meredith poured and Field circulated with liqueurs, Rachel moved sinuously between their chairs mocking his movements, strings of tiny coloured beads swinging from the circlet binding her head.

The party broke up early; had really been falling apart since the first moment they were all assembled. The meal, excellent as it was, counted for little but garnish to the central action, and no one was in doubt about that. Prurient curiosity might have kept them together longer but there was a limit put on their voyeurism by the lovers' clear impatience.

Uncritical, barely embarrassed, the guests permitted themselves to be implicitly dismissed while the pair were still only marginally out of control. They said goodnight loudly on the doorstep, calling out to each other as they dispersed to either side of the Goodwins' gateway.

Field made no pretence of leaving, simply stood in the kitchen doorway, jacket off and a tea towel tucked into the waistband of his braided trousers, ostensibly poaching on the duties of a perfectly efficient Bosch dishwasher.

Colin left, trailing behind mother and sister, obliged to see them safely indoors before he should double back and follow Gayle. She, pulling her coat collar high about her ears and relieved that the disagreeable evening had ended so soon, turned into the unlit driveway of Polders. And was instantly, intuitively, aware of being watched.

Someone was waiting ahead, invisible in the shadows under the trees. She kept to the far side, moving on swiftly past the danger point. She heard a rustle of dry leaves and the tearing sound of thorns as some larger body thrust through the undergrowth. She began to run, and was fearfully half-way to the safety of the porch light when he lumbered up behind and gripped her shoulder.

A huge man. The one she'd glimpsed against the passage lamp when he followed her from the station. On the night of the murder.

'Please,' he said throatily. 'Please, you must help.' And his grip was a steel vice.

Dr Goodwin sat wanly waiting for the moment to move. It was perverse, but for tonight he granted himself that one indulgence, that Meredith should stay unsatisfied. He waited for the clatter in the kitchen to cease, then got up slowly and went through to them. They were locked together, breathing hard, Meredith bent backwards against the sink, Field's hands already fumbling in her skirt.

Goodwin stood in the doorway to let himself be noticed. It was unreal, like watching some scene on television when these gropings held up the plot: time to toddle off and put the kettle on, come back for the car chase and the villain's bloody finish.

He saw horror rock the man back, breaking through his alcoholic haze. Meredith, raising a hand unsteadily to her head, seemed to be waking after deep narcosis.

He spoke from another lifetime. 'I'll lock up,' he told her. 'Leave everything and go to bed, my dear. You're tired. The dinner was a great success.'

There was a silence when it might have gone any way. But normality broke in, habit stronger than present folly. Meredith moved apart, wiping moisture from her chin with the knuckles of one hand. Field had no choice but to release her.

Goodwin saw him out. Shattered by the confrontation, Field fought to contain a fury he felt burning to explosion point. He stumbled off, mumbling drunkenly, away from the direction of his home.

Her lover was still reflected in Meredith's distracted eyes. Cheated of her climax, she was off balance, between two worlds in collision. But she reached out for a familiar pattern. Under this roof she was still a wife.

Goodwin doubted she would sleep at once and was filled with pity for her. He might have gently kissed her then but held back. It could have told her too much.

Meredith started to speak but he held up a hand. 'Not now. Tomorrow perhaps.' He smiled at the irony of his own words.

She drew a long breath, said goodnight and left the bright kitchen, in unnatural control. He heard her moist right hand squeak faintly on the polished banister rail as she went up. He put out the lights, stood silent a moment in the dark, then rattled the door bolts, snibbed up the deadlock and quietly let himself out, pulling the door shut against the ball of his thumb.

The dank chill struck through his dinner jacket. In the right-hand pocket his fingers encountered the little packet. He moved on into the shadows of neighbouring trees, took the track through no. 1's side garden, brushed his way past the spinney and scrambled down to the river-bank.

At roughly the point where only days before he had bent over a young woman's lifeless body, he paused and sat a while on the damp grass. Now there were no plastic tapes to keep the place private. Time had moved on. Before long her death would be forgotten.

His heart was heavy for what she had suffered, in life and in the losing of it. If he had been a religious man he would have prayed for her.

But he wasn't, so instead he quietly wept; for her, for himself, for Meredith, for the whole human condition.

Eight

After Monday the police presence in Mardham was to be scaled down. From any viewpoint results had been disappointing. The villagers' brief period of cooperation was over. They wished it to be on record that they'd volunteered all they could; meaning all they'd intended.

As ever, there were those who instinctively scuttled away from any questioning, and a few others who yearned to be identified, however uselessly, with the scandal of a murder case. Two opposite kinds: the guilt-ridden and the self-righteous, Yeadings assumed. Or simply the self-effacing and the pushy?

In the two pubs, in the Tea Shoppe and on the street, gossip offered several versions of what the fingertip searches had yielded. Some were scabrous, others merely comic, because everyone knew what went on along the river-bank, and that apart from larking youngsters and the occasional Peeping Tom there had been no previous scavenging of the area.

As a result a range of miscellaneous objects from the mundane to the frankly unpalatable had been collected, bagged, numbered, dated and solemnly signed for at the Area station. Of those submitted to expert examination some

131

were retained against a slender hope of future usefulness and the remainder discarded. Overall locally there was negligible progress to date.

Within the forensic pathology department tests continued and Petri dishes were brooded over. Nevertheless little was now known of the dead woman beyond her general health: the accelerated wear and tear expected of her apparent mode of life, the markedly carbon-coated lungs of a heavy smoker and early evidence of varicose veins. She was not pregnant and had never given birth.

Superintendent Yeadings, still neglecting his desk to circle the locals like a benevolent sheep-dog, was obliged to accept that when the case sparked into life it would probably not do so at the Mardham end. The dumped body appeared to have no links with the village, and such trickle of help as the Incident Room had received was drying up. It might as well be closed down and made available for serious crimes flourishing else-where in Thames Valley. He regretted that it was DI Jenner he had directed towards what now appeared the active end of the inquiry.

So it was a startling message that reached him at the Feathers during 'supping up' after closing time on Monday. Yeadings took it himself on the landlord's private phone.

'Who?' he demanded brusquely, covering his free ear with a large paw to cut out raucous noises from departing drinkers.

'Gayle Dawson?'

That was the young student Z had mentioned: long blonde hair; blue eyes; five feet eight or nine; played the flute in some London youth orchestra. Most notably, had complained of being followed home late at night from Mardham station. On the very night of the Sheena woman's murder!

'So . . . What?' He could barely make out the repeated details. 'Poor young woman. Where? Right, I'll be over just as soon as I've contacted Littlejohn . . . No, don't. I'll speak to him myself.'

This time they would have to call in the pathologist in person to confirm death. Anything else was out of the question.

Always mindful of his own womenfolk, Yeadings was sickened at the thought of so hideous an end to a quiet evening walk in the country. But why had the girl chosen that place, already infamous as the haunt of a killer? Hadn't she learnt better from her earlier scare?

One thing he could be glad of: that it had come to notice so soon, not waiting like the first corpse for discovery in daylight. With Beaumont and Z on the spot and an exclusion zone marked off sharpish, there was every chance of traces to be picked up. Most murderers left a signature behind, but it could take a deal of luck and dogged hard work to fit it to the hand that made it. Far too often wasted time and the rival demands of other investigations allowed the outlines to become obscured.

He caught Dr Littlejohn at home, on the point of going to bed. 'Thought an early night seemed too good to be true,' the pathologist grunted. 'Not still raining out your way, is it? You can expect me along in thirty minutes.'

'Gayle Dawson,' Yeadings repeated to himself, settling into his Rover for the few hundred yards he had to go. Not to the river-bank but to the house in Orchard Close. Which was the one with a name instead of a number, he remembered from the reports.

Polders — that was it. He could safely leave the body to his two sergeants. For himself the first essential was to discover just why a girl recently scared by a stalker should invite danger by walking alone in such a lonely and dangerous place. But perhaps not alone. So who would she have been in the company of?

He frowned, trying to recapture from rapidly scanned notes what the woman's name was that Gayle lodged with. As he drew up at the stone pillars of the driveway it came suddenly back to him: Mrs Olive George, an elderly widow.

Poor old thing; it would be a shock for her too.

The lady was in her night gear, a warm fleecy dressing-gown rather shorter than the daunting starched garment underneath. She wore her frizzy grey hair in a single plait down her back, and stray tendrils teased out over her ears to show she had already been to bed when disturbed by the policewoman still in attendance.

'What's happened?' she demanded in a rush,

as soon as Yeadings had introduced himself. He fielded the question by asking for her student lodger, but Gayle wasn't back yet.

'She went out to dinner with Dr Goodwin and his wife next door. It was kind of Meredith to arrange for the young people to meet one another.'

'Does she have children of the same age?'

'Oh no, it seems they can't have any of their own. It's been a great grief to them. But the Fields, on their far side, have nineteen-year-old twins, a boy and a girl. So Meredith invited them all, to help Gayle settle in.

'I suppose I should have done something of the sort myself,' she regretted, 'but I rarely do any entertaining nowadays. I don't even provide meals for Gayle. She's supposed to share my kitchen and cater for herself, but I find she gets most of her meals out.'

She was chattering too much, one sure sign of shock. Yeadings had the impression that, normally living alone, she had become unaccustomed to balanced conversation. But a kindly lady. Gayle had been lucky over that.

'And when were you expecting her back?'

'I wasn't. She has her own key, you see. I mean, she *is* twenty-one and she always insists I shouldn't wait up. Actually, this is the first time I hadn't done.' Mrs George blew her nose to prevent her tears showing.

'After the policewoman came and told me Gayle had found this other body, I wanted to ring the Goodwins, but it seems I shouldn't. Fancy her going for a walk at night. Surely she wasn't alone? And nobody will tell me who it is that's been killed.'

She stopped to draw breath. 'I really don't understand. If Gayle left at the same time as the others, the party must have ended early, before eleven.'

'Was that unusual?'

'Oh yes. They're so hospitable. They'd normally go on till two or three in the morning. Especially since Dr Goodwin became semi-retired. Meredith is a wonderful hostess, and her brother helps. He's living there with them at present.'

'His name?'

'Barrow. Maurice, I think. No; no, I'm wrong. It's Malcolm. He's in his mid-thirties but doesn't seem to go out to work.'

'Tell me about Gayle.' Yeadings led her back to the main subject. 'Was it her habit to walk alone at night?'

'Indeed no. She has a little car, but after all — going just next door. It would have been silly, wouldn't it?'

'But she'd had an unpleasant experience only a few days ago. Didn't she tell you about that?'

'Unpleasant? Do you mean she'd seen something to do with that terrible murder?' Mrs George pulled her dressing-own closer and shuddered.

'It was the same night. Someone followed her

back from the station, after the last train down from London.'

'She said nothing to me about it. I do remember she seemed a little flushed when she came in. I put it down to excitement over her music. Or from hurrying. Her car hadn't come back from its servicing, so she'd been on foot, you see.'

To reassure the old lady, Yeadings assumed his comfortable teddy-bear face. 'Perhaps it disturbed her less than we supposed. Which might account for her strolling down to the river tonight.'

'I couldn't say at all,' Mrs George assured him. 'She's not a rash young woman. But it doesn't seem very sensible to me, in view of what happened there only last week.'

'No doubt she had her reasons. Perhaps we'll find out about that from my sergeant.'

'You haven't told me who it was, this — body that she's found. I mean, is it someone I'd know?'

'I won't say for the present, Mrs George, until we've learnt a little more.'

He declined the offer of a hot drink, assured her that Gayle would be back before long, took his leave and drove to the bridge over the river, noting that Dr Littlejohn had not wasted time. His car was already parked on the verge behind Zyczynski's.

From that vantage point he saw repeated the scene of early last Friday, with white overalled figures slowly moving in the glare of arc lights. He made out the pathologist's bulky figure bent over the black huddle on the ground. Even soaked in river water, the triangle of white dress shirt stood out against the black of the rest.

Formally dressed for dinner, Yeadings noted. For dinner and then death. Poor devil.

And no sign of Gayle. She'd still be with Zyczynski in the caravan. Time he went there himself and found out what it was all about. What on earth had possessed the girl to take such a risk?

The hard fingers had bitten into her shoulder. Instinctively Gayle's arms flew up to protect her face. But the expected blow didn't come. She stood cowering, yet even then ashamed of her own fear. She tried to steady her voice as she croaked, 'Who — who . . . ?'

But she saw, once she swung round. It was the man who lived next door with his mother. Harry Snelling. A bit simple, though no one had actually said so: the Snellings were still fairly new in the district, and judgement was being reserved. Yet there was a feeling of distrust, and Jasper Wichall had once described him as a lunatic.

And certainly this was the man she'd glimpsed under the lamplight, the one who'd frightened her before.

He let go of her now like a hot coal. 'Kittypuss,' he said. 'She's run off. Got lost, like as not.'

She didn't know whether to believe him; he looked distressed. Or mentally disturbed? It could be a trick. But there came a soft wail from somewhere in the shrubbery, followed by the rustling of dry leaves.

'There!' he whispered urgently. 'Got to catch her. She's only a tiddly wee thing.'

He seemed to expect her to help. Surely there was no harm in the man? Already he had crashed back into the undergrowth, bent on retrieving the kitten. Which was bound to tear off ahead, terrified at the lumbering pursuit.

She could head it off, try coaxing it to her. So she'd gone ahead a little way and begun to approach from the opposite direction, through bracken and brambles that Mrs George had allowed to grow wild behind the taller rhododendrons.

And the little grey shape had darted off full tilt back across the driveway, round the east side of the house towards the open water meadows beyond. There was a back fence there at the far end, but no door in it. The kitten was up and over in a flash, and they were left empty-handed behind.

The man moaned aloud, then shambled off under the pergola dripping with tangled branches of untrimmed rambler roses. Gayle followed more slowly and saw him lifting out loose boards from the fence between the two properties. It must have been an access he'd used before. In his own garden he blundered towards the rear. Only posts with two strands of wire marked its end and he forced his way between. After that were a few yards of tussocky grass and then the gloom of the spinney before the river-bank. He plunged on, calling, 'Kittypuss! Kitty!' Gayle hesitated, relieved that he'd left her alone, once convinced she would help.

Surely his mother would hear and come out to fetch him back. But perhaps, like old Mrs George, she sometimes took a sleeping tablet and was already well under. The way the man had stumbled across the uneven terrain in the dark, he could easily trip and get injured.

Despite herself she followed, and heard his triumphant, 'There! I seen her!'

Her coat caught up by snagging brambles, she was some seconds behind him as she forded the ditch before the higher river path. His huge silhouette loomed over her. She saw his arms humped across the squirming form of the kitten which he held close to his chest.

His face was turned away as he stared at something in the water, a dark shape that bobbed slowly some three feet from the bank. 'No,' he begged it, backing away. 'No!' Then before she could get close to see what alarmed him he had turned and fled, stumbling along the path towards the bridge.

The dark bundle gently rose and dipped, rose and dipped with some surface disturbance of the water. Gayle went close, shivering in the cold. She bent and reached out a hand but the thing was too far off.

She remembered the dead woman and how afterwards the river bed had been dragged here. A cramping fear paralysed her for a moment. But she had to make sure. She couldn't run off now and be haunted forever.

She clambered back along the bank, looking for some broken-off branch to hook the object with. The trees there were all young and sappy, resisting her efforts to break parts off. Then she stumbled on an object in the grass. A walking-stick?

No, it was one of the posts which the police had used to mark off the zone with tape. Bollards, she'd heard Jasper call them, making it sound like a swear word.

It had a blunt end but she managed to hook it under one corner of the floating bundle and eased it slowly, heavily, to the water's edge.

And it was what she'd dreaded seeing. The body of a man. But, far worse, because when she rolled it over it was someone she knew, had talked with, and had rather liked for his old-fashioned courtesy. But how had he come to fall in here, out in the dark, and so near to home? Only minutes after she'd left him there!

Through the waterlogged cloth his body was still warmer than the water. But quite dead. One of his eyes had failed to close and stared up through a trailing strand of weed in an obscene wink. His mouth was set in an agonized rictus. Perhaps this was a stroke? He would have hated to be seen so.

It was unbelievable: Dr Goodwin, who had barely drunk anything all evening, the only one sober apart from herself.

'I had to leave him on the edge,' she explained tearfully to Z who was first to follow up her 999 call from the phone box by the bridge.

'He was too heavy to lift out, with his clothes all waterlogged. But I checked he wasn't breathing. Well, I knew, you see. He'd been face down in the shallows, half-submerged. Oh, I'm so sorry, poor man. He seemed such a nice, gentle sort of person.'

'You'd met him?'

So had Z. She remembered him from the earlier death. He had left the murder scene before she arrived, but she'd been to see him later with Jenner: an under-sized man with a melon-shaped head in which small, screwed up features looked lost in the middle; wire-framed half-lenses; a few wisps of dark hair smeared across a high receding forehead. Physically unattractive, to her mind. But yes, she'd agree he seemed gentle enough, even abstracted.

With the arrival of a patrol car, Z had left the uniformed branch to set up the exclusion zone. Her concern was to get Gayle into the comparative warmth of the Incident Van and stave off the effects of shock with a hot drink. Better there, isolated from others' reactions, than take her immediately back home. What a witness said in the first dazed moments was often of greater value than when there'd been time for reflection. And a sudden death could turn out to be more than it seemed on the surface.

The constable on night duty there produced a blanket, switched on the kettle and set out mugs for the universal remedy.

'Now,' Z told the girl, 'when you're ready, tell me how you happened to find him.'

'There was a dinner party at his house.' Gayle paused, frowning. 'Mrs Goodwin wanted me to meet some neighbours, the Fields.'

'That was kind of her.'

'I thought so at first, but . . .'

'Go on. Wasn't it really like that?'

'Oh, she introduced me around. I'd met Colin and Rachel already.'

'Wasn't there another young man? I saw four of you together yesterday.'

'Jasper Wichall. He hadn't been invited. Maybe the Goodwins don't know him so well. He lives at the far end of the Close.'

'Sorry, I interrupted. There was this dinner party. It wasn't quite what you were expecting.'

Gayle was silent, then shook her head. She was fighting with some kind of repugnance. It seemed to Z that she felt ashamed of something. Then suddenly she broke through her reluctance.

'It was horrible. I couldn't understand what was going on. After a while it was as if everyone else knew something I didn't. Things they said seemed to have a second meaning. They were getting at each other somehow. Everyone except the doctor, that is.'

'He was odd man out?'

'Not exactly. I was the outsider. He seemed to

143

understand what was going on, but he didn't take part. Meredith — his wife — she's very beautiful, you know.'

Gayle stopped there as though that was a complete explanation.

'A good hostess?' Z prompted.

That seemed to throw the girl. 'She — the food was really good, yes. A lot of wine and that, too much really. But I never have more than one glass. It doesn't suit me.'

'Everyone else was drinking?'

'Even the twins, who were supposed to be on cola. But they'd hidden a gin bottle under the table. Dr Goodwin left his wine untouched, but he poured himself a large brandy just before we broke up.'

'So who did most of the drinking?'

Gayle shook her head again. 'They were all about the same. The Fields, Meredith and her brother, I guess. Maybe I've given the wrong impression. I mean, nobody was falling-about drunk, just sort of — larger than life. And they all lived locally. No one needed to drive home.'

'They do say "in vino veritas", so maybe you got a true picture of these people. Did you like them?'

The last question came suddenly and caught the girl unprepared. 'I — like I said, Meredith was very attractive.'

She hadn't actually said that. Only that she was very beautiful. Z gave a little smile. 'So, like all the others, you were attracted.'

'Mrs Field wasn't.' Gayle spoke abruptly. Z couldn't miss the sudden distaste in her voice.

'Neighbourly jealousy perhaps?'

'Not really. It was — more scornful than that. I can't explain. As though she had the laugh on her. You'd have thought she didn't care.'

'I don't understand. Care about what, Gayle?'

The girl shook her head. 'Her husband being so besotted.' The words came tumbling out, wretchedly.

'Was Mrs Goodwin teasing him on?'

Gayle gave a short bark of laughter. 'Not teasing, no. Nothing so lighthearted. There's no polite way of putting it. If we'd stayed on longer, I think she'd have torn her clothes off in front of everybody. They could hardly hold back from each other; Meredith Goodwin and Mr Field.'

'I see. So how about Dr Goodwin in all this?'

'That was strange. He seemed very fond of her — Meredith, I mean. He couldn't help but see how things were. But he must have known about it, because he did nothing to stop it going so far. He was just — very sad, I think.'

Sad enough to end it by taking his own life? Z suppressed a shiver. 'Were you the last to leave?'

Gayle straightened and accepted the mug handed her. She clasped her hands round its comforting warmth, relieved at the shift of subject. 'We all left together. It would be about a quarter to eleven. They'd had a village girl in for waitress service. She'd left some time before, soon after serving the coffee.'

'And Dr Goodwin saw you all off at the door. With his wife.'

'Yes.'

But they hadn't all left. Barrow, Meredith's brother had previously sloped off upstairs. Gayle remembered too Donald Field lounging in the doorway to the kitchen, jacket off and a tea towel tucked into the waistband of his dress trousers. And now she recalled something that hadn't quite registered at the time. Behind him the dishwasher had just clunked to a stop. There was nothing left to help with but their last set of glasses.

Z saw there was something else, and that Gayle wasn't going to admit it. Perhaps later. So continue the story from there. 'Did the Fields see you home?'

'No, we went opposite ways. It was only a few steps, but when I turned into the drive —'

'At Polders?'

'Yes. It's a bit spooky there. All those trees and that wall of evergreens. I heard — or felt — somebody in there watching me.'

But she'd left Goodwin at his house, and the others had turned off to go the other way. Someone else, then, who hadn't been at the dinner party.

'It was Harry Snelling. He'd lost his cat in Mrs George's garden. It really was there. I saw it, heard it. Only it escaped into the fields at the back. And we went after it, through the garden of no. 1, where Harry lives, because there's no way out at the back of Polders . . .'

'You chased it right down to the river?'

'It wasn't all that far. One corner of no. 1's garden stops just short of the trees. Then there's a drainage ditch and a bank up to the path. Harry had got the cat in his arms by the time I got there and was staring into the water. It was quite dark but I could see something floating.'

'And Harry?'

Gayle pulled the blanket closer round her shoulders. 'He ran away.'

'Once he knew you'd seen the body? Leaving you alone?'

'Yes.' Her voice was low.

'Anything else?'

Gayle looked up, horror mirrored in her eyes. 'I recognized him, you know. The man who followed me from the station last Tuesday; that was Harry Snelling. I'm not sure, but last night —'

'You think he was waiting for you in Polders garden, and the cat business was just a ruse?'

Gayle hid her face in her hands. 'I don't know. It could have been.'

'How long did all that cat-chasing take?' Beaumont demanded, when Z had escorted Gayle back into Mrs George's care at Polders and the three Thames Valley detectives had met to compare notes.

'She couldn't say. Checking the time is not what the general public do in moments of panic. But the 999 call was logged at 11.21 P.M. Say a minimum of seven or eight minutes for the girl

147

to pull the body in and run the fifty yards to the phone box. which just gives leeway for Goodwin to have left the house, gone directly across the fields at the rear, and reached the river while Gayle and Snelling were hunting through the gardens.'

'With time enough to kill himself, or meet someone and get killed? To my mind that's running it a bit close.' This was from Yeadings. 'How did he die?'

'Littlejohn's not saying officially,' Beaumont offered, 'but he looked a bit shattered at recognizing a colleague. Sniffed at the man's mouth, so my money's on poison. Something very rapid.'

'We could have a suicide,' Yeadings said thoughtfully, 'but if so it's an unusually business-like dispatch. People normally like to linger a while and consider, blur the edges of their going.'

'Which he may have spent the whole evening on. Gayle described him as "withdrawn" and "sad",' Z reminded them. 'Perhaps' he'd taken a tranquillizer first, with whatever would provide a speedy end later. As a practising doctor, he'd have had access to all kinds of drugs.'

'And he could have done it on the river's edge, so that he'd topple in and hope to sink. Going with the flow, sort of thing. We'll know soon enough,' Beaumont said. 'Littlejohn's doing the post-mortem in the morning.' He looked at his watch. 'At 11 A.M. That's today now.'

'Meanwhile, we have to inform the family,' Yeadings said heavily. 'I'll do that myself. I have a WPC standing by, to stay on with Mrs Goodwin if necessary, but I'd like you along too, Z. With eyes and ears wide open. In view of the girl's account of Meredith Goodwin's behaviour earlier tonight.'

Nine

It was Malcolm Barrow in pyjamas who answered the door, leaving the chain on. He was sharply suspicious of the three night visitors, but when the WPC moved forward and the porch light shone on her uniform hat he froze in alarm. 'What's up?'

Yeadings identified himself and asked to speak to the man's sister. Apprehensive, as the questions he fired were left unanswered, Barrow unchained and let them in. By then Meredith was already leaning over the hall gallery to listen. She came downstairs unsteadily, tying the sash of her satin bathrobe, her eyes heavy with sleep. She seemed at first unable to take in what the quiet voice was telling her.

'Stanley? But he's in his room upstairs. You mustn't disturb him. He's been unwell.'

Yeadings signalled to the woman's brother. 'Perhaps you would make sure?'

'Something's happened,' she said suddenly, making an effort to bring her wits together. 'That's what you've come about. Something's wrong, isn't it? Someone's been hurt. Who — ?'

'Stanley's not here,' Barrow called down. 'His bed hasn't been slept in.'

Even then she didn't believe. 'But he locked

up and came upstairs right after me. I heard him. I — think.'

Then both hands went up to cover her face. She shot up out of the chair Yeadings had led her to, and went rigid. 'Oh, dear God, no! What has he done? *Donald!*'

The policewoman moved swiftly forward to support her as she swayed, but Meredith gave her a savage glare and raised an arm to thrust her off.

Yeadings, an old hand at delivering bad news, was taken aback. She was Lady Macbeth struck centre-stage in a dramatic pose, the huge eyes flaring and the proudly held head framed in russet curls that tumbled about her shoulders. Histrionic, yes; and yet he felt sure her shock was genuine.

Or were his loins mocking his head? Now that was a question he'd not needed to ask himself for long enough!

Discreetly Z had taken over. 'Can I get you something? Brandy? Tea?'

The woman already had some kind of hold on herself, perhaps too rigidly. Her voice came through clenched teeth. 'I've had enough alcohol tonight. Tea, then. Malcolm, will you see to it? . . . No, go along. I'll be all right on my own.'

She sank back into her chair. 'What has Stanley done?' she asked hollowly.

'It's bad news,' Yeadings told her. 'The worst, I'm afraid.'

There was a silence through which the long-case clock dragged its slow ticking. Yeadings became aware of the stillness of the room they were in, disordered with evidence of last night's entertaining: cushions crushed; ashtrays unemptied; a stack of records on the floor by the music centre; by the side of an armchair a half-full bottle of Courvoisier.

'Dead, then? It's *Stanley* who's dead?'

Who else was she afraid for? This Donald whose name she'd cried out in anguish? He'd be Field, the man she'd been making a dead set at, according to young Gayle. Had her first thought been that her husband had gone out after him with murder in mind?

Again she surprised him, rocking over her knees, arms clasped tightly across her breasts, lips and eyes pursed. Only a thin thread of sound escaped from the back of her throat, a muffled keening.

To ease his own tension as much as hers, Yeadings started talking in a low voice, explaining how Gayle had gone to the river to find the Snellings' cat. She had seen Dr Goodwin floating in the shallows where he must have fallen in.

'Drowned?' Meredith asked on a painfully indrawn breath, unbelieving.

'We can't tell yet. Dr Littlejohn's there. He'll find out what happened.'

Meredith sat up stiffly, her face a tragic mask. 'I know what happened. He's killed himself. I don't want to hear any more. I can't stand it. *Sta-a-a-nley!*'

From Barrow they found out the name of her

own GP and rang his number. He promised to be across as soon as he'd dealt with a local emergency. His wife would get a room ready for Meredith if she wished. It seemed she had no scarcity of friends.

Yeadings and Z withdrew, leaving the WPC. The grieving woman seemed as unconscious of her presence as of their departure. She had closed her eyes again and the anguished rocking restarted.

At the front door Yeadings demanded of Barrow, 'Has she a friend you can get to look in until Dr Forrest gets here? Maybe the woman from next door?'

Fleeting expressions crossed the man's face. His voice, when the answer escaped him was gravelly with sarcasm. 'What, Hecate herself? God, that would be real trouble!'

And his brother-in-law's death wasn't? Yeadings' dark eyebrows soared.

'Heckitty?' Z queried as they went out again into the night. The name sounded vaguely familiar. Some comic character out of Dickens?

'The Queen of Witches,' her boss said shortly.

'Now what,' he demanded of her in the car, 'did you make of all that?'

'Complicated relationships,' Z said sombrely, thankful for once that her own were so simple.

'These are the bare facts,' Littlejohn said offhandedly much later that day. 'Yours the task of fleshing them out. I'm glad to have no part in it.'

He had none of his usual bonhomie on producing his findings. This new brusqueness covered a personal hurt. He had worked alongside Goodwin and admired his calm dependability. Yeadings was sure he could have told more than was there on the page of initial notes.

He had merely indicated the poison found to have killed within minutes. As he'd guessed on first sight of the body, Goodwin had used cyanide, uncommon enough. It belonged to an earlier age, with the suicides of wartime prisoners. Prescribed drugs were more usual in these days, and easily on hand for a doctor. But Goodwin hadn't chosen to die in his own bed, slowly succumbing in his sleep. He'd left his house and opted — if indeed this was a DIY job — for a rapid, painful and anonymous end in a place where the first to come across his body would most likely be strangers.

Littlejohn had set aside liver, spleen and brain for further study. There was a very small volume of fluid in the lungs, not necessarily from the river. Later analysis would decide its nature.

In general the doctor had been sound in wind and limb. There was no heart disease. No abnormal cell formations, either benign or malignant, had been found. The liver tended towards cirrhosis but its condition was not critical. He had consumed a meal some two and a half to three hours before death. There were scattered naevi, particularly inside the nostrils, indicating that he had probably been subject to sudden nosebleeds.

'Was he an alcoholic?' Yeadings enquired mildly.

'No,' was the short answer. 'To my knowledge he rarely drank; recently not at all.'

Except one large brandy which he poured for himself at the end of the evening, Z recalled from Gayle's account.

'Drug abuse?'

'Certainly not.'

There was still something missing, the Superintendent thought. Littlejohn was holding back. But he couldn't do so indefinitely. There would be further analysis of organs, blood, and body content, and it might be useful to get hold of the late doctor's medical record.

He had a notion that nosebleeds and a dodgy liver were connected, but he hadn't knowledge enough to put a name to any condition. He'd try it out on Nan when he got home. She always claimed her nursing experience was antediluvian, but he knew she read avidly whatever medical news came out. Once a Nursing Sister at the old Westminster, you never gave up entirely. And bodies, after all, were still constructed on the same model.

'Sir.' Z was frowning over some problem of her own. 'Dr Goodwin went in from the very spot on the river-bank where the dead woman was found. Any significance in that, would you say, sir?'

'Her murder could have been weighing on his mind. He'd been called there to confirm she was dead, but we can't yet assume he was connected

155

with the woman in any other way. And thought of a recent violent death might loom large if he was about to take his own life.'

Yeadings paused, then went on. 'But we don't know even that for certain. He was in low spirits, but he could still have arranged to meet someone at that specific spot, uneasy about some aspect of the earlier killing. He could yet be that person's second victim, though it's hard to imagine how the poison could have been administered. Leave it for the present, Z. We haven't enough on the man's life to start guessing about its end.

'It seems he was in a small joint practice with two other GPs. I want you to tackle his partners. Find out as much as you can about his recent professional conduct. We can't assume it was only his wife's apparent passion for another man that sent him over the edge. He could have been expecting trouble from a different quarter. Doctors are vulnerable in many ways. See what you can achieve with womanly wiles and sympathy. They'll fob you off with protestations of professional discretion, but in the first shock of receiving the news something useful may slip out.'

'You don't suppose he was overcome by guilt?'

'For having strangled and battered this Sheena woman? It's just possible, though it doesn't sound his style. No, the idea doesn't excite me.'

'If his wife had turned her back on him and he'd looked for sex elsewhere — ? After all, this was a prostitute who was killed. She had to have *some* connection with Mardham, sir.'

'It would close the case tidily, I agree. But I've a feeling in my water, Z, if you'll pardon the coarseness. This isn't a simple case. There's a labyrinthine whiff to it. Or it may be the rural drains. But let's keep our minds open, ready for a whole menu of options.'

For all he'd damped her enthusiasm for the theory, it remained with him. It was perfectly feasible for Goodwin to have gone to London with the intention of recouping his lost sex life. And suppose the woman had discovered his identity — perhaps gone through his pockets while he slept after coitus, found his address and the fact that he was a respectable family doctor. He could have seemed a well-heeled subject for blackmail.

Her most likely gambit would be to confront him here, near enough to his practice and family to underline the danger to his reputation. She'd been strangled, then beaten with a blunt instrument. No premeditation in that; it implied the desperate actions of a person under sudden unbearable pressure.

Yeadings had told Z the idea didn't excite him, but it was beginning to take a hold. He went in search of Beaumont to try the theory out on him.

He found his senior sergeant in the Incident Room, its function suddenly restored by the new death. Beaumont was bringing his notes up to date by hand before feeding them to the computer wizards. He stopped writing to listen, and grunted noncommittally afterwards. Yeadings gathered from his attitude that the sergeant had an alternative theory.

'Littlejohn appears to be holding back,' he cued in, and waited for Beaumont's reaction.

'Covering for one of his own kind. Doctors go glutinous at any hint of scandal within their circle. Cling together like swarming bees.'

'So what scandal?'

Instead of answering directly, Beaumont swivelled in his chair and eyed his chief evenly. 'I've been talking to the Fields. Just the woman and the twins, that is. Mr Donald Field has gone to work today as usual. I suspect that's in order to keep out of everyone's way, because there's one hell of a volcano due to erupt in that family.'

'Because of his behaviour last night at the Goodwins? Since the doctor's been found dead, is Mrs Field lashing out wildly or keeping a savage silence?'

'A bit of both. In spurts. The kids are jumpy, for once admittedly out of their depth. Their mother started off tight-lipped but she couldn't pass up the chance to brand Meredith Goodwin as a scarlet woman.'

Yeadings remembered how Barrow had called Mrs Field Hecate. 'A spiteful woman who has to have the last word,' he suggested.

'Conclusive,' agreed Beaumont, heartlessly punning.

'Ah.' Yeadings twirled a straight-backed chair and straddled it to consider this. 'So she's come down from the sardonic heights she adopted last night? Gayle Dawson described her as coldly scornful. Has she had time for second thoughts about her husband's behaviour, or is it the good doctor's death that makes the difference?'

'The two together, I'd say. With Dr Goodwin removed from the scene it does leave Meredith a widow ripe for the taking. Not that she hasn't been taken already, if we accept common opinion. And Phyllida Field, the third side of the triangle, is by no means last night's mocking bystander. Today she has a mighty head of steam up. Perhaps now facing her husband's option to divorce her and remarry.'

'Wasn't that on the cards before?'

'It depends. Particularly on Meredith's feelings for her husband.'

'I'd like to be more certain of everyone's feelings for each other.'

'Gayle Dawson's an outsider, and in a position to pick up the state of play better than those on the pitch. She believes she saw real affection between the Goodwins; at least the man's compassion for his wayward wife. It's not the way many men would feel, openly humiliated in his own home, but suppose he understood her needs and was unable to satisfy them himself —'

'It would take a saint. But if we can believe he was one, he might have turned a blind eye.' Yeadings nodded. 'And his wife might have been having a mere adventure, keeping enough tenderness for her husband not to want a total break.'

'But such philandering couldn't go on forever

in such a close-knit neighbourhood. Not without some kind of unpleasantness breaking through. Marriage still counts, and some conventions have to be observed, among people of their kind. The affair was building to a climax, and suddenly there's a resolution. Once she's done grieving, there's only one bar now to Meredith Goodwin becoming Mrs Donald Field II.'

'And that's Mrs Donald Field the First.'

'So if that lady's suddenly out of her mind, it could mean she sees Donald riding high, more than ready to dish her and make the exchange.

'So,' Beaumont summed up, 'as a motive for eliminating Goodwin, we needn't look further than next door, at the widow's lover — Donald Field. And Phyllida's mental state could be partly due to suspecting her husband. Of collusion with Meredith in murder.

'I rest my case, m'lud,' he offered in pseudo-courtroom tones.

Yeadings gave a wry grin. So much for the adversarial system. Beaumont's new theory had made a strong case against Z's. The truth hung on Goodwin's reaction to his wife's overt unfaithfulness. Either the man had gone elsewhere for what he was deprived of — and become embroiled in blackmail — or accepting the role of complaisant husband and relegated to being some kind of house eunuch, he'd been removed by his successful rival.

So what of the suicide theory? As Beaumont had said, the weaker role wasn't one many men would accept. But then in Goodwin's case there might have been a special reason for self-effacement, such as impotence or failing health — and Littlejohn's findings to date hadn't entirely ruled that out.

And, according to Gayle Dawson again, Goodwin had seemed withdrawn and unhappy. So perhaps he had already made up his mind to end it all.

Yeadings sat pondering the options. He found all of them depressing, but murder was, in a way, more acceptable to him then than a man choosing to take his own life.

There was a further possibility — that elsewhere in Mardham Dr Goodwin's death had proved necessary for some other person's peace of mind.

He'd been a doctor, after all, with access to secrets nobody else had been privileged to share. Secrets which his professional ethics might require him to bring to light. Doing so could threaten someone's security. Now that he was dead that danger was at least postponed, if not eliminated.

London's West End Central had received DI Jenner with unflattering calm, but he was eager to mark up brownie points for himself on the strength of the Met's efforts. An address had been traced for the murdered woman but as yet no surname to back up the 'Sheena'.

By scouring the pubs and less salubrious haunts

in the area between Oxford Street, Regent Street and Shaftesbury Avenue, various references to her activities had been turned up. She appeared to be a freelance, unlike the majority of girls run by a pimp or the proverbial madam.

It was from a whiskery old wino who slept nights in a doorway in Dean Street that they learned she had rented an attic room above a video shop towards the Oxford Street end. The central floor of this cramped house was by day the work-room of a rapid-service tailor late of Hong Kong.

It was evident from the spicy sweet-sourness of the stale air in the house that oriental food was prepared on the premises. It had penetrated the very fabric. As he climbed the creaking wooden staircase Jenner's questing nostrils flared with distaste. Unsure of the rickety handrail, he reached out to the flaking distemper of the opposite wall. And felt something small and scaly scuttle away in the dim light. He shuddered, visualizing a Hieronymus Bosch creature from a nightmare hell.

And Hell was a reality he'd been raised as a child to believe in: a physical structure created from one's own evil living. Eighteen years of police experience had shaken some of his certainties, but he retained a superstitious fear about that one. What else, indeed, could suitably reward a debauched harlot in squalid city surroundings, far distanced from Bicester's simpler sinners?

The small square room was lit only by a skylight, until the bedside lamp, shaded with grubby pink satin, was switched on. Its folds were then revealed furred with fluffy dust. Dust and fluff were the decorative theme throughout. Sheena's taste had run to violent pinks which failed to match, in grimed curtains, damp-stained wallpaper and frilled nylon bedspread.

Either the woman had been phenomenally untidy or the room had been trashed. Jenner stared round at gaping drawers spilling items of underwear which she'd presumably thought seductive. Over the threadbare donkey-brown cord carpet were strewn a few paperback books; a plastic tray with the remains of a takeaway meal; a heap of cheap jewellery comprising several strings of coloured glass beads, glittery brooches and earrings. As he moved forward his shoe slid on loose pearls and he almost lost balance, saving himself with one hand that landed in a pool of face powder spilled on the makeshift dressing-table.

The Met sergeant he'd accompanied was turning over junk on the floor with the toe of a Doc Marten. He gave a grunt and hunkered to take a closer look. 'Seems someone emptied her handbag here. So where's the bloody thing been dumped? You say it wasn't with the body?'

'Nowhere in the vicinity.'

'How about the river?'

'It was being dragged when I left.'

The sergeant grunted and began pushing items into a large manilla envelope with the end of his ball-point pen. 'Plenty of rubbish to go through here. We'll let your lot have it.'

He completed his collection by upturning a tin wastepaper bin. The contents were mainly used face tissues, and Jenner detected some malicious humour in the man's actions.

The plastic bag used as a lining had stayed in the bin. Caught in its crinkled folds Jenner spotted a glint of something white. He reached down and retrieved a small triangle torn from a sheet of notepaper.

There was no handwriting on it, but he could make out fragments of two words typed or printed in capitals: 'HARD C'.

Hard cheese, he said to himself. Wasn't that the slang expression people used as mock consolation?

Nothing there to work on.

The Met sergeant tweaked it out of his fingers and dropped it in with the rest. 'More treasure,' he said sardonically. 'I'll get you to sign for all this.'

Ten

With Jenner's return Yeadings called all person-
nel involved in the Sheena murder inquiry to the
commandeered canteen at Amersham, and
briefly stated why the Incident Caravan was to
remain stationed at Mardham.

'There's a chance,' he said, 'that the locals will
be more helpful about one of their own. And Dr
Goodwin's death could connect in some way with
this earlier case. We have to stay open-minded
for the present over whether it was suicide or
murder. But in view of the toxic substance used,
we can pretty safely rule out accident.

'I want you all to keep eyes and ears open for
the slightest hint of tittle-tattle or of unusual activity in the area.

'We still find no link with organized crime. And
just as one swallow doesn't make a summer, two
deaths don't indicate there's a serial killer on our
patch. Nevertheless people will be getting nervy,
looking over their shoulders. See what direction
they're looking in. Make yourselves available for
their confidences and be sure you put in a full
report. On *everything*. No detail is too small to be
passed on. If not relevant to the present case, it
may still be of use elsewhere. So don't make your
own judgements on the importance of any fact or

rumour. Leave that to the experts who hold the other pieces. And remember that in a situation like this we stand to harvest useful information on all manner of dodgy local practices.'

He left a list of specific inquiries within the village's confines for the Allocator to arrange. His next concern was to gather his own team in a private room of the Feathers at Mardham where the landlord's wife had promised a log fire and an almost continuous service of coffee and sandwiches. Jenner was invited to open proceedings with a report on his findings in Soho.

Apart from the bag of trash now having its contents listed by two uniformed constables from Area, he had brought nothing back. The woman had possessed no papers that could identify her and there had been no correspondence found in her room. It was possible that she'd carried a savings book or medical card in her handbag, which was still missing. If not, it must be assumed that her permanent home was elsewhere.

The Met were continuing to seek out known clients of the dead Sheena, but it seemed she'd had few regulars, relying on one-off services to visitors found rubber-necking outside the strip clubs.

The street door to her staircase was independent of the video shop, but shared with the tailor on the intervening floor. This ethnic Chinese, who was a legitimate immigrant but scared out of his wits and his command of English by police interest, appeared to keep his eyes on his sewing-machine by day, and was absent at night when the woman would be most active.

Yeadings checked through Jenner's written notes while Beaumont reported on the finding of Dr Goodwin's body on the river-bank. Invited to suggest a scenario, he pointed out that the immediate beneficiaries of the death were Goodwin's widow and her lover.

'Assuming that Field wants to divorce and the lady agrees to remarry,' Yeadings warned.

'You see the man Field as a killer?' Jenner demanded in schoolmaster tones. 'Motive's not enough on its own. Had he the means? Had he the opportunity?'

'He's yet to be interviewed,' Yeadings said calmly. 'He left the house early for work this morning. I've arranged an appointment for you and Sergeant Beaumont to see him at eight this evening.

'Sergeant Zyczynski, let's have a word from you. Do you still favour Dr Goodwin's committing suicide?'

Z hesitated. 'I'm not so sure as I was. I was basing it on a presumed connection between the two deaths: that Goodwin could have killed Sheena after she attempted to blackmail him as one of her clients.

'We have only Gayle Dawson's view of the doctor as a quiet, sad man who had accepted his wife's unfaithfulness. Secretly he might have felt humiliated and resentful. I'd like to know how often of late he'd driven up to London, and what he got up to there away from local prying eyes. Did he wander round Soho looking for someone to restore his wounded pride? Was he one of this Sheena's one-offs that DI Jenner spoke of?

'If his photograph was circulated by the Met would anyone recognize him? That vagrant, for instance, who slept in a Dean Street doorway and knew where Sheena lived?'

'Good point,' Beaumont said generously as she finished. 'Sir, can you cap that?'

Yeadings scratched behind one ear. 'I haven't prepared a case, so let me ruminate out loud. What do we know about the dead man, apart from the marital angle? He was a sober professional who needed to keep up a discreet front, because trust was essential for him to function; to earn his living, if you like.

'A doctor gets to know things we don't divulge to anyone else. So suppose he gained some knowledge which, broadcast, could threaten the security of one of his patients, a person of precarious stability — knowledge that he might feel professionally bound to share with colleagues, and which he was intending to pass on to the right quarter.

'Looking around at apparently respectable members of the community, is there one who's concealing such a secret?'

'Some crime? Or a dangerous notifiable disease?' Z asked.

'HIV,' Beaumont decided. It could well be that; some poor sod half out of his mind — his/her mind — desperately trying to hang on to a little more time before everyone must know . . . But someone far enough gone to think he'd nothing to lose, so that even murder became more than necessary, actually acceptable.

'Can we fit the prostitute into some such frame?' Jenner spoke with distaste. 'If *she* was HIV positive, the cause of someone in Mardham becoming infected, that could provide a motive for revenge. And there'd be an incentive to remove Goodwin too because he'd diagnosed the local person's condition. This way we'd be looking for one killer for both crimes.'

'According to the path. report she wasn't infected,' Yeadings said flatly. 'But that doesn't rule out someone having reason to think that she was.'

'Medical records,' Beaumont groaned. 'It takes an earthquake or more to get those released for a living body.'

'In a single given case it's possible,' Yeadings assured him. 'But no power on earth will open up the entire records for all patients in Goodwin's practice. We need a name first, a specific reason and then some medical muscle behind us. Without it . . .' He shrugged.

'There's nothing to stop us asking his partners for a list of his patients,' Z said hopefully. 'That's a legitimate line of inquiry after a sudden death.'

'One you can follow up,' the Boss granted. 'Use your charm, Z. There's one elderly male partner and a young woman not long out of medical school. See what you can come up with. But

169

remember, the person we're looking for need not be on his list. He/she could have approached him privately, or Goodwin could have observed some condition by chance in an acquaintance or a neighbour.

'But again I could be barking up a wrong tree. We need to keep Field in the frame, and take a good look at Malcolm Barrow. See if he has a motive, because nobody can vouch for his going to bed as he claimed. So far everything we've discussed is supposition. As I've mentioned before, we could all get faster results and make a deal more money scriptwriting for the cinema.'

After the experiences of last night Gayle had been lying in late that morning, and had no intention of going to college. When she appeared in the kitchen at a little before 10.30 A.M. to make some toast, Mrs George announced that Superintendent Yeadings had phoned and would like an appointment. Accordingly she dressed and rang back, offering to visit the Incident Caravan.

She found him waiting, seated at a VDU, pecking at the keyboard with an index finger. As she came in he folded the programme, blanked out the screen and sat back with a sigh.

'I suppose to your generation dealing with these gadgets is second nature?'

'They save a lot of time over notes and essays. I just wish we could use the thing's memory bank when we sit our finals.'

'And how do you feel about computerized music? Synthesizers replacing wind and string instruments?'

'Not so happy. Fortunately there's no comparison in the sounds — unless you've got cloth ears.'

'A lot of people must have, just as others go about with their eyes closed. Shall we find out how observant you are? I'm sorry to repeat what you've already discussed with Sergeant Zyczynski, but I think we'll discover you saw more last night than you realized at the time.'

'One important thing is that I'm sure now about Harry Snelling. He *was* the one following me from the station on Thursday. But that time I sprinted, and got away.'

'Did you feel confident you could do the same last night?'

She hesitated. 'Unconsciously, perhaps. I was quite scared at first, but then I accepted he really was trying to recapture the cat. I heard it crying among the trees, and then it dashed past. But I never saw it after it leapt our back wall at Polders, until he'd got it in his arms. That was on the river path when we found — the body.'

'Let's go over it all in detail. Tell me everything as it happened and exactly what you felt at each point.'

'Apprehensive mostly, but I didn't want to be mean to him, in case — well, he's not like other people.' She frowned, recalling her entry into Polders driveway and the sense of being watched. She described minutely all the events. When she reached the point of catching up with Harry on the river-bank, Yeadings stopped her.

'I get the feeling you're uneasy about something there.'

'It wasn't exactly suspicion, but it did occur to me then —'

'Yes?'

'— that he'd been not so much chasing the cat to catch it, as driving it ahead.'

'What made you feel that? Can you remember the moment it came into your mind?'

'I think it was the way he held the cat. As though it had done what it had to, and now he would reward it and take it home. Only that sounds fanciful . . .'

'Was this before you realized there was something floating at the water's edge?'

'Yes. He was facing me, then turned and looked down that way. That was when I saw it.'

'So I have to ask you, Gayle, in view of what you've just said, do you think now that Harry was leading you there to see something he already knew about?'

She was silent a moment, but not in any way astonished.

'You have thought that already,' Yeadings said.

'It did seem possible.' Her voice was low. She didn't want to make trouble for Snelling.

'The reason I asked,' Yeadings said, to reassure her there'd been no betrayal, 'is that a number of large footprints have been found near where

172

you both stood. They could be identified as from Harry's boots. And there are far too many of them to fit the story as you told it at first.'

She looked squarely at him, the blue eyes troubled. 'You mean he'd found Dr Goodwin shortly before he saw me come in Polders gateway? And what I found so alarming was *his* fright? I sort of caught it off him?'

'Does that seem reasonable?'

She nodded. 'But why was he *there,* waiting for me?'

'He was hiding. Like a frightened child. Until he saw someone he felt he could trust to deal with the situation. You said that once you'd recognized what it was in the water, he ran off.'

'Yes. Without another word.'

'Not very good with words probably.'

'But this doesn't mean he was the one who —'

'Probably not, but who knows? Only Harry perhaps, and we'll have to be very careful trying to question him. Wasn't his upset over the elusive kitten a bit overdone? Perhaps he'd been disturbed by an earlier experience — such as finding the body. Or seeing the death. How far he felt responsibility depends on the state of his mind.'

'Whether he's sane, you mean?'

'Whether he's clear about the right and wrong of his own actions. Things like that.'

Gayle said nothing for a moment, then, 'I wish it hadn't been Harry found the body.'

'And I wish it hadn't been you.'

She smiled then. 'Thanks. So do I.'

173

He let her leave, doubting she'd feel lighter, but at least she had shared one doubt.

He must now arrange to question Harry, but first contact Social Services to find out the lad's official standing. And a qualified worker would have to sit in on the interview to provide the special protection to which people with learning difficulties were entitled.

Leaving the caravan, Gayle recognized familiar shoulders hunched over the bridge wall: Colin Field, craning to see what was going on in the taped-off area along the river-bank.

'Hi, there,' Colin said disconsolately, turning at the sound of her footsteps. His fine brown hair was damp and lay sleek against his head. It made her think of a frightened horse with its ears flattened back.

'Hullo. What can you see?'

'Just another search going on. At least this time anything they find can only have been there since Friday morning.'

Four days back, she reflected; but it seemed half a lifetime. So much had happened, everything distorted. The more she got to know the people here the more she believed she'd been deceived by the pleasant-seeming village. There was evil abroad in Mardham, and coming uncomfortably closer.

'It's awful,' she said. 'Poor Dr Goodwin. He seemed such a nice little man.'

Colin scowled down at the water. 'Last night

was bloody awful all round,' he admitted. He turned on her abruptly. 'You found him.' It was like an accusation.

Immediately Colin covered it with a hollow laugh. 'I mean, rotten shit. And then all the police hassle.'

'They have to ask questions. He might not have done it himself.'

'What did you tell them? Do they think someone else was involved?'

'They found some footprints.' She broke off, unwilling to pass on suspicion of Harry Snelling.

Colin looked shattered. 'Whose?'

She shook her head. 'I don't know,' she lied.

He turned away and stared sickly towards where the group of dark figures worked close to the ground above the river. 'They'll be taking plaster casts.'

'I guess so.' He had surprised her, so genuinely upset. True, Goodwin had been a neighbour, but she wouldn't have expected Colin to be so disturbed by what had happened to him.

Rosemary Zyczynski found the elder of Dr Goodwin's surviving partners more easy to charm than the young one, but he had the disadvantage of a short concentration span unhelped by interrupting phone calls.

'Now where was I?' he asked, wiping his halflenses, then inspecting her over them. 'Stanley's list? Well, I could get a printout for you, but it's not really up to date. We've had to make quite a lot of — er, amendments over the last month or so.'

'Why would that be, Dr Parfitt?'

'Reorganization, you know.'

That was merely a restatement of his earlier words. The man was hedging. Time to be steely, Z decided. 'Can you tell me why that was necessary?'

He gave her a hapless stare. 'Stanley had expressed a desire — er, yes, a desire — to move sideways into management. We were in process of — er, making the adjustment.'

'Do you mean that his patients were being transferred to your list and Dr Fennell's?'

'Some of them. That is, we had only got so far with the — er, adjustment.'

'I see.' She didn't. She believed that managers of medical practices were well paid, but surely Dr Goodwin hadn't needed to supplement his salary? If she probed too far now, she believed Dr Parfitt would clam up on her, and she did need that list. So she smiled as if satisfied, and reminded him of the printout as she rose to go.

'I'll get our receptionist to send it to you. At the caravan, is that right?'

'I'd like it now, please.'

It clearly displeased him, but she couldn't risk any alterations being made during the delay. The Boss had seemed to think he smelled paydirt there.

Dr Parfitt fielded another phone call transferred from reception and then requested the

176

printout to be handed to Z as she left.

At the door she added as an afterthought, 'May I ask if the Snellings are on your own list, Dr Parfitt?'

He blinked. 'Snellings? I've no one of that name. Do they live in the village?'

'Fairly recent newcomers, I believe.'

'Oh, no doubt Alison's got them then. That's Dr Fennell. You could ask about it at the desk.' Relieved that she was leaving, he rose stiffly to his feet and summoned a smile.

Z thanked him and left.

Dr Littlejohn was having some trouble catching up with Superintendent Yeadings. The constable on duty at the caravan offered to have him traced and promised he would return the call.

'It — could be important,' the pathologist said testily.

Receiving no answer from Yeadings' car radio, the constable was inspired to ring the Feathers, where the message was relayed to the sitting-room where the Boss was working through a stack of reports without visible success. He assumed the invitation to ring Littlejohn held some promise, so wasted no time.

'Mike,' the pathologist confessed. 'There's something of possible interest which was overlooked at first go.'

'Which body?'

'Oh, sorry. Goodwin's. He wore a dental half-plate, upper set, which my idiot of an assistant put to one side before we opened up. I've just come across it.'

'And it has traces?'

'More than that. It has a lump. Of what appears to be chewing gum. I think on analysis we'll probably find some residue of the cyanide.'

Yeadings hummed. 'Is this a variant on the wartime cyanide pill?'

'I'm assuming so. And leaving you to draw any further conclusions.'

'Right. You'll let me know more when you've conclusive results?'

'Instantly. I regret the delay, of course.'

As well you might, Yeadings thought, ringing off. Littlejohn must have been more than a tad distrait not to have asked for the dental plate when he found teeth were missing in the upper gums.

A pity the oversight was of something that could be vital to the case. The question of how the poison was administered had been exercising him enough. No container was found on or near the body. A small bottle of some kind could have remained embedded in the river mud, denying the divers' efforts to find it. Now, it seemed, there need have been no more than the paper off a strip of chewing gum. Which Goodwin might have prepared himself with cyanide to crunch up as he chewed.

Or he could have accepted the gum in good faith from someone he met on his final walk.

Yeadings ran a hand over his dark bush of hair.

He was still left with the alternatives of suicide or murder, but a body of information on the death was slowly beginning to build. He reminded himself that it took a lot of grains to make even a sandcastle.

Prompt on the thought came Rosemary Zyczynski with her offerings from Goodwin's medical practice: a list of the dead man's patients, some of the names starred, with the words Fennell or Parfitt added afterwards. She explained the significance of this.

'So Goodwin was gradually edging out of the practice?'

'Into management.'

'So you were told.'

'I believed it.'

'Hmm. So if all these starred names have something in common, it could indicate a reason for shunting them off him.'

It sounded an acceptable theory. Z waited for more to come, but it didn't.

'You might as well knock off now,' the Boss told her. 'Jenner will be phoning a report to me at home after he and Beaumont have seen Field. We'll meet here tomorrow at 8.30 A.M. to discuss what comes out of it. Anything else?'

'I don't think so. Except that the Snellings don't seem to have signed on with a doctor since they moved into Mardham. They've no transport. It struck me as awkward if they have to continue with their previous doctor at wherever they came from.'

'Do we know where that was?'

'No.'

'Ah well, I'll get it tomorrow from Social Services. They're bound to have something on Harry. Thanks, Z. Goodnight.'

Yeadings made up his own notes, considered and declined Mrs Goodge's offer of Irish coffee and went out to his car.

A fine drizzle had begun, and old-fashioned street lamps were casting barley sugar patterns on the black sealskin of the macadam road. He drove slowly, wary of pools of shadow between the brighter patches.

There were half a dozen cars haphazardly parked outside the path to the Baptist Church Hall. As he looked, the double doors were opened for a loaded pram to be trundled in.

Some kind of junketing on hand, he thought, catching a glimpse of lights inside and bustling activity. With the instincts of a sniffer dog he braked, got out and wandered up to satisfy his curiosity.

Inside, there were trestle tables with garments being sized and labelled, then transferred to large cartons. In a chair by his elbow a little dumpling of a woman waved a clipboard at him and demanded in refined tones, 'Food or clothing?' When he hesitated, she added, 'Only men's clothing this time. We don't get the same demand for women's, you see.'

'You're stocking up for a jumble sale,' Yeadings beamed.

'Oh no. Dear me, no. It's the London Run.' And she waved expansively at a hand-painted poster with just those words on it and a date sticker for two days' time. A crude sketch below showed a huddled figure slumped in a street doorway and reaching out for alms.

'This is all new to me,' Yeadings confessed. 'Could you tell me about it?'

Every four weeks, she explained, a collection of warm garments and foodstuffs was taken by volunteers to the homeless in the capital. There were three delivery points where those in need gathered for hot drinks dispensed from the van and received sandwiches, pies, tinned foods and supplements to their inadequate clothing: the Embankment by Temple Gardens, Lincoln's Inn, and St Anne's Court off Dean Street.

'Our little effort,' she cooed, 'towards making life more tolerable for those who have fallen on hard times.'

He didn't doubt she meant it, but looking round he was more impressed by the systematic nature of the operation as garments were inspected, categorized and sorted into piles with almost conveyor-belt speed. The women involved were dedicated organizers, not least the chief examiner who was a hard-faced blonde harpy in her early fifties wearing a white overall and rubber gloves. Her charity, Yeadings thought, would be cold, dispensed hygienically and at no cost to herself. He took a further look at the poster and decided to withdraw before his new winter overcoat was required of him to bring up numbers.

Getting back in his car, he reflected that this London Run was a physical connection between Mardham and Soho that no one had yet considered. How many more were there, he wondered, which had yet to come to light?

Eleven

At home Yeadings found his normally calm wife in something of a tizzy, and remembered that today Sally had been due for her measles inoculation. At school the doctor had offered her the option of taking the child home for the rest of the day.

'I knew this new stuff was dynamite,' Nan admitted, 'but even then Sally's reaction has rather rocked me.'

'Where is she?'

'In bed asleep. Within an hour or two she started running a fever. When her eyes began to puff up and she wanted to go on reading I decided to knock her out with paracetamol.'

'How about Luke?'

'He doesn't qualify for a shot until he's five. He was climbing on his frame in the garden until it started to get dark. Since then he's been playing his electronic keyboard. I'm nearly round the bend with Jingle Bells and Little Brown Jug.'

Yeadings loosened his tie and went upstairs to change. He looked in on Sally, but across the darkened room could see little but a hump in the bed. He sat on a corner of the duvet and leaned close.

As ever he was amazed at the heart-aching

beauty of the blunt little Down's Syndrome features, but now her face and neck were flushed, the pursed lips emitting a tiny moist popping sound each time she breathed out.

So vulnerable, and therefore so very precious. It would be unbearable if anything happened to shorten this little life threatened from before birth.

Nan had left a wet square of towelling in a bowl on the bedside cupboard. He squeezed surplus water from it and gently wiped her forehead and neck. The child murmured wordlessly, but it was a comfortable sound. She turned on to her side and he rearranged her covers after kissing the exposed shoulder.

Poor Nan, she had agonized over the decision for or against the injection. All her past training as a nurse insisted on the need for universal immunisation. But your own child was special, and Sally more special than most.

When he had left the house that morning he had had to switch off family feelings, but Nan had had no such relief. On top of the earlier apprehension she must now face the possibly adverse results and ask herself if she had made the wrong choice. Would Sally prove to be one of that very small minority who just couldn't take it?

When he went back downstairs Nan had made tea and Luke was clamouring to be read to. Yeadings worked through his zoo book and joined loudly in the animal noises as each was identified.

It was rewarding, if sometimes frustrating, to be coping with so young and rumbustious a child at his mature age.

He and Nan had long delayed trying for a second child after Sally's birth, partly from fear of a repeat of Down's Syndrome but also because monitoring Sally's progress was so time-consuming for Nan. Then Luke had suddenly announced his intention to join them, so they'd been saved from making the decision. And Luke, when he arrived, had been gloriously normal and lusty.

So Mike, swopping notes with other new fathers in the job, had felt transported back to his own early days on the beat and jauntily rejuvenated — except on mornings after the inevitable nights disturbed by teething and colic.

Tonight, by the time the little boy was bathed and bedded, Nan was in need of hugging happy again. It wasn't until he was switching off the bedroom light that Yeadings remembered Dr Goodwin and asked her about a tendency to nosebleeds.

'Epistaxis,' she said. 'It can often be controlled by cauterizing the septum.'

'And a connection between liver trouble and nosebleeds?'

'Cirrhosis,' she said. 'When the liver gets badly diseased it affects the clotting ability of the blood. Was this man an alcoholic?'

'According to those who knew him he was almost teetotal.'

'Teetotal is what a reformed alcoholic needs to

185

become. Of course, there are other possibilities. Hepatitis, for instance. With chronic active hepatitis you find naevi, and these —'

'Naevi. That was the word!' Yeadings exclaimed in the dark. 'This man had them in his nostrils. That's what Littlejohn was telling me without actually naming the disease.

'So maybe Dr Goodwin had the Hepatitis B virus, which is highly contagious through body fluids, and that's why he was dropping any of his patients he might need to use minor surgery on. He must have informed his colleagues in the practice. And Littlejohn could have heard unofficially. The path. tests on it haven't yet been completed.'

But that was only part-explanation of Goodwin's actions. Would knowledge of having the disease cause him to withdraw from more than his medical practice? — from life itself?

Beaumont had had enough of DI Jenner long before their joint appointment to interview Donald Field. The long coffin-shaped face with its cheesy pallor had not endeared him to locals who were finally turned completely off by his cold and patronising manner. There must be some senior wire-puller at Bicester, Beaumont decided, who contrived to off-load the man when a stand-in was needed in other Areas of Thames Valley force.

Yet it seemed the Boss had asked for the outsider by name when DI Mott was temporarily transferred. Since Jenner's track record was nothing remarkable, it could only be that it gave Yeadings an excuse to oversee the case more closely himself, detached from total desk-work.

But Yeadings didn't have to suffer being yoked to the insufferable man day-in day-out, and Jenner's pairing with Z had been sadly short-lived. It was Jasper Wichall's wisecrack Beaumont had to thank for that. He would like to get that young man for something.

They had pulled up outside no. 4 Orchard Close a few minutes short of eight o'clock on Tuesday evening and waited in the car. Jenner proceeded to explain his plan of campaign to a sceptical Beaumont who believed in playing most inquiries by ear. His role, he learned, was merely to observe and record. DI Jenner would be starring as the latter-day Perry Mason.

It was young Rachel Field who let them in, slinking ahead to show them where to wait in the lounge until her parents were available. When Field entered, wiping at his mouth with a linen napkin, he left the dining-room door open, and Beaumont dutifully observed that he had eaten alone.

From the look of the daughter she was anorexic, possibly bulimic. He could imagine her stuffing herself with face tissues for bulk and then regurgitating them to retain her skeletal lines. But surely the son didn't opt out of meals?

Field was apologizing for his wife's absence. She had returned from sorting jumble and would spend the next hour or so recovering in a scented bath and suchlike. His words were meant to be humorous, but their tone barely disguised his disdain.

He was a tall man, darkly handsome if you overlooked the heavy structure of the upper jaw which made his mouth too prominent. The lips were full and muscular between deeply scored lines from nostrils to cleft chin. A hard face, a strongly male face.

Sexy? Beaumont asked himself, recalling that this was the man who had won Meredith Goodwin away from her more modest-seeming husband. Yes, why not? Mick Jagger was considered very sexy. Field's face had something of that other's, but with less aggression. A solicitor by profession, he'd needed to cultivate a smoother exterior.

The house indicated that his career was a successful one. Not that it was over-furnished. Its simplicity was evidence of a sophisticated taste, but everything the sergeant's eyes lit on was certainly pricey, from crystal chandelier and swagged velvet curtains to rich-piled Wilton carpets, not to mention the porcelain knick-knacks on display in slender glass-fronted cabinets.

'Now how can I help you?' Field asked loftily, waving them to be seated.

This was Jenner's cue and he went straight in on it.

In reply Field said that last night's dinner party had been a modest neighbourly affair, but as ever

Mrs Goodwin had presented a delicious meal. The idea had been to introduce young Gayle Dawson, a newcomer to the village. His children had already met her and found her charming. Asked for his opinion, he considered her a rather shy girl.

'Not taking a large part in the table-talk?' Jenner enquired.

'Not really, no. Apart from mentioning her studies and background.'

'So where was she from?' Beaumont bluntly put in, abandoning his restricted role as observer.

Field opened his mouth with all confidence to reply and was struck dumb. 'She did say. Now where was it? Slipped my memory, I'm afraid.'

Never took enough interest to register it. Concentrating on something quite different, according to Gayle's version, Beaumont thought.

'And when did the party break up?' Jenner demanded.

'Quite early. Well before eleven. Nearer half-past ten perhaps? A weekday affair. Most of us had to work next day.'

'But I believe this was unusual. Was there any particular reason why it should end so early? Who was the first to move off?'

Field had to think, corrugating his forehead impressively. 'D'you know, I really couldn't say. There was a general movement. Not that it hadn't been a delightful evening.'

'You haven't mentioned Dr Goodwin,' Jenner reminded him. 'I find that curious, since you must have heard by now what occurred so shortly after you all left.'

Muscles became taut along Field's jawline as he clenched his teeth. 'Respect for the dead,' he said tightly. His eyes were coldly reproving. Even Jenner halted a moment in his attack.

'Had the doctor seemed to enjoy the social occasion?' Beaumont asked mildly.

'How could he, if you believe he took his own life straight after?'

'From your own observation,' Jenner pressed.

'He — really I do find this most . . . indelicate, Inspector. The man was a close neighbour of mine, a friend.'

'Please answer my question, Mr Field. I am sure you wish the police to use all possible diligence in finding out what happened.'

Field abruptly stood up and went across to a drinks cabinet. 'Can I get you gentlemen anything?' He gestured with a cut glass decanter, but barely waited for them to decline. While he poured himself a large scotch he kept his back turned.

In silence they watched him return to his chair and place the drink untasted on a table beside his right hand. He crossed his legs, twitching at the knees of his immaculate trousers, and assumed a new gravity.

'I see I must be quite frank with you, Inspector. For some months now Goodwin's state of mind has given us all — has *disturbed* those of us who were closest to him. Lack of concentration, depression, withdrawal: all symptoms, I fear, of mental deterioration. I'm no medical man, of course, but I cannot deny now that he must have been more seriously ill than we supposed, and in need of specialist help.'

'So was he getting it? As a friend of the family observing this deterioration, you must have discussed his condition. With his wife perhaps? His brother-in-law?'

Field reached for the whisky. Beaumont watched the knuckles whiten as his hand tightened round the tumbler. 'Meredith had mentioned her alarm at his condition. I tried to reassure her. The brother, Malcolm Barrow, is a relatively new acquaintance of mine. I have never discussed anything of a personal nature with him.'

'Mrs Goodwin must have relied heavily on your support. Did you convince her that there was nothing seriously wrong with her husband?'

Field gulped whisky before answering quickly, 'She was willing to be convinced. Eager, even. How could I increase her distress by suggesting that anything like this would ensue?'

'Did you think it might?'

'Of course not! Nothing so ghastly!'

'Have you been to see Mrs Goodwin since it happened?' Beaumont put in almost casually.

'I — no. I called at the house on my return from work, but was informed she was resting.'

'And had you phoned?'

'Earlier, yes; from my office. With the same result.'

For long seconds, with narrowed eyes, Jenner sat watching the man's barely hidden discomfiture.

'And were you close enough to know if Dr Goodwin had enemies? People who might wish to do him harm. To get rid of him, for example?'

They hadn't done so badly between the two of them, Beaumont thought. Jenner had definite viperish worth as interviewer. And he himself had found some openings for subtler questions. Despite all his legal wariness and assumed sang froid, Field had stumbled over some of his statements.

In particular he claimed to have returned promptly home after leaving the Goodwins' house, then contradicted himself when reminded that his family had denied this. As correction he remembered he'd gone for a walk, turning right into Mill Lane and out of the village by way of the railway bridge. In the opposite direction from the river, if that was to be believed.

Beaumont withheld total faith in the revised version: Donald Field had displayed uneasy symptoms of guilt.

'Guilty as hell!' the DI echoed his unspoken thoughts with relish. He clipped himself into the passenger seat aglow with success.

'Guilty of what though?' Beaumont wore his wooden puppet face.

Jenner was pulled up short. 'He's our man,' he declared defiantly.

'Meredith Goodwin's man,' the DS said crudely. 'It's enough to shake any woman's lover when the deceived husband suddenly tops himself. Maybe it's true he went for a country walk alone after Goodwin gave him short shrift. Field's not likely to admit that to anyone, nor that he was staying out late to spite his wife who must assume he was making out with her next-door neighbour.'

Jenner's indrawn breath was audible, his thin nostrils flaring over compressed lips. 'We'll see what Mr Yeadings says when I get Field in for questioning. For the moment I want those notes made up straight away, for debriefing first thing in the morning.'

Mike Yeadings' waking thought was of Sally. He rolled out of bed in the dark and went padding to her room before the sleep was properly out of his eyes. She was sitting up listening to a tape on her headset. He pulled out the jack and as the music went public she looked up and smiled. He lifted off the earphones, kissed her forehead, went over to the window and raised the floral blind. In the light of day he saw the feverish flush had almost left her face and her eyes looked normal. 'Feeling better?' he asked, a lump in his throat.

She nodded. 'I had a prick. In my arm. It didn't hurt.'

'They get good at it,' he said. 'I expect they've done hundreds. Thousands.'

'Can I get up now?'

'Better wait till Mummy says.'

Nan was in the shower. He rolled back the door to poke his head through. 'Sally's all right.'

Nan shook back wet hair, reached for him by the ears and pulled him in to be kissed while water ran over both their faces. 'She should be,' she said weakly, 'after all those prayers!'

At breakfast they were all together. Nothing special, Mike told himself; you shouldn't fuss so. She's a strong little girl despite the bad beginning.

It would have been good to take the day off by way of celebration, all four go skiving, but he'd promised himself to look in on Amersham Social Services. Questions had to be asked about the Snellings and he couldn't entrust them to Jenner, because Harry Snelling might be a special case too.

In the event he was forestalled, because the DI asked for an early debriefing over the previous evening's interview with Donald Field.

He'd started softly, Jenner claimed, then worked up to the point of actually charging him with being Meredith Goodwin's lover. And, after first denying it vehemently, the man had been broken down. And also admitted being out and about at the presumed time her husband had died. Jenner made it clear he considered him to some extent or other responsible for the doctor's death.

Yeadings listened without expression as Jenner

194

marked up his personal success. 'Nevertheless, let's not hurry over pulling him in. I'd like him to stew a while,' he said.

The DI had excluded Beaumont from the meeting, having sent him on further quests for witnesses for the events of the previous Thursday.

'He'd mentioned the possibility of poachers,' Jenner explained offhandedly, 'so he may as well follow up the idea. I've brought along the notes he made on my questioning of Field.'

Yeadings looked past him through the glass door-panel to see Rosemary Zyczynski hovering in the corridor outside. She evidently had been warned that this was a one-to-one meeting and wouldn't break in. He held up his right hand, the thumb and forefinger crooked into a reverse C, the acknowledged invitation to coffee. She came in and he nodded her across to the filter machine.

'Let's restore our caffeine level before we hit the road,' he said. 'Rosemary, I'd like you along with me this morning. I need your gentle touch.'

One advantage of official inquiries being pursued at a higher level, Z reflected, was that the answers came rather more promptly. The Boss was known by reputation at Social Services. There was a deal of discussion of other matters before the subject of the Snellings came up. And then immediate recourse to the computer produced a blank.

'I can't understand why the referral isn't entered,' the grey-haired woman said. 'According to our records the Snellings don't exist. Let me ring through to the Family Health Services Authority and ask them. They'll know whose list they're on, and where they came from originally.'

Again there was no result. 'It just means they're from outside the county and haven't re-registered,' she said, apologetic for the data gap but in no way overwhelmed.

'This is ridiculous,' she said after further researches. 'If the mother is a widow and had been receiving any kind of benefit she should have notified her change of address. Then normally, in good time, her details would come through to us from her local authority. This sort of slip up does happen, of course, but I'd have expected her to contact us for assistance by now, for her son if nothing else. We do have day centres for rehabilitation and special requirements. In fact we're rather proud of what we manage to do on our restricted budget.'

Yeadings turned to Z. 'I've looked through the notes on your visit with DS Beaumont to the Snellings. You learned they'd been in Mardham eight months. That should have given the mother time to get sorted out.'

The woman official clicked her tongue again at the computer screen. 'Still nothing. However, not to worry, Mr Yeadings. Thanks to you, we know where they are now. I'll send someone out to visit them. Then we'll get all the information direct.'

'Which could take days to reach us,' the Boss told Z as he drove away. 'We'll steal a march on Social Services, and drop in on the Snellings ourselves, after lunch.'

An early gloom had set in, the drizzle barely discernible now. Yeadings felt they were moving through gently sprayed vapour. Glancing into Polders garden as they passed he saw solid blue-grey shadow massed under the older trees. The few leaves still on the chestnuts drooped motionless like damp yellow bunting. There was a sweet, dank scent of rotting vegetation.

From the ground-floor living-room of no. 1 Orchard Close lights shone out. Inside they could make out a woman's head bent over a sewing-machine. Her hands moved, turning some heavy fabric under the needle. As the door-bell shrilled she looked up startled, pushed her spectacles up into her hairline and pressed a hand over her eyes.

It took her a few moments to open up. The two detectives waited, hearing her muffled voice and the sound of an inner door closing. Shutting her son away, Z supposed. It was the woman's habitual protectiveness.

'Yes?' she said doubtfully on seeing them.

'We're from Thames Valley Police,' Yeadings told her. 'You've met Sergeant Zyczynski before.'

He observed the tension in her hands, and a vertical frown line appeared between her brows. 'I've already made a statement. I don't know anything to help. I'm sorry.' She was going to close the door on them but Z said quickly. 'Did you ever meet Dr Goodwin, Mrs Snelling?'

It surprised her. 'The gentleman from no. 3? Yes, he gave me a lift home once. From the grocer's. Is something the matter with him?'

'There's been an accident. Didn't anyone tell you?'

'I haven't been out.' She clawed at the neck of her cardigan, defensively. She didn't need anyone else's bad news.

'Perhaps we could come in for a moment and talk?' Yeadings asked mildly. He was using his bulk to loom, Z noticed; not threateningly but leaving the small woman no choice. She backed into the narrow passage and felt for the door of the room she had just left. The other two followed her in.

'Moccasins!' Z said, lighting up. 'How clever of you.'

She looked at the half-filled cardboard carton on the floor beside the work-table. 'You've quite a home industry.'

'It's for a firm where I was once forewoman,' Mrs Snelling admitted. 'They deliver the sheepskin cut out to the right sizes and I just make them up.'

So actually she still worked, but from home now instead of in a factory.

'You don't carry that great box to the post, I hope,' Yeadings sympathized.

'No. Someone comes to pick them up when they're filled.' The questions were making her nervous, but there was a hint of pride in her voice. Self-employed, so it meant she could watch over Harry and still make enough money for them both to scrape a living. Less need for help from Social Services in that case.

'Won't you sit down?' the woman invited.

Z managed to stumble against the carton on her way to a chair. Her hand knocked its top flap closed and she caught a glimpse of the label. The company heading wasn't clear, but the final line of the address, in block capitals, was High Wycombe.

The Boss was explaining about Dr Goodwin, still making it sound as though his death in the river could have been accidental.

'How awful. He was a kind man,' Mrs Snelling said, adding almost to herself, 'not the sort to pry.'

A curious remark. She evidently lived in fear of other people's unwelcome interest.

'He wasn't your own family GP?' Yeadings asked.

'No.' She sat at her machine, half-turned to face him, fists doubled in her lap, shoulders tense.

'So who's your doctor locally?' He still made it sound conversational.

'I — we haven't decided yet. It's early days.'

199

'You're obviously very healthy people.' He stood as if to go.

'Yes. Luckily.'

'Did you have a good doctor before? What was his name?'

Again her hands went to her throat, clawing at the cardigan. 'I — yes. It was in — Gloucester. Dr Fos . . . Fairchild. I guess he's dead now.'

Yeadings smiled, the door open in his hand. 'Well, we won't keep you from your work, Mrs Snelling. Just thought you ought to know about this latest sad news.'

'Thank you.' She stood helpless, hands hanging down at her sides. 'I suppose I should send a card or something.'

'If you think you should. It's not obligatory.

Harry was standing in the opposite doorway as they went out. A really big man. Even an inch or two taller than himself, Yeadings reckoned; but carrying a lot more weight. His broad face was puckered with uncertainty.

'Mum, you got it wrong.' He went a few steps after them. 'It was Dr Gardner. You remember her, Mum. She was nice to me.'

Twelve

In the car again, Z explained about the moccasin carton coming from a firm in High Wycombe.

'Which is where we'll doubtless find there's a lady doctor called Gardner,' Yeadings assumed. 'So the Snellings haven't moved far; they're still in the same county. I'll leave it to you to check Dr Gardner with the Family Health Services Authority.

'Somewhere in the background I think there'll be a genuine connection with Gloucester. Maybe Mrs Snelling lived there as a child: I thought I detected a hint of West Country burr in her voice. But the name Fairchild was a nick of time recovery. My guess is she was starting to invent a Dr Foster but realized it would sound phoney in that context.'

'How much do you need to know about them?' Z asked cautiously.

'Ah, you think I'm probing for the sake of probing.'

'No, sir. I guess we have to clear them off our slate.'

'Z, I don't expect their background to be anything very sinister, but the woman is secretive to the extent of deliberately lying to the police. Let's know why.'

'Yessir.'

They were trickling along the Close in second gear. 'What's Beaumont up to this morning?'

'Still chasing poachers for DI Jenner.'

'Then there's one of two places he'll be: the Feathers or the Barley Mow. Either of which I'd vastly prefer to where we're off to now. I'm afraid it's more than time we had another talk with Mrs Goodwin.'

The woman's pallor was alarming, more vivid because of the contrast with her bright copper hair which today was severely pulled back in an elastic band. She was dressed and attempting to be about her daily tasks, but the effort was pitiable. In her eyes Yeadings recognized the dawning of ever increasing horror. When he spoke she turned her head and seemed to stare through, rather than at, him.

'I'm asking you to forgive our intrusion, Mrs Goodwin,' he told her, 'but there are questions that must be answered before we can leave you in peace.'

Barrow began again to object. He had blustered on the doorstep, trying to block their entry, but his sister had called from the kitchen and agreed to the interview. Now she sent him to make coffee, cutting harshly across his objections. He was the sort of man, Z thought, who expects women to be subservient. Now that his brother-in-law was gone perhaps he hoped to run things his way. But in Meredith he'd find more than his match.

'I need to be clear about the sequence of events

at the end of your dinner party,' Yeadings said comfortably. 'There were just the three of you here last night, plus the four Fields and Miss Dawson; is that right?'

'Yes.' Her voice sounded distant, but she made an effort to centre her mind. 'Phyllida and the young people left together, at about half-past ten, I suppose. Stanley was resting in the lounge and Donald Field offered to help me clear up in the kitchen. Actually there wasn't much to do. Betty from the village had put all the china and cutlery in the dishwasher. We rinsed the last glasses, then Stanley came out to say goodnight . . .' She closed her eyes and lay back in her chair.

'Are you feeling all right, Mrs Goodwin?'

'Yes. It's just — that was the last thing he said to me. That I was tired; the dinner had been a success, and I ought to get some rest.' She paused, then went on again.

'I went upstairs and Donald left. Stanley locked up, and I thought he'd followed me. His room is at the back of the house. I should have heard his door close, but I realize now that I didn't.'

'So perhaps he'd slipped out after Mr Field. Or *with* him?'

'After, I think. I'm almost sure. I heard Donald say goodnight, and then the sound of the bolts being shot. But Stanley must have just rattled them to make it sound like locking up for the night.'

'So he had some reason to go out, and he didn't

203

want anyone to know.'

'Didn't want me to know. Didn't want me disturbed.'

'And why would that be?'

'He — was going to kill himself. He wouldn't do it at home, didn't want me to be the one to find him. He . . .' She rocked forward over her knees, her hands covering her face. 'Oh God, to think! He was so — alone! Nobody knew; nobody cared!'

'You never guessed?'

'I'll never forgive myself. Never!'

She stopped rocking and sat slumped with her arms crossed on her lap, frowning at the carpet, fingers biting through her sleeves into her flesh. She made a visible effort to go on.

'I knew how much his work meant to him; that he'd never find it enough just as a manager to the practice. He'd once wanted to go on, take his FRCS. He had the hands for it, and the brain. But that was way back, when we'd just met. He gave up the chance, to go into general practice and settle down. He said — he said then that our marriage was more important.'

Ambitions to be a surgeon. And he'd continued coping with small surgical emergencies as a family doctor. Until just recently. It was bitterly ironic that those skilled hands with potential to save life could have become a means of passing infection. It was increasingly clear that once he knew he'd caught the virus himself he'd been faithful to his Hippocratic oath and removed himself from risk of passing it on. However carefully he handled a scalpel, no doctor could be totally sure of not nicking his fingers through the latex gloves. That was probably how he had become infected himself. And he knew that it then cut him right off from performing the work he loved so much.

An honourable man, as well as a loving one. But his wife hadn't specifically mentioned any disease. Yet it seemed she'd known.

Meredith's thoughts had taken a different direction. Her face was twisted with bitterness. 'Our marriage,' she repeated in a whisper, 'was more important.'

'Well, wasn't it?'

'You know, don't you? Someone has been talking.' She stared at him with anger, high spots of colour suddenly in her cheeks. At last she was coming alive.

'It's my business to listen to what is said. But I can select what I believe.'

'And what do you believe?'

He saw no reason to mince his words. She was an honest woman who would prefer the truth. 'That you and Donald Field were lovers, and your husband was aware of it.'

'Not *lovers*, no! We had an affair. Simply that. There's a big difference. Not love; just a physical need. Stanley understood. He was able to accept it.'

She had to believe that. Anything more would be beyond endurance for her now. Because it seemed she'd loved her husband, in her way. At any rate believed at present that she had done.

Yeadings stirred, examined his hands. 'And later that night, after they'd all left, what did you do? Did anyone return to this house?'

'My mind was in turmoil. I felt — frustrated. And I'd had far too much to drink. I took a shower and went to bed. I didn't expect to, but I fell asleep instantly. They woke me to tell me Stanley was dead. You were here then yourself, I remember.'

'And you think he died by his own hand?'

'What else?'

'It never occurred to you that some other person could have caused his death?'

'If anyone did it was me.' The words were almost too low for him to catch. He discounted them.

'Could someone have *wanted* to kill him?'

'Stanley? No! He was the kindest man ever.' Her conviction was heartfelt.

'Just two more questions then, Mrs Goodwin. To your knowledge, had he access to cyanide?'

'Cyanide? *That's* what he took? But that's hideous!'

She sat a moment with bowed head, then looked up to consider the question. 'I rather think cyanide was used when we had a wasps' nest under the eaves. It was last year, but I never noticed any among the gardening things in the outhouse.'

'I see. And finally, did he ever chew gum?'

She looked at him in astonishment; clearly considered it an uncivilized practice. 'No, never!'

Yeadings rose and held out his hand. 'Thank you for your patience. You have my sincere sympathy, Mrs Goodwin. Please let me know if there is anything you feel we can do to help.'

'No one,' she said hollowly, 'can do anything now.' And she saw them to the door, the coffee tray lying untouched where Barrow had deposited it before she nodded him out.

Beaumont had stood a round for the old gaffers in the Barley Mow. The extension of licensing hours had provided them with this more congenial alternative to the small branch library as refuge from unretired wives. It was equally warm and a deal more welcoming. Here the rumble of their spasmodic conversations provoked no bookish backlash.

They were superannuated minor rogues, but sufficiently trusted to draw their own draught and leave the right money by the till when staff were absent on cellar duties. There were advantages to tight communities, Beaumont reflected, where a clear code of what was, and was not, permissible still held good.

He sipped companionably, grunting at the right points in the lethargic reminiscences. The few observations he offered were meant to identify him as a copper of the old school, gifted with a blind eye and an occasional willingness to cut legalistic corners. But he knew these people still wouldn't be entirely open with him.

He made some mention of his old 12-bore, complained that living in town he'd not the time any more to go out and pot bunnies.

'Haven't done none of that meself for long enough. Happy days them was,' one of the oldies muttered.

'Doan' you go harkun back to 'em, Charlie,' advised another. 'Never could shoot straight even when you 'ad two good eyes.'

The others chortled, drank and wiped their mouths with the backs of their hands. In unison, like a bloody stage chorus, Beaumont marvelled.

But the concerted gesture had been a cue to launch the next round. They were all looking expectantly at him. 'Mine again already?'

'It surely is.'

'Right then. Charlie, you fill 'em up since it seems you're not that good at seeing the top of the glass, and I'll hunt out some change.'

More cackles. They were warming to him.

'So where you dun your shootun?' enquired the one referred to as Woody.

'Now, that's asking. Let's say I didn't waste time on targets. The wife's a bit of a cooking buff. Got a taste for a nice plump bird now 'n then. In season, of course.'

'Har. In season, right enough. Doan' want no townees takun the younguns off the nest.' This met a chorus of assent.

'S'not just townees these days,' one mourned into his pint. 'Them Pottersfield lot . . .'

Beaumont affected not to hear, nor to notice how the man's two neighbours leaned in and firmly shouldered him into silence.

'Mind, I'm a beef and spuds man meself,' he said dreamily, and led them on to comparing their favourite Sunday dinners. Which was mostly nostalgic fantasy: the toothless in pursuit of the uncrunchable.

He heaved himself from their company, regretting there was constabulary work to do, and hung a while over the bridge by the caravan to clear his head and help waft away the evidence of his afternoon's occupation. As he'd feared, DI Jenner promptly materialized beside him demanding to know the outcome of his researches.

'I've had a definite tip-off,' he claimed. 'But the folks I'm interested in are on day work. After six I'm more likely to catch them at home.'

'It's dark by five these days,' the DI warned severely. 'You could miss them by hanging around. Get in there as soon as you can.'

Fretting over overtime, Beaumont told himself. The old scrimshanks was tightening the purse-strings. He waited for Jenner to move back to his paperwork, then made off to Yeadings' sitting-room at the Feathers to compare notes with Z.

He found her scribbling on a notepad, with the phone's receiver hunched between shoulder and chin. The Boss at ease in a chintzy armchair had his empty pipe clamped between his teeth, which signalled an attempt to centre his mind on some problem.

'Perhaps I could come over and have a quiet word with you?' Z was saying tentatively as she laid down her pen. She was clearly meeting some resistance at the far end of the line. Well, an appearance in person would probably get her what she was after. She could give a deceptive impression of demure cooperation.

'Blocking you?' Yeadings enquired as she rang off.

'The usual professional reluctance. Dr Gardner will see me at 4 P.M., after ante-natal clinic.'

'Don't you go catching anything from that lot,' Beaumont warned.

Yeadings gave him a withering stare and removed his pipe. 'It seems the Snellings came from High Wycombe. Z has been contacting their earlier GP. Who didn't appear to have heard of them at first.'

'Until I described them,' she explained. 'Then Dr Gardner said I'd got the wrong surname. They were May and Harry Varley. And after that she clammed up on me.'

'An alias,' Beaumont said. 'Which explains why they've not re-registered here with Social Services. There'd be no records to back up the new name.'

Yeadings stood up, frowning. 'If they go to such lengths, depriving themselves of financial benefits and medical help, there has to be something they desperately need kept dark.

'After seeing Dr Gardner, Z, have a word with

Wycombe Area's Collator. The name Varley rings a distant bell. I feel I should remember something about it.'

'Right, sir. I'll get off there now.' She collected her notes, stuffed them in her shoulder bag and left.

'Anything new from Mrs Goodwin?' Beaumont asked the Superintendent.

'We went over how her dinner party broke up. Her version seemed to tally with Field's. He'd been the last to leave, and Goodwin pretended to lock up after him, but apparently slipped out and made for the river. Whether to meet someone or be on his own, we don't know.

'Gayle Dawson had already left and almost immediately ran into Harry Snelling. So Harry hadn't seen the body before he caught up with the kitten. The large footprints at the river were probably some oaf of a policeman's, ignoring caution rules.

'Mrs Goodwin has accepted her husband's death as suicide, but where before she seemed to blame only herself, she now attributes it partly to the ending of his active career. She didn't refer specifically to any disease he had. But I think she knew well enough why he'd given up on minor surgery. And on sex too, which a less cautious man might not have done.'

Yeadings turned to his DS. 'You dealt with the rest of Field's family. Was there anything the young people said that might cast light on Goodwin's final movements?'

Beaumont pulled out his notebook and turned back the pages. He read through silently, then grunted. 'The three agree they left the Goodwins' house together, by the front door, while Field stayed to help in the kitchen with clearing up. Colin saw his mother and sister to their door and then peeled off to catch up with Gayle who'd gone in the opposite direction.'

'So we've got young Colin loose in the Close about the time Goodwin must have left by his back door.'

'But the lad says he reached Polders gateway and started up the drive without seeing Gayle. By then she must have been in the shrubbery hunting Harry's kitten. When he got round the bend and had a view of the whole front of the house he assumed she'd sprinted home and was already indoors. He hadn't wanted to disturb old Mrs George, so he turned back and went home.'

'Directly?'

Beaumont pulled at the lobe of one ear. 'We didn't get round to that. Too taken up with Mrs F's imminent fireworks,' he admitted.

'Find out from Rachel just when he got back,' Yeadings suggested. 'If he didn't return immediately she'd have presumed he was with Gayle. She'd have felt enough sisterly curiosity to be checking up on the time he returned.'

Beaumont reached for the phone pad on which the Close numbers had been noted. The Boss waited while he rang through. He was lucky; it was the girl herself who answered.

'Hello,' he said amicably and identified himself. 'How are you?'

'Fluffed off,' she said dispiritedly. 'Did you want to speak to Mother?'

'Not really. I'd maybe get more of what I want from you.'

'You should be so lucky!' It came out brassily and Beaumont's mouth twitched. Till now he'd been treated to the languid lily act. Underneath, it seemed, she was a normal teenager.

'I could have put that more delicately,' he admitted. 'What I'm actually about is still asking official questions. Much the same ground as before: about Monday night, after the next-door dinner party. Did you happen to go out again after you got home? After all, the night was still young.'

'Too late to fix anything else up. Nuh, I just hung around waiting for Colin to get back. When he didn't I put on a couple of videos.'

'Any good, were they?' He thought he'd overdone the matey tone because there was a marked silence before she replied.

'I can imagine what you're thinking. But I'm not into blue movies, you know.' Her voice went icily superior. '*La Fille Mal Gardée* and *Giselle*. They're ballets, for your information.'

'Ah, nice,' he commented. 'Don't care for the fairy prince stuff, but I've fancied having a bash at that clog dance. Your brother into ballet too?'

'I told you, he was *out*. Chasing after the Dawson girl. For over two hours!' Rachel was talking down her nose, clearly peeved by her twin's defection.

Beaumont wound up and cheerfully rang off. 'Spoilt brat. That child needs a good spanking,' he growled at Yeadings.

'She needs parents who would notice she's there. What did she give you?'

Beaumont repeated her end of the conversation. 'But we know her brother wasn't with Gayle, because she'd joined Harry Snelling on the cat chase. So where was he?'

Yeadings frowned. 'I don't see Colin Field and Doctor Goodwin having much in common. They would hardly take an evening stroll together.'

'Unless there was something extremely private they had to discuss. Like results to medical tests. If Goodwin was managing the practice he'd have first access to reports when they came in. I'd like to know if he was the GP the Field family were registered with.'

'You think those two could have met by previous arrangement? What about Colin's claim to have been following Gayle?'

'Fictional cover-up. And plausible. Who's going to query the boy-chases-girl story? Most natural thing in the world.'

Yeadings shook his head. 'He'd have been short on time: meeting up with Goodwin, hearing what he had to say and then passing him the strip of chewing gum ready prepared with a cyanide implant. It's as far-fetched as moon-dust. And you can't wipe out diagnosis by killing off your doctor.'

'You can postpone publication.'

'So, having disposed of Goodwin in the river, how do you suppose the boy spent the rest of the two hours Rachel says he went missing? If he stayed anywhere near the river-bank he'd have got involved in the police activity. Someone would have seen and challenged him. There was too much light introduced for him to have watched from under cover.'

'Maybe his sister was wrong about the time he returned. Or he could have gone walkabout to turn things over in his mind.'

'We've too many isolated characters wandering loose round that neighbourhood at the time. Gayle with Harry Snelling, Colin Field, his father, and Goodwin himself. Can we believe that none of them met up? Or is everyone lying, to make it harder for us?'

'In collusion?' Beaumont suggested gloomily. 'That's all we need — Mardham village in a combined murder conspiracy. How long before the gutter press blazon the idea? Ah well, time I got off to visit my Pottersfield poachers. See the level I've sunk to!'

Yeadings watched him go with a stab of envy. Any avenue of inquiry would be welcome to him at that moment. With inactivity he felt his mind had stagnated. Even the normally perky Beaumont was affected. Such stalemate had set in after the finding of the first body as he couldn't remember in any recent case.

Case? he questioned himself. Wasn't it rather

cases, plural? Two bodies: one female, strangled, an active tom working independently, an outsider to Mardham. The other male, poisoned by cyanide, a steady medical man, well known and liked in his home village. Nothing in common but the fact that they were both dead. It wasn't even clear whether the second had died by his own hand or not.

Two cases then. Dare he go further and say definitely there was no connection?

His pondering was interrupted by the arrival of Jenner who had at last run him to earth. 'We've had an update from Soho on the woman,' the DI announced importantly.

'And?'

'There was a husband. Probably still is, but they haven't caught up with him as yet. Name of Chadwick, Lancashire man, came originally from Wigan. Unemployed glazier. He visited her a couple of weeks back, when he got made redundant, but she didn't let him stay. Sent him packing, according to drinkers at a rat hole where she used to pick up punters. Made him sleep in his van, parked in Carlisle Street.'

'Van,' Yeadings picked up. The man had quarrelled with his wife. He'd had transport. A Mardham drunk had mentioned seeing a large truck on the night of the murder. Glaziers' vans weren't that big, but they often had tall frames attached to the sides for securing sheet glass. Viewed from the ground and fairly close . . .

'And the van has a history, went missing at the

216

same time as Chadwick. Reported stolen, but it hasn't been spotted, so presumably it's got another set of licence plates by now.'

Yeadings' mind took a glorious, hopeful leap. 'Could be interesting,' he said, outwardly calm and noncommittal. 'Let's hope they pull him in soon. Meanwhile I'd like more on the man, whatever description they have of him and his transport.'

'There's a shout out for him,' Jenner offered. 'The details are circulating. We should hear before long.'

Yeadings left for home soon after, to avoid Jenner's grinding comments on earlier reports. He needed peace to juggle this new detail into the overall picture. If the dumping of Sheena's body at Mardham had been purely fortuitous, there could be no connection with Goodwin's death. Which left a better opening to prove the doctor had taken his own life.

If only he'd written a letter explaining his intentions. A seemingly kind man, why hadn't he made it that much easier for those left behind?

At home Yeadings found Nan finishing the transfer of heaped dead leaves into sacks for making compost. Sally, well wrapped in coat, scarf and gloves, was sitting on the idle swing, recovered from her brief fever but short on energy. Luke, she told him, had gone to tea with a friend from play group.

'Tea,' he echoed. 'What a mavellous idea,' and

217

he shepherded them indoors.

At a little after six there came a phone call from Z.

'I'm still in High Wycombe,' she told him, 'at Area station. There's quite a lot on Harry Varley. Including a good reason why he changed to his mother's maiden name.'

'You're telling me he has a police record? Was it for violence?'

'Six years back the original charge stood as murder, later reduced to manslaughter. But it never went to court. He was sectioned under the Mental Health Act and committed to a secure unit at Fenstone Institute; later released into the community, just eight months ago.'

Thirteen

First thing on Thursday, a week after the woman's death, the details of Harry Varley's police record would be waiting for Yeadings at the caravan in a sealed envelope marked Confidential. He anticipated it with a sense of revulsion.

It was a crisp, bright morning, the pale blue of autumn sky streaked with only a few isolated veils of cloud. On such a day he should have been heading somewhere pleasant, hearing welcome news, sharing in the brisk impression of well-being of the village people he drove past as they headed for work.

He nodded at Gayle Dawson cautiously steering her old Triumph out of Orchard Close, and she waved back. At least one thing was satisfactory. She had her car back, so no more scares walking home from the station in the dark. That would be tonight, after her orchestra rehearsal in London. A whole week since the unknown woman's body had been found.

But the body now had a name — Sheena Chadwick, and her estranged husband was an unemployed glazier from Wigan; who had a stolen van which might, or equally might not, be the one seen in the pub forecourt at the critical time.

Yeadings drove his car on to the grass verge by

the caravan. Z and Jenner were inside waiting for him. He sent them off for a more detailed account of the van observed locally, with little hope of mending the memory gap of an elderly drunk. But it ensured he would be alone when he read the bad news.

And it had to be bad, because if what Z had discovered from Wycombe showed that Harry Snelling had a record of violence, he would have to be questioned. And that came too close to home personally, dealing with a suspect who was mentally disadvantaged.

Z had given the Superintendent the outline over the phone. Now he went into the written report. But it was still incomplete. He would need a transcript of the evidence against the man, witnesses' statements, background, the lot.

It wasn't unique, Harry's case. Case which wasn't a case in the end. A dead file.

Harry had done it, no doubt about that. Three separate eye-witnesses; matched blood samples; verbal confession. And then, rightly enough, the custody sergeant observed his behaviour in the cells, had his doubts and sent a second time for the police surgeon who had already patched up the superficial head wound. After that came two medicos, one of them a shrink, plus the required social worker, and Harry was found unfit to be detained or questioned. Sectioned under the Mental Health Act, he was committed to Fenbridge Institute as a severe manic depressive.

The police file had been closed and left to

gather dust. No Crown Prosecutor either then or later would consider it safe taking such a case to trial. But Harry Varley had benefited from treatment, and six years on was released as safe to live at liberty in the community. Subject, presumably, to social and medical guidance as an outpatient.

But his mother had promptly upped her roots, changed their surname and disappeared with him into oblivion, to subsist without welfare benefits; and, despite her claim, more seriously, without any access to continued medication for Harry. What kind of protectiveness was that? The only known connection with the past that she'd kept on was with her original work place, because she and Harry needed money to live on.

So what charge would have been brought, had Harry been considered fit to plead? Yeadings re-read the man's police record. Originally murder, later reduced to manslaughter. The victim was a young skinhead, manually strangled during a violent street battle between National Front and ethnic Pakistanis.

Strangled. As Sheena Chadwick had been strangled. But not in the same way. Sheena had been attacked from the rear. In the heat of the street affray Harry had leapt on the six-footer, torn away his pickaxe handle and strangled him, kneeling on his chest. A big man could underestimate his own strength. And Harry was very big, carried a lot of weight. Hands like hams? More like a steel vice.

There was little detail given about him. He'd been only nineteen at the time of the offence, which made him twenty-five or -six now; a good bit younger than he looked. He'd been working then as a machinist for a furniture manufacturer in Wycombe.

Yeadings put the papers together and slid them back into the envelope. If he wanted more he could get it from the man's mother. The Snellings were available, and Harry was now deemed responsible enough to live normally in the community. This time there was no excuse why either should avoid questioning.

All the same, there were precautions to be followed. Yeadings reached for the phone and demanded an outside line. Overstretched as they might be, Social Services must send him a qualified worker to stand by against requirements in case there was occasion to interview Harry himself.

Gayle Dawson had acknowledged his nod as the big detective drove by. She guessed he would be on his way to the Mobile Incident Room. By tonight it would be a week since the unknown woman's murder, and as yet there'd been no mention in the news of an imminent arrest. Perhaps there never would be: the victim wasn't from around here and the press said she had been killed elsewhere. The body could have been dumped from a car.

But why in Mardham, and why bother to take

it along the river path when it could have been dropped in over the bridge?

Strange, she thought, what a difference the passing of time makes. I've started to think of it just as a puzzle. I must be getting thick-skinned.

Half-way along School Lane she recognized two figures hurrying ahead in bomber jackets, jeans and trainers. Colin and Jasper, making for the station. She would have passed them but Jasper suddenly turned at the distinctive rattle of her car, pranced into the road and grinned at her through the windscreen. 'Hi, maiden.'

It wasn't funny forcing an emergency stop on her. It really set her neck hairs bristling. She tooted, waiting for him to give way. He loped round to the driver's door and pulled it open. 'Going to town, feller?' he demanded.

'No. To college.'

'Uh. Shame. Change your mind and join us.'

'Jasper, come on,' Colin urged from the pavement. 'Train's due in five minutes.' He looked shamefaced. Because of his friend's brashness, or from memory of the last time they'd met? She'd managed to avoid the Field twins since that embarrassing dinner party and its tragic aftermath.

'Hell, the dame could drive us there.'

This calm assumption was the final insult. 'Get lost!' And she slid into gear, gunned the engine and spun the wheels as the handbrake came off.

Even if it hadn't been a college day, he knew

she used the train for her trips to London, so why did he assume she'd give them a lift? She never drove herself there. The dense London traffic scared her and there were never any places to park.

'Hoity-bloody-toity!' she heard sung after her. As the car jerked forward the door slammed itself shut.

Silly display of temper, she told herself. No need to make enemies. Especially in front of Colin who'd tried to act civilized. There weren't many people of her age on this side of the village, and a time could come when she needed company.

In the mirror she saw them both loping behind, at the double now because their train would have been signalled. She could at least have given them a lift to the station. Next time, she promised herself, however patronizing Jasper gets, I must play it cool.

The social worker provided for Yeadings was a Ms Morrison and she wasn't available until 2 P.M. It was only because he had stressed the critical lack of cover for an after-care mental patient that she agreed to fit in a visit then. He had first considered taking Z along because she had already established a relationship with Harry, but that would have denied Jenner's prior right as senior officer. The man was touchy enough about his standing with the team. He took Yeadings' own presence at field level on the case as heresy enough.

But, the Boss decided, Ms Morrison and himself must suffice. A third person — and Jenner at that — could too easily look like harassment.

This time when he knocked there was no light in the front sitting-room. When May Snelling answered the door, after the customary delay, she wore a cotton overall and there was a smell of baking. There was no sign of Harry.

'We've come to bother you again, I'm afraid,' Yeadings led off.

The woman held her ground. 'I'm sorry, but I've decided. No more questions. I don't know anything that would help. And it upsets my son, all this prying.'

'Just as you like, Mrs Snelling. If it's inconvenient now, you can both come down to the station. Only I thought you'd rather not. All those uniforms.'

She picked it up at once. 'Uniforms? What do you mean?'

'I think you know.' He watched her from sad eyes. 'They could revive bad memories for Harry.'

She gasped, holding on to the door edge.

'Shall we come in then? This is Ms Morrison, from Social Services. She's a little worried because you've lost touch with them.'

Mrs Snelling started retreating and the other two followed her in. She went to a different room this time, stood a moment as if to bar entry with her body, then abruptly gave way. The door

225

opened on the sound of familiar music, but the name of it escaped the big detective. He waited until the end of a phrase, then leaned across and pushed the tape-player's stop button. Harry Snelling, sprawled on the worn cotton covers of a settee, looked up, perplexed.

'Doan' do that. I was listenun.' But he wasn't angry.

'Can we talk first?' Yeadings asked mildly. 'Then we can hear the rest of that tape.'

'Mum?' he appealed, sitting straight.

'Let's do what the gennelman says, Harry.' She had got a grip on herself. Ready perhaps to face the worst. Which must mean the overthrow of all her careful plans to cover her tracks and keep her son safe from outside interference.

'Please sit down, Mr — er —'

'Yeadings,' he reminded her. 'And Ms Morrison from the Amersham office. I don't expect you've met before.'

The two women made wary sounds of greeting.

'Would you rather I called you Mrs Varley or Mrs Snelling?' Yeadings asked, exposing his hand.

She kept her head down, inspecting her knotted fingers. 'It doesn't matter.'

She sounded hopeless. She had made her bid for freedom and lost; she'd run and they'd caught up with her. Worse, they'd caught up with Harry.

'I don't think,' Yeadings ventured to say, 'that you have anything to be afraid of in me.'

The woman looked up, and this time her mouth was bitter. 'Questions,' she said. 'I thought all that was past, but it seems not.'

'I hope I don't need to do anything like that again,' Yeadings told Ms Morrison as they walked back to their cars.

'I thought you handled it very tactfully.'

'I wasn't sure what we'd got there. Harry, I mean. It's one thing to be talking to someone with the educational age of eight and quite another to have to cope with a mentally disturbed person.'

'It's complicated,' she agreed. 'I'm not qualified to say which he is, if he's either. And I can't just accept every word his mother says about him. All I can do is report back that I've met him, he lives here and he's our responsibility to check on. Then it's up to the appropriate experts to assess him. You know, his mother had a widow's pension. She hasn't been drawing it since she reverted to her maiden name. That will all have to be sorted out. Eight months' arrears.'

She seemed more concerned by the paperwork and finances than by the woman's selfless motives.

He held her car door open while she tucked her coat ends in and belted up. He detected a smell in the confined space compounded of peppermint and dry-cleaning fluid.

'Is there any *real* likelihood that he has killed

again?' she asked, tapping at the wheel.

So perhaps she wasn't just a walking calculator. He tried to make a fair assessment of the possibilities. 'All we know for sure is that he recently followed a young woman home in the dark but she managed to outrun him. That was on the same night that another woman was murdered. And a few days later he led the same girl to the body of a possible suicide. It's of note that the girl is a striking natural blonde, and what hasn't been released to the media is the fact that last Thursday's dead woman had a switch of her bleached hair cut off and removed.'

'So maybe you're looking for a fetishist? And I understand that woman too was strangled.' She shivered, starting the engine.

Yeadings nodded. 'And as we know, years back, in the excitement of a racial affray, Harry caused the death of another young man. He escaped being charged only because he was declared unfit to face trial. He's been released for just eight months after six years in a secure unit as an inpatient controlled by drugs.

'I don't want to assume anything at this point, but for everyone's safety, including his own, we do have to monitor his recent movements carefully.'

'And check back on previous diagnosis,' she said grimly. 'We have this on-going problem: so many cases being released into community care as economies are forced on institutions and many

228

of them closed. It makes our workload unbearable, tied to restricted budgets ourselves.'

He assumed that was her last word, smiled and shut the door on it. Now she could go back and complete her paperwork, juggle with figures, make the too-familiar complaints to her colleagues. He sympathized, but whatever was the outcome of the inquiry he hoped he'd not, like her, get to see Harry more as a case than a person.

DS Beaumont had dropped in on Mrs Madeleine Crick. As he had guessed, the night-watchman was still in bed asleep, but a couple of textbooks and a block of lined paper were laid out ready for his use before supper and a return to work.

'Do you call it supper, or breakfast?' the DS asked, watching her polish the cutlery as she set up the table.

'Depends what we eat. Bacon, eggs and sausages, we call it breakfast. Bit of lasagne or a shepherd's pie with veg, and that's supper. We're easy. I got used enough to turning the day upside down when I was on ward duty. That's when Rup got himself this night-watchman job. It's not leading anywhere but it brings in some money till he breaks into the real thing. You want to stay on a while and take pot luck with us? It'll be another half hour.'

'Thanks a lot, but I'll have to move on before then. Was actually hoping you could tell me about other people's night activities round here.'

She regarded him with her head tilted. 'You want me to soil my own nest?'

'Look, I'm not interested in who does what with their buckshee pheasants or salmon. Just where they'd go to get 'em and whether, while there, they saw anything connected with the recent deaths.'

'And do you really think they'd be telling me?'

'No, but their wives might.'

She let out an unexpected whoop of laughter. 'There speaks a married man! You think I got nothun else to do with my time but chat over the back fence?'

'Spot on. Just like my wife spends the day spread out on the settee wolfing chocolates and sherry!'

She shrugged. 'Ah. Well, I won't deny there are some sharp fellers savun on the housekeepun money hereabouts, and Galley Woods are overgrown enough to keep most nosey folks away.'

'Galley Woods?'

'Along the river, upstream a bit. Not Buckman's Shoot side: right opposite. If anyone was puttun down a handful of corn for the birdies there —'

'Out of kindness to wild animals . . .'

'Like you say, Mr Policeman. If they was there, they mighta seen somethun. But no one's said. Not to me leastwise.'

Beaumont considered this. 'If you should hear

something, anything . . .'

'You want me to keep my ears open? Mebbe get the talk round to funny things that go on at night? Man, they're not stupid. They'd know at once I was listenun for your lot.'

'Well, you could always explain that your husband's the number one suspect for murder to date, and neighbourliness cuts both ways. Nobody's going to bother about a spot of poaching when we're after big game.'

She smiled. 'Ah'm sayun nothun, mind. But you follow your nose the way it's pointed and you might learn somethun. Not next door but a couple along.'

Nan Yeadings observed the deep line between Mike's eyes as he switched off the late TV news. He stood watching the little spot of light diminish and disappear, and then went on scowling at the dark screen.

'No real progress yet?' she asked sympathetically. He hadn't spoken of the current murder case since he got home.

He sighed, gave her a lopsided grin. 'A whole week, and we haven't a solid clue that leads anywhere. Unless . . .'

She waited.

'There's this young man. Difficult to say what his problem is. One card short of a deck, as Beaumont would say; or else a violent sociopath. Maybe both, if that's possible. Even the experts don't seem to agree about him. He's had six years in Fenbridge and now he's out without control drugs. Lives with his over-protective widowed mother. Gets out and roams about at night. And he just could have strangled that woman.'

'Difficult. Have you access to his case history?'

'Just police records so far. We'll have to go through the usual kerfuffle to see medical ones. Meanwhile —'

'Something else could happen?'

'I hope to God it doesn't. We've got uniform officers patrolling at night, but not enough for a full surveillance. And I have this gut feeling that there's more to come; that things won't make sense until there's been another death.'

The last train from London slid into Mardham Halt. This week only five passengers got out. Three, chatting together, turned right and started walking up the hill to the main road. A solitary man took the footpath opposite the station exit. In the precinct Gayle Dawson tucked the file of sheet music under one arm, to dig in her coat pocket for the car keys. Holding them ready in one hand and the flute case in the other, she walked past the empty stalls for the bicycles, went down the sodden wooden stairs and into the car park.

Her yellow Triumph was isolated under trees at the far end, because she had driven it in after college but before the rush hour of returning commuters. The whole area, now bare, had then been crammed with vehicles. Sometimes a slot occurred near the ticket office, but not today.

Either because the time switch was faulty or the stationmaster was economizing on power, the far single sodium lamp wasn't on. Her heels struck a defiant beat across the tarmac. She stayed alert for any echo but none came. With relief she fitted the key to the car lock and slid into the driving seat.

Nothing moved outside in the dark. She started the engine and switched on the headlights, began to reverse out — and the car lurched bumpily, out of control, tilting over on its far side.

It couldn't be a flat. She'd had all her tyres checked to the right pressure only yesterday. Yet one of them was clearly dead.

There was a pencil torch under the dashboard. She scrabbled for it, got out and went round to investigate.

Not one, but both on the passenger side. Totally flat. A coincidence; or more? She ran a hand round the wheel's metal edge. The dust caps were off, and by poking with a finger she could feel that the valves were missing. It was deliberate, and must have been done some time ago because the wheels were right down on their rims. If she drove away like that the tyres would be slashed to ribbons and the wheels themselves damaged.

But how — ? No accident. Someone had wanted to —

She had to get safely inside, lock the doors.

Screaming silently, as in a nightmare paralysis, she managed to reach her door again.

And suddenly wasn't alone. There was someone behind, a hand clamping her shoulder. She couldn't cry out — her throat muscles had contracted — only struggle to get loose. Was almost inside the car and felt her scalp torn back as scissors slashed at her hair.

Abruptly her head came free as the hair was severed. She fell forward on her knees on the seat, curled small, pulled the door after her, felt it bounce off her shoes. Wriggled round and reached for the handle again, desperate. Found it. And heard the door slam. Pushed the lock down.

God, she'd got away. Even though she dared not move the car in this state, she'd never leave her safe little box until morning and the station opened up.

She thought the man — the shadow — had run away, but no. He was behind now, leaning on the far side of the boot. And as she peered at him in the dimness of the driving mirror he started to rock the car, just like she'd seen done to cars on TV in the riots, before they set fire to them.

It creaked and crunched with a steadily mounting rhythm as she hung on to the useless wheel.

He'd have it over. This morning she'd filled the tank up at the pump. If the rusted metal sparked, if it went off —

Suddenly now she *could* scream. The sounds

tore at her throat. Of its own volition her hand slammed on to the horn, went on pressing. She'd go on and on hooting until somebody heard and came.

Or the maniac managed to get her outside.

Fourteen

Despite her determination to stay awake, May Snelling had nodded off. She'd known, as the television voices receded like distant seashore sounds, that she was drifting, but Harry looked so settled in his chair, really content, that she told herself, just a minute: I must close my eyes for just a minute.

Then suddenly she was awake, to gunfire pinging off corrugated iron, and horses rearing, wheeling, and being whipped out of some dusty shanty town while guns blazed and men fell from saddles. 'Harry!' she shouted.

But it was too late. She could feel the cold draught from the back door left open. He always did that, as if to warn her, or scare her; she didn't know which. It was enough that he had gone wandering abroad, and she'd promised herself, promised the big detective, that he didn't and couldn't get out at night.

The trouble was that keeping watch meant her turning nocturnal too, but with all the things she had to do by day she got tired. In a flat like this with a neighbour overhead you couldn't use a vacuum cleaner or a washing machine at night. And there was shopping to fetch and always the quota of moccasins to keep up with. It was a special concession from Aziz that they'd pick her stuff up, so if she fell behind on their orders it wouldn't be worth their bothering with her.

There was little comfort in the fact that now she had been found out her pension would be restored, because her security was threatened elsewhere. There would be a constant watch kept on the house. If Harry overstepped . . .

In her slippers she ran out into the garden, for a moment unaware of the chill. 'Harry,' she beseeched him, softy but urgent. 'Harry, come along in. I'll make your hot cocoa. Harry! Harry, love.'

How had he managed to get out? She knew she'd shot both bolts on the back door, locked it, and taken away the key. She could feel it still, hanging on its cord against her breastbone. He must have the second one, which went missing weeks back. She should have had the lock changed after that awful murder, then she'd have been sure. Not that she doubted him. Harry wasn't like that. Other people might say terrible things, but she *knew* . . .

'Harry,' she appealed again, tears in her voice. 'Oh my God, Harry, how could you do this to me?'

But he wasn't coming. He might have gone out only a few minutes back, and he could stay away for hours, a night wanderer. He felt better after dark, because he had the world to himself. And the animals. It was people he was afraid of. And he'd every reason.

She went across to the old rabbit hutch where he kept his snails. His farm, as he called it. There were hundreds of them in it. Fortunately the baby ones got out through the wire netting or it would be a plague. Probably already was a plague in neighbouring gardens.

But Harry wasn't there feeding them. She went back indoors, chilled to the bone, rubbing the backs of her upper arms to renew her circulation. They didn't take newspapers so she'd no way of knowing how long this TV programme had been running. When she'd nodded off it had been something about whales. Harry would have lost interest when it finished, and looked for something else to amuse him.

There was nothing else she could do but sit and wait. There was no knowing in what direction he'd gone, so it'd be folly to try following him. If he came back and found the house empty he'd panic for sure.

She wondered what the big detective would think if he knew. In a way he had seemed to understand, but there were limits. Pray God nothing went amiss tonight that they could blame poor Harry for.

In his silent house Yeadings lay awake. The mattress had gone lumpily hard against his stiff shoulders, and Nan had managed to curl up with almost all the duvet wound round her.

Tea, he thought. Maybe a cuppa would help get me off. He lowered his legs gingerly, scuffed about in the dark for his slippers and padded downstairs.

Seated in his favourite winged leather chair, a hot mug steaming between his hands, he felt more awake than ever.

His body, over-ready for sleep, was balked by the orbiting of his mind which buzzed on like a blowfly that wouldn't settle when you were waiting to swat it.

It was the conversation he'd had with May Snelling that still disturbed him. Harry hung on in his brain.

So think it through, he told himself. Go over everything she told you. When it's all docketed and pigeon-holed it may stop bugging you. Or the effort may weary you enough to knock you out.

She'd talked about Harry as a child, an ordinary little boy but always big for his age, attending the local church school. He hadn't been much of a scholar but he hadn't been a dunce. And good at music, learned piano and recorder.

Because of his size older boys picked fights. There was always the physical challenge, and he was a gentle lad, would rather walk away, only they wouldn't let him.

Which didn't suit his Dad. Varley senior had the same build; a beautiful body, May Snelling had said. But not an easy man to live with. And she'd talked at some length about him.

Yeadings could see him, the actual man behind her idealized portrait: an enormous, overbearing character — superb physique, self-indulgent; no compunction or compassion for others; forever assuming his own superiority, going out of his way to seek physical conquests, both male and female. Adrenalin stimulated by success after conflict; voracious, without commitment. Unbeatable.

Fine while it lasts. And dangerous as hell.

There comes a time with such a one when conquests cease. He reaches the point of non-success.

So was it in his son that he first met failure? — his only child, intended to clone himself? And had he fought him to try to put him right?

He had started to teach Harry to box. The hard way, by knocking him down again every time he tried to get away. Until he learned what was required of him. Harry had been sent along to the local gym and had taken on the bully boys there.

And he had the body for a future amateur heavyweight. So strong. When he was only seventeen, single-handed he'd lifted the rag-and-bone man's horse when it fell on ice and broke the cart shafts. And soon after, he'd been set on in the street by a group of muggers, fought them off but was brought down by a blow to the head by a length of lead piping.

After that and a period in hospital to mend his skull, there was no more visiting the gym for training. He had trouble with his balance. But his father hadn't understood, couldn't accept it. He kept on at the boy until eventually Harry had turned on him and knocked him out cold.

Then Varley senior had to face the truth. The career he'd planned for his boy was ruined, because Harry had dissolved in tears, was a great blubbing baby now who'd rather take any punishment than use again the fists he'd broken his father with.

And the father *was* broken, pathetically. Always the centre of his own universe, he saw he wasn't so now for anyone else. Even his submissive little wife had become a champion for the useless son against him. Accustomed to driving others' lives, he found he had lost the energy to pursue his own. He started to drink heavily, lost his job as a storeman because his timekeeping was unreliable and his accounting became inaccurate.

May had persuaded him to take a break with his sister in Cardiff. But just four days after he got there he was killed along with his brother-in-law, a heavy goods driver, in a jack-knife crash near the Severn Bridge.

Six months later, in a street fight between skinheads and Asians, Harry had gone in when he saw a youth using a pickaxe handle on a young Pakistani, and went over the top. Kneeling on the man's chest, his hands couldn't be prised away from the other's throat. Onlookers said his head was bleeding and there had been froth on his mouth. Afterwards, arrested for the murder, he hadn't been able to remember a thing. In the police cell he'd run amok and screamed for his Dad.

Evidence had been offered of previous unstable behaviour, and from then on he suffered sporadic loss of memory, emotional surges, *petit mal*. Instead of appearing in court on a serious charge Harry had been sectioned, remaining as an in-patient under medication in a secure unit. On release after six years, life in Wycombe among neighbours who remembered what had happened would have been insupportable. So his mother reverted to her maiden name, and they had moved to Mardham eight months ago. For peace in the country.

It was not quite the way the police reports told Harry's story, Yeadings conceded; but then there were two sides to it. He was forced to see both, being a policeman and also father to someone similarly disabled — but not equally, thank God.

Eventually he would have to think out what to do about Harry. But not yet, while he felt so much.

The local constable, Jeffrey Bond, had an arrangement with the lads who'd drawn the short straw for the graveyard shift. Since both Mobile Incident Room and canteen van were closed at 11 P.M., a spare key to his own back door was left hidden above the lintel outside. A kettle and tea things were available in the kitchen, the inner door of which was secured against anyone penetrating farther while he and Jeanie slept.

He had no idea of the hour, when a heavy thumping on its panels and a voice shouting his name brought him suddenly back to earth. Not waiting to pull on slippers or dressing-gown, he went crashing downstairs to voice a righteous complaint.

'What the blazes — !'

'There's been another attack. Down the station car park. CID's been called.'

'Did you get him?'

'Nuh. He bolted. There's a girl —'

'Who, man?' God, it could be someone he knew this time!

'Dunno. Girl in a car, got off the train. You're to come down. They've put her in the station waiting-room.'

'Ambulance been called?'

'She won't have any. Says she'll be all right. Shut herself in the car, so he didn't get to touch her.'

Bond didn't stay for more, scrambling upstairs. 'Don't wait!' he shouted down as an afterthought. 'I'll come on me bike.' More than that, he'd scour the lanes around before he made it to the station; see what houses still had lights on. Third time the maniac had gone for a woman here. He had to be local. It could even be the same girl, he realized: the one who'd got away before. The student lodging with old Mrs George.

Gayle was white-faced, with a lump already discolouring her forehead where she had struck

243

the steering wheel in the buffetings of the car. She was in an excited, talkative state but the sergeant hunkered beside her bench had insisted she should keep her story until CID could hear it fresh from her. An ex-marine, he had provided the universal remedy from his own flask of coffee laced with rum, and his uniform tunic was wrapped round the girl's hunched shoulders as she sipped.

'I'm so glad you came,' she exploded. 'I was so scared. The tyres —'

'Don't you worry none,' a woman PC said comfortably. 'Bob's gone down to take a good look. He'll see no one lays a hand on your car till Fingerprints've been all over it.'

There came a sound of wheels on the gritty surface of the station approach. A car door slammed and in came DS Zyczynski with a civilian in tow. She turned at the door as if to wave him back but he gave a puckish smile, with one finger pushed his spectacles up the bridge of his nose, and claimed, 'First-aider.'

'If you say so.' It was mildly ironic. 'Gayle, how are you?' Z moved in on more urgent matters.

'All right, I think; once I stop shivering. No, I'm going to be sick!'

The DS whisked an arm round the girl and steadied her to her feet. 'Can you make it to the loo?' Already they were moving off. The others hurriedly cleared a way.

A constable came in from outside. 'A real nutty character,' he growled. 'I just had a good look

244

what he'd done. Wasn't enough to take all four tyre caps off. Had to superglue them on top of the bonnet, hadn't he? No sign of the two missing valves, though. Too much to hope he'll have them in his pocket when we nick him, eh?'

'SOCO shouldn't be too long with some lights,' the sergeant said crisply. 'See where we can run the cables from. And I don't want anyone else walking near that car before everything's been photographed.'

He sized up the civilian who had come in with Z. 'You made it pretty nippy, sir. Rally driver, would you be then?'

The man smiled. 'DS Zyczynski requires no chauffeur, Sergeant.'

'Right, sir.' He switched on a noncommittal expression, as if he wasn't curious who Z was dating. It was clear as the red nose on a toper's face that neither had been home yet that night. First-aider indeed! He'd heard that one before.

The policewoman was staring at the stranger. 'Met you before, sir, I think. That hit-and-run at Beaconsfield*. Weren't you the reporter who linked it to the Met murder?'

'You flatter me. That was Mr Yeadings' deduction. And I'm not a journalist. A columnist: much more of an armchair character.' His voice was laid back, to fit the description, but the eyes were sharp, crinkled at the outside edges with humour lines.

* *Past Mischief*

'Max Harris.' The sergeant recalled the name now. He hadn't been on that case, and didn't know the man's face. So Harris was still hanging around. Around DS Zyczynski in particular. Need to be careful there, because however he preferred to describe himself, the man worked on a newspaper. And newspapers were trouble for everyone.

The two women came back, Gayle still unsteady but now with a better colour in her cheeks.

'Shall we talk here and now? Or would you rather get home?' Z asked. 'I'm thinking of Mrs George. Will she be waiting up for you?'

'No. This time I persuaded her not to. After all, I had the car. I should be safe enough!' Her voice cracked on the attempt at humour. 'Let's get it over straight away. I don't want her dragged in. Tomorrow's soon enough.'

'It's tomorrow already,' the sergeant corrected her. '12.42 A.M.'

'Only that? It felt it had gone on for hours.'

'Did you see who it was?' Z demanded.

Gayle frowned. 'Not really; just a dark shape looming over me. There wasn't any light in the car park . . .'

'Bulb shattered,' said the constable who'd been looking around out there. 'Someone chucked half a brick at it.'

'. . . and I was trying to get away; inside, for safety. I was a terrible coward. I — I'm sorry. I panicked, did all the wrong things.'

246

'Not a bit of it. You're here safe, aren't you? Hooting fetched the cavalry.'

But wasn't it providential that the Boss had laid on a patrol for that night, Z thought thankfully. Otherwise there could have been another death. Already four officers were circling the village in pairs alerted for a lone figure on foot. Two patrol cars were making a wider sweep. There was a chance they might get him. But if he lived nearby he could be at home by now, in bed, ready to swear he'd been there all night.

A new arrival put his head through the waiting-room door. 'SOCO,' he reported. 'Want the overalls now?'

'And a blanket,' Z said shortly. When they were handed through she laid them on the table. 'I'd like everyone out now while Miss Dawson changes. Gayle, I'm sorry, but we need your clothes, the outer ones anyway.'

A pity the sergeant had lent her his tunic: there might be traces passed. She lifted it carefully off the girl's shoulders.

'And a hair sample, I'm afraid.' She stood by with an envelope ready.

Gayle slammed both hands against the sides of her head. 'Hair! That's what he did. He had scissors or something. He slashed my hair off!'

It had suddenly hit her, the extent of her physical abuse.

And she didn't know about it being the second time he'd gone for blonde hair: that she'd been part-way to the murdered woman's fate.

PC Bond had twice been passed by the patrol car when he encountered the infantry. 'Was it the Dawson girl?' he demanded of the constable he'd just seen using his handset. By now there had been time to consider the message that had wakened him.

'Seems so. It's her car they've taped off down at the Halt.'

'Smashed in?'

'Nuh. Just immobilized. Two tyres let down.'

'That's all?'

'Enough, isn't it? *She* thought so. They're laying on the full works; Scene-of-Crime team; that Polish bird questioning her; and a message through to the Superintendent. He'll really care for that, tucked up all snuglike.'

'Have you done the Close?'

'Close? What Clo— ?'

'Orchard Close, where the girl lives.'

'Not yet. We've been —'

'Don't bother. I'll take a look.' Bond swung his leg back over the saddle and pedalled creakingly off.

'Living up to his name,' said the humorist wanly. 'Dig his state-of-the-art transport.'

'Typical Thames Valley force,' his partner appreciated. 'Pared to the bone. We'll have to fight to get our overtime on this.'

Bond was asking himself as he furiously pedalled just why the Close had sprung to his mind. The girl wasn't there herself. The action had been elsewhere, so why this urgent hunch?

Was it because she seemed a quiet youngster who hadn't spread herself like some kids did nowadays? — had been here only a few weeks, probably knew no one beyond her nearest neighbours?

But someone had noticed her, had picked up her Thursday habit of leaving the car at the Halt. That same person had followed her on foot just a week back, and would be galled that she'd got away that time. After this second failed attempt, how would he be feeling now?

The thin tyres screeched as Bond braked at the corner into the Close. He pulled up under the unlit streetlamp. After 12.30 that fact wasn't significant. In the house to the extreme right, facing him, there was light showing behind the curtains of a downstairs room. But that wasn't where the girl lived. Hers was next door, the big old house hidden by trees.

He remounted and pedalled across to the stone pillars of the driveway. Inside he took the turns at speed and the house came into view. A heavy coach lantern illuminated the square portico in readiness for the girl's return. But there were lights on inside as well, both at the upstairs landing window and in the hall. As he dismounted and leaned his bike against a column the front door opened and a dumpy little lady stood there pulling a coat round her shoulders. 'Gayle? My dear, you're —'

Bond stepped forward. She saw him and froze.

'Oh no, something's wrong! I knew it. It's because of Harry, isn't it? I heard his mother calling and calling, but he didn't come. Oh, this is awful! Whatever has happened to Gayle?'

Fifteen

DS Beaumont cursed the force five wind that sprang up before first light. It disturbed the accumulated leaves and debris in the car park making the search more difficult. From a distance he watched the white-overalled figures bagging the yellow Triumph in billowing plastic before it was ferried off for expert examination. The two missing tyre valves hadn't turned up. Their superglued rubber caps still marched erect across the top of the car's bonnet, mocking all efforts so far to remove them.

Four caps off, but only two valves removed, he thought: now why? Had the attacker needed to hide on one side of the car as he worked on it? Or been disturbed and left the job half done? Not disturbed by the girl herself, though, because it would have taken some considerable time for the tyres to go flat. So perhaps it was done much earlier while others were about, coming off a train?

There was a bit of mathematics promised for the scientific experts. Gayle claimed she'd checked the tyres the previous morning and they were made up to full pressure. So, knowing what that was, it would be perfectly possible to reconstruct the act and discover the minimum period it took to deflate them completely. Which would give the latest point of time at which the interference could have taken place. But there was no clue to how early it could have been done. The car might have stood like that nearly all day. He would need to question everyone using the car park to see if anything had been observed.

For himself he inclined towards a later time, because the overhead light had been shattered. That could be as much to hide the attacker while interfering with the car as to set the scene for the girl's return.

And on consideration he could see another viable reason for tackling only one side of the car. Deflating all four tyres could leave the car more stable than fixing only one side. The attacker hadn't intended Gayle to travel any distance at all before realizing that something was amiss. He'd wanted to immobilize it so that he could get at her right where he'd planned; therefore maximum lurching when she tried to start off.

What attacker? he asked himself. Such planning didn't seem much in Harry Snelling's line if Harry was as slow a reasoner as was generally supposed. Or had he been left with a modicum of native cunning, enough for survival as the vicious animal which Jenner was determined to prove him?

The plastic-wrapped car was being hauled off, and the fingertip search almost complete. Nothing here, the DS decided. And an equal blank had been drawn in the fenced passage where Harry, already questioned, claimed to have picked up the hank of cut hair. Just a single loose strand caught on the rough woodwork or among the fallen leaves might have borne out his story.

No; it appeared more and more certain that the hank had passed straight from Gayle's head to Harry's pocket. But in that case what had he done with the knife or scissors he'd used to chunk it off? Every inch of the gardens to either side of his way home would have to be beaten, to check if he'd thrown anything over before they caught up with him. And a needle in a haystack would be nothing compared with looking through the woods.

The interview arranged for 10.30 A.M. had to be left to Jenner. He was the investigating officer, and the most Yeadings could properly do was sit in on part of the questioning. It would be taped and on camera, with a member of Social Services present. Rosemary Zyczynski would be alongside the DI to give details of the arrest.

At a few minutes before 3 A.M. they had caught up with Harry as he emerged from woodland along Buckman's Shoot. He had stood blinking in the glare of the headlights, and, although reluctant, came peacefully enough when she offered him a lift. But he had picked up the others' tension, for all they'd been warned to play it cool, and his eyes never left their uniforms all the way to Amersham nick.

Once inside, he'd begun to display open alarm, barely holding back panic when asked to empty his pockets. The little pile of his treasures on the custody sergeant's desk was pathetic: no money, but two tap washers, a handkerchief, a length of twine, a key, the empty plastic box from a tape of Strauss waltzes and half a tube of peppermints.

'Is that all?'

He nodded. 'Why d'you want to know? I dun nothun. I di'n hurt no one.'

'Any inside pockets?' The sergeant nodded towards the anorak and a constable slid a hand in, searching.

Harry suddenly stepped back, fists balled. 'You don' touch me.' It was getting to him: the uniforms, the way they all stood round him. He remembered how it had gone before.

'My God, it's in there! I felt it.' The policeman moved after him, but Z had stepped between.

'Hang on,' she cautioned. 'Harry, is there something you haven't shown us?'

He defied her a moment. 'It's mine. I found it.'

'May I see?'

Resentfully he looked round at the others. 'It's private.'

She nodded at the uniform men to draw back. 'Things you find have to be handed in and we put them on our list. They could belong to someone else. If nobody comes to claim them, then we'll return them to you. That's the way it's done. Do you understand?'

He nodded slowly.

'You can trust me.

He said nothing but pushed a big hand inside his anorak and felt around. It came out with a thin hank of blonde hair which he held protectively against his chest.

Z closed her eyes briefly. 'Write it down,' she told the custody sergeant. 'We'll have to look after this, Harry. It's to be handed back to you if not claimed.'

She stayed on while he was cautioned and walked with him to the cell which he entered in a haze of incomprehension.

Then she went into the CID room and rang the Boss.

On arrival in the cell, Harry first asked for his father, then remembered he was dead and changed it to mother. He hadn't wanted a solicitor, but Mrs Snelling brought one when she came in almost an hour later. Unsurprisingly, it was their neighbour Donald Field.

The man had sat in on the interview later that morning, and Yeadings, fearing the numbers in the small room might overwhelm Harry, waited in his office, teeth clamped on the tobacco-free pipe he still turned to in moments of tension.

The interview tape was harmless. Listening to it for the second time after lunch, Yeadings breathed more freely. Forewarned, Jenner had held off, but his excitement came through in the jarring tone of voice, the tightness of the bitten-off consonants.

Harry had agreed that he knew Gayle Dawson,

the girl who had come to live next door, but he hadn't known her name. She was pretty, he said. She'd helped him find Kittypuss. When? — he wasn't sure. Perhaps it was yesterday, or before then. No, he didn't know what day of the week today was: nobody had told him.

Did he know whose hair it was he'd had in his pocket?

This had upset him. The solicitor had advised him not to answer that question.

Where had he found it? — with the same advice, but Harry had overridden it. The hair had been on the ground. The ground where?

Clearly Harry didn't know the street names in Mardham. Z had intervened to ask if he could describe the place where the hank of hair had been lying. He said it was in the passage. With fences. He knew she went home that way because he'd seen her there once before.

' "She",' Jenner repeated tightly. 'There is only one passage in Mardham. It leads from the station to Mill Lane,' he said for the tape's benefit.

'Did the young lady have a car?' he asked. And Harry had nodded. A yellow one. It rattled a bit. He always knew when it went out.

Had he seen it tonight? No. But he'd heard it leave before breakfast, and again just after tea. He seemed quite proud of his own observation.

Had he known where it went that second time? No, because he didn't go out until much later.

How late? It had been after the telly.

Did he remember what was on the television? Yes, it was about the sea. Whales and dolphins and that.

Had he gone anywhere near the Halt station? No. He went over the bridge.

Which bridge?

Again he didn't know its name, but was able to explain that it crossed the railway line, and then the road went out into the country. Where there were badgers.

And which was on the far side of the village from where eventually they'd picked him up. 'Harry,' Jenner said slowly with emphasis, 'how could you find the hair in that passage when you were out past the railway track?'

Again the solicitor warned that he didn't have to answer, but Harry frowned over the recollection. 'I had to get there, didn't I?'

'Do you mean,' Z put in, 'that you found it on your way to see the badgers?'

Harry had nodded, then was asked to reply aloud for the tape recording. 'On my way to the badgers,' he agreed.

Jenner sat back with a satisfied hiss. 'That passage wasn't on your way, Harry. Coming out of Orchard Close you would've turned right and gone straight along Mill Lane to the bridge.'

Harry didn't argue, frowning down at his huge hands on the table before him.

'He doesn't know the names of streets,' Z reminded the DI.

Jenner's nostrils flared as he breathed in over

tightened lips. The stupid girl was spoiling his interrogation.

'Perhaps,' Field said on his client's behalf, 'you would point out the route on your map of the village.'

Z swivelled the map for Harry to see it from the direction he would have travelled, and pointed with her pencil. 'Look, here's the bridge and the road over it. Do you remember which way you went to get there?'

She thought he might not manage to understand the diagram, but without hesitation he laid a thick finger on the passage from Mill Lane into Lower Church Road. She described his action for the tape.

'That leads away from your home,' Jenner growled, 'and away from the bridge.' He frowned over the diagram. 'The direct route . . .'

'Isn't necessarily the way he'd go,' Field put in quickly. 'He was out for a night walk, Inspector.'

'I allus go that way.'

'So where after Lower Church Road?'

Harry hesitated, confused.

Z looked at her map. It had all the drawbacks of a flat plan. But Lower Church Road was a hill. 'When you came out of the passage did you go uphill or down?'

'Uphill,' Harry said, nodding. 'To go over the bridge.'

'So tell me this then,' and Jenner leant close, fixing Harry with a menacing eye. 'If you came out by the passage, you were quite near the station car park, just above it. Didn't you hear anything, see anyone?'

'Heard an owl.'

'No car hooting?'

'No.' Harry frowned. 'Saw some policemen. Two and two. But I hid.'

'But they caught up with you much later.'

He nodded. 'Going home. My Mum worries if I stay out.'

'You were picked up down Buckman's Shoot, behind your house. That wasn't the way home.'

Harry merely nodded. 'I allus go round the back. I'd got me boots dirty, see?'

Jenner shook his head. 'Useless,' he said. 'He doesn't know one path from another. Just show me again the whole route you went.'

Slowly, doggedly, Harry traced the route with his forefinger.

'You're sure?' Z asked. 'You went along this path here?'

'Yes.' He didn't seem to recognize he'd won a point.

'Which is where you picked up the bunch of hair?'

'That's right,' he said. He looked up, worried. 'It's her hair, isn't it? The pretty lady next door.'

He shook his head in wonder. 'Why'd she want to go and spoil it?'

Before Donald Field left the Amersham nick he had asked to speak with the Superintendent. When he was shown into the temporary office,

Yeadings was struck by the greyness of his drawn face. Events in Mardham were certainly taking their toll of the residents.

The suggestion Field made was quite proper, that being a neighbour to both victim and suspect, he should transfer the Snelling defence to his partner, who was in any case more familiar with criminal charges. Mrs Snelling had said she was agreeable.

'I see,' Yeadings nodded, waiting for whatever else was to come.

Field reached the door before turning to ask, affecting sudden recollection, 'Has there been any development concerning Dr Goodwin's — er, death?'

'The inquest will be opened on Monday. We shall be asking for an adjournment. You won't be required to attend at this stage.'

'I see. Just a formality then.'

'Evidence of identity and circumstances of discovery. Some medical facts. No more.'

'So your inquiries are continuing? But I trust the family may make arrangements for the funeral. Unnecessary delay can be most distressing under such circumstances.'

By family he obviously meant widow. From what Yeadings had gathered from his team, Meredith's brother was hardly grief-stricken. And the widow had gone to friends, was seeing no one. Even if he was the Goodwins' authorized legal representative, Field wasn't in an enviable position, shunned by his mistress, and surely bearing more than the usual measure of guilt felt by survivors after a sudden death.

'Is there any particular evidence you wish to present yourself?' Yeadings probed.

The question shocked the solicitor. 'No, no! Nothing. I merely . . .' He made a helpless gesture with his hands. 'If there is anything I can do to make it less painful for the family . . .'

'I'm sure they will let you know. As to release of the body, that decision will naturally rest with the coroner.'

The man nodded, resumed the saturnine mask of his profession and took his leave.

'Mmm,' murmured Yeadings. 'Now where the hell is Beaumont? He could have gone to the moon for all I've seen of him these last days.'

Donald Field again tried phoning Meredith at home and heard the ringing continue unbroken. Even the answerphone had been turned off. With little confidence he rang the doctor's number where she had taken refuge, and a woman answered. He identified himself and was told that Mrs Goodwin was recovering but could not be disturbed.

'As the family solicitor,' he insisted stiffly, 'I am empowered to take care of the legal implications. Today I have consulted with Superintendent Yeadings of Thames Valley Police and learnt that the inquest will be held on Monday.' He went on to point out the necessity of speaking with his client before then to protect her interests and avoid her exposure to unpleasant publicity.

The woman let him talk himself out, then said quietly, 'Mrs Goodwin has left strict instructions that you should not attempt to contact her again, Mr Field. She will be represented in future by Martensen and Silver of Aylesbury. They will be writing to you regarding the transfer of any documents you may be holding for her or her late husband.'

Shattered, Field replaced the receiver without another word.

The evening newspapers were on to the incident with shrieking headlines: Hair Fetishist Strikes Again; Mardham Killer Stalks Blondes.

Beside the paparazzi a television van and crew had arrived at Mardham Halt and were interviewing commuters off their trains. Householders were brought to their doors and had microphones thrust under their noses. Women with hair even remotely describable as fair were being asked for their feelings about walking the village alone at night.

'Who leaked it that they both had their hair cut off?' Yeadings demanded. 'We had the wraps on that aspect of the Sheena murder.'

'I heard there was a newspaperman present when the girl was brought in,' Jenner accused. 'Perhaps someone there shot off his mouth. His or hers.' He stared tightlipped at Z.

Beaumont didn't bother to speculate. It would take only one of their number to mention cut hair in the canteen for it to become common knowledge within the force: a saleable property. One had to be realistic these days. This was the Era of the Profitable Leak. For some a way of life.

But yesterday, at the time of the attack on Gayle Dawson, it hadn't been public knowledge that some of the murdered woman's hair had been cut off. That one fact, known only to four police and the pathology department, had been carefully kept under wraps. Which should rule out a copy-cat crime. He considered the implication.

'This has to be the same man striking at Gayle who killed the woman from Soho. And that implies a local, or someone who has visited Mardham at least twice . . .'

'. . . and who knew of Gayle Dawson's use of the station,' Z added. 'So we should look again at other commuters, her neighbours and college friends.'

'Harry Snelling,' Jenner declared with confidence. 'He fits the bill in every way. And we've caught him redhanded with the hair on him. He's admitted using the path that leads from the station. I don't believe he was going out to the bridge. Some witness may have seen him down in the car park. We'll get a confession once we start questioning him about the earlier strangling. It's in his record. We don't have to search any further.'

It did look bad for Harry, Yeadings admitted. But it just didn't smell right. And he always trusted his nose on these matters. It hadn't often let him down.

On the other hand he knew he could be prejudiced, because privately he carried a torch for a certain kind of person.

Sixteen

Next morning a telex from the Met reported that the glazier's van stolen by Martin Chadwick had been traced to an unofficial fishmonger lodging in Acton.

'What makes a fishmonger official?' Beaumont marvelled, taking elaborate care over the pronunciation.

'Ask them,' the Boss invited.

It appeared that the man was involved in a syndicate, using the van to ferry thawed frozen fish from northern markets to hawk it door-to-door in the south, prepackaged as fresh fish. The Geordie entrepreneurs, miners made redundant, considered Home Counties housewives incapable of telling the difference between fresh and dubious. Their glib spiel boasted direct service, middle-man cutout, low overheads, therefore lower prices than in local shops. But in case taste-buds or abdominal cramps should disillusion conned customers, the door-to door service never covered the same route twice.

The ex-glazier's van was part of a fleet of five. It had been used in the fish scam for almost a fortnight now, having been bought at a London street lot only three days after Chadwick absconded with it from Wigan.

'Which rules it out as the van in the pub yard, unless Chadwick is in with the Geordies or borrowed it back . . .' Beaumont began.

'You're right,' Yeadings gave as his opinion. 'Alive or dead, the woman's body hadn't been contaminated by fish. Even wrapped in polythene there would have been some trace when the covering was removed. Littlejohn is thorough enough, with a surprisingly fine sense of smell.'

'Anyway,' Jenner said decisively, 'it's more likely the woman hitched a lift with some unknown man and arrived alive, then happened on Snelling — Varley, if you prefer — who then killed her.'

'But why should he kill a complete stranger?' Z demanded.

'If she was soliciting, that could be reason enough. The man could have felt threatened by his own sex urge. It's not as though he's of normal mentality.'

Yeadings stirred out of his chair and wandered to the window where he leaned, looking out on the village street. 'I had a phone call from Miss Dawson half an hour back,' he said flatly. 'She's pretty certain now that the man who attacked her was not Harry Snelling.'

'How certain?' Jenner demanded sharply.

'She didn't quantify her impression, and the only reason she gave was that he wasn't big enough and he moved too quickly.

'I suggest we shouldn't rush to connect the murder with this attack on Miss Dawson, which was malicious but — beyond the haircutting — seemed primarily intended to terrify her.'

He turned back and faced the team. 'Think, now; Gayle's attacker had the advantage of surprise. Yet he didn't cover her mouth, didn't threaten her with a weapon, didn't pinion her arms. Didn't drag her into nearby bushes to rape or beat her.

'And he didn't speak. Which suggests to me that he feared she might recognize his voice. He let her get back into her car, holding her only by the hair from behind as he chopped at it. Under the microscope the cut ends show he used scissors. The murdered woman's hair, in contrast, had been removed close to the scalp, by a sharp knife or razor.

'We know that Harry Snelling had no cutting instrument on his person, and searches have so far failed to turn up anything of the sort between the car park and where he was arrested.

'But, before we entirely rule him out as the attacker, I want a search made of his home to discover whether any scissors have gone missing over the past week or so. Perhaps you can spare Sergeant Zyczynski for this, Inspector, as she is familiar with Mrs Snelling's craftwork. As soon as she returns, if nothing has been found, Harry Snelling will be released.'

Jenner darted Yeadings a black look, then nodded grimly in Z's direction. 'See that you're thorough. I'll authorize two constables to help. If the woman insists on a warrant, ring in and stay with her until it arrives.'

In the short silence that followed, Beaumont moved restlessly. 'Sir, anything more on Dr Goodwin's death? He's looking like the odd one out.'

'Because he wasn't given a short-back-and-sides?' The Boss's harsh tone revealed his distaste. He must be rattled to have come out with humour that black.

'Also Goodwin's photograph pulled a total zero in Soho, round Sheena Chadwick's haunts,' Beaumont added. 'I had a call from a newspaper hack wanting a copy. He must have got scent of that inquiry and thought he was on to a profitable line. I turned him down, warned him there could be a defamation suit from Goodwin's family if he drew the wrong conclusions. Goodwin remains whiter than white, the perfect family practitioner and faithful husband.'

Yeadings nodded. 'You're right, of course. He doesn't fit in. I think we have to accept that he killed himself, unusual as the method was. I'd be a lot happier if we could turn up a suicide note. It could be that there was one and it's been suppressed for some reason.

'What other photographs should we be sending the Met?' he asked. 'A lot of Mardham folk must go up there shopping or on business from time to time.'

'Get a selection,' Jenner snapped at Beaumont, reasserting his control of the investigation. 'And see what comes out of it. Include both Snellings,

Malcolm Barrow, Field. I want you to examine again everything we've got on the Chadwick woman. It's all on disk. Have another look at the listed stuff I brought back from her flat. There has to be some connection either with her husband or with someone at Mardham. And start up another search for the missing handbag.'

He turned to Yeadings thrusting out his bony chin in defiance. 'Is there anything else, sir, you think we should be concentrating on?'

Yeadings lifted his overcoat off the chair where he had dropped it on entering. 'You could list and ponder all the vital bits that are missing: the handbag, the van, a suicide note, a pair of scissors. They're negative, but clues just the same, because there's a reason for each being missing. If we knew why, and could lay hands on the damn things, we might see a way out of the blind alley we've been led up.'

The others watched him leave before moving off themselves. As so often, his final words, seemingly thrown away, had struck Z with a new blazing possibility. '. . . blind alley . . . we've been led up.'

That was a concept she'd never imagined: that somewhere out there a criminal mind was conscious of police efforts and planning their frustration. Nobody at all like Harry, but a devious intelligence bent on deliberate evildoing.

They went about the routine tasks allocated, and although none of the declared missing items came to light something else did, an unconsidered scrap of paper which, on finding, had reminded Jenner of a slang expression. But Beaumont, his mind free-wheeling as he turned over the bagged junk retrieved from Sheena Chadwick's bedroom floor and the contents of her waste bin, did not read the print as HARD CHEESE.

It was a torn fragment from a sheet of stiff notepaper, and he saw its context in an instant. The capitals HARD C were part of the words Orchard Close. Someone from Mardham *had* been in touch with Sheena Chadwick. It rested with him now to identify the notepaper and trace the number of the house.

The capital letters, the experts informed him, weren't from professionally stamped stationery but produced by an electronic daisy-wheel printer. Leaving them to run experiments for comparison, along with paper analysis, Beaumont armed himself with a list of residents of the Close and set out to discover which of them possessed word processors. In these universally computerized days he guessed that could be everyone.

In the event he was able to eliminate no. 1 and Polders. If the alcoholic Ibbott had ever owned a PC it would long have gone the way of half his furniture in order to sustain his habit.

The Snellings had no need. From their open front door Beaumont glimpsed Z in the kitchen searching drawers. Jenner was a daft bugger, to imagine you could prove something *wasn't* there, unless the household cooperated over what was there originally. The Boss had suggested it just to provide a let-out for Harry.

But Mrs Snelling was distressed enough, with Harry held at the nick. She wouldn't have the heart to lie, even if she understood why scissors were important.

Mrs George next door also had no state-of-the-art aids to writing. Gayle Dawson owned an electric typewriter incapable of such even reproduction as the HARD C sample. She was familiar with computers, but had access only to those at her college.

The door of no. 3 was opened by Malcolm Barrow slightly the worse for drink at eleven in the morning. Beaumont, who had passed through bad moments himself and recognized the occasional need for a hair of the dog, was able to excuse this. He was taken through to Dr Goodwin's study and with a bad grace shown machines shrouded in tailored covers of soft plastic. It was a German system which Beaumont had encountered in brochures, through his teenage son's expensive but unrealized ambitions.

'I'll need to run something off,' he told Barrow who shrugged and slouched away to the kitchen, perhaps to recover his pick-me-up. The DS switched on, selected a clearly marked start-of-day disk and sat to operate the keyboard. He typed an unoriginal event in the life of the quick brown fox, followed by the house address. The printer was individually switched, and while he waited for it to deliver he ran an eye over the alphabetically arranged disks. One, which came after MEDICAL, was labelled MEREDITH, and he reached for it, weighing it thoughtfully in one hand. On an impulse he exchanged it for the used disk and pressed E for EDIT.

There was a single entry, undated and unattributed. It appeared to be in verse.

Such beauty, beloved,
Such passion, cannot be contained;
I would rather try
To beat out a heath fire with a feather!
And I so cold no longer dread
The onset of my winter.
Sterile, its shroud blots out
The darkness and the doubting;
Guilt that gathers with the gloom;
Ghosts of angry words, the shouting
Of passionate obscenities,
Then tears . . . And now
The necessary ruptures left behind.

That was all the disk contained. 'Gawd,' Beaumont said shakily. Not quite a suicide note, it had to be something close. An intimate letter to his wife, which perhaps she hadn't caught up with.

Exactly what it meant wasn't immediately clear, but then all poetry had the taint of obscurity to him. This would be more in the Boss's line. Let him work it out. All he could do himself now was take a copy and put the disk back where one day, sorting through her husband's effects,

Meredith might come across her name, and curiosity would do the rest.

There had been nothing in the poem that seemed to refer to the Sheena Chadwick business, but all the same, since the two deaths were chronologically and spatially so close, Beaumont could not discount a connection. So he requested, and obtained from a still sulky Barrow, samples of all notepaper in use by the household. Again there was printed stationery, some bearing the doctor's name and surgery address in black Roman font, and for private use two boxes of quarto loose sheets with the house address die-stamped in blue script.

Beaumont folded the papers away in a jacket pocket and went to be let out. In the hall Barrow faced him with narrowed eyes and a sly smile. 'Someone writing poison pen notes then?' he supposed. 'Nothing'd surprise me in this miserable dump. Lot of par-parsimonious, self-righteous nit-pickers. Such nice folk full of nasty thoughts. Small wonder the saintly Stanley topped himself. Not that he was any better, sod him.'

'You didn't get on with your brother-in-law?'

'Oh no, you're not getting me to say that. He was heavy, thassall. Now he's gone . . .'

'Well? Now he's gone, what?'

Barrow stared back foggily, his open mouth sagging. He shook his head slowly, then put a shaking hand to his temples. It seemed that was the doubt he had been seeking to drown. He just didn't know; had hoped things would be easier,

273

with just himself and his sister to enjoy the fruits of the dead man's labours. But then he'd had second thoughts, perhaps remembered his sister's passion for Field, and saw he'd be out in the cold more than ever.

'Life's a bitch,' Beaumont told him, easing through the door held ajar. Some people had work to do; and his wasn't the easiest, at times pretty gruesome. It left him scant sympathy for jerks leeching on to others' efforts. Maybe Dr Goodwin had felt much the same, had even pondered the effect on Barrow of sudden deliverance from dependence.

At no. 4, Donald Field, marking Saturday by still being in his dressing-gown, denied all knowledge of electronic gadgetry, clearly considering this ignorance a distinction. At his Amersham legal practice things like that were 'left to the girls'.

The Field twins shared an early Amstrad PC system with a slightly worn printer. Their mother also used this for various lists connected with charity work, claiming that floppy disks offered no security from interference, so 'private matters' were not included among her data.

Along with a printout from the machine she volunteered a sample of her own notepaper which was a polished bond headed at the centre with her name and address embossed in bright green. Her personal typewriter, surprisingly, was a manual Adler. With a disdain matching her husband's she claimed she had never learned to touch-type and found electric models 'too fast'.

Beaumont wasn't surprised to find Zyczynski waiting alongside his car. 'Finished at the Snellings'?' he asked, uplifted from gloom by her shining face.

'There was little enough to go through. Mrs S was quite a needlewoman once. She had a full manicure set, a little case with three pairs of scissors for fine work, a pair of tailor's shears which she also uses for wallpapering, and some kitchen scissors with serrated edges. They were all present and correct. In Harry's room I also looked through his little box of "treasures". There was no hank of hair, Sheena Chadwick's or any other.'

'Good. I didn't notice the two constables Jenner ordered.'

'Well, fancy that! I hope you aren't going to tell tales.' She grinned mischievously. 'He imagines all the Close houses are vast mansions. It was straighforward enough, and I felt Mrs Snelling had seen enough of uniforms lately.'

'So they're cleared, and now Harry will go free. Are you off to tell the Boss?'

'No rush. It's just come through from control that he's been called to Kidlington. I can't see Jenner authorizing Harry's release in a hurry, if it's left to him.'

'Join me then? I've two more houses to visit.'

She fell in alongside, humming under her breath, the breeze teasing loose a brown curl from under her red bobble cap. There was no doubt where her sympathies lay in this case. Clearing the Snelling household of obvious involvement had lifted her spirits.

'I hope you're not getting personally involved,' he said, more grumpily than he felt.

She grimaced. 'You misread me. Actually I've just had an idea, the first positive one since this dead-end case started. It was something the Boss said this morning.'

'*His* idea then?'

'I suppose it was, but I doubt if it's seeped through to his consciousness yet.'

Beaumont groaned. 'Not another touch of his old Welsh granny? I couldn't stand your antennae picking up his signals too, Z.'

'Seriously, remember he said that if we knew the reason for certain items being missing we might find our way out of the blind alley we'd been led up?'

'Yes. Go on.'

'That's it. A blind alley we've been led up. Someone playing with us, masterminding the game. A joker in the pack.'

Beaumont stopped in his tracks and stared at her. It was just a form of words the Boss had used. 'Blind alley': OK, that's where they'd been for a matter of days. But 'led up'? Had the Boss been talking loosely, or had he subconsciously stumbled on a truth? And Z had been the one to pick it up? He'd have to watch out for his own seniority if the new sergeant and her superintendent were going to leak things to each other at spook level!

'So what do you think?'

'Dunno yet.' He hunched his shoulders and trudged on. Miffed; he admitted it. Z could have stolen a march on him; snatched a theory while he was groundhogging. Still it *was* only a theory. He reminded her of this.

'Agreed. So let's knock it around.'

'As soon as I've finished this chore. Here we are, no. 5.' He consulted his list. 'Eustace Potts, 68, and housekeeper Ena Judd, 37. We've heard little enough of them so far. This could be new ground.'

Both were at home. Miss Judd opened the door to them, beaming: a bespectacled, comfortably rounded brunette with a peachy complexion. 'I thought you might be from the police,' she said when they had identified themselves. 'We were just about to have coffee. A bit late, but we had rather a long run this morning.'

Sight of Mr Potts, clinging to the sitting-room door made this hard to believe. He was no jogger, not far off a crutches subject, and his heavy tweed suit was crumpled from long sitting. Maybe, Beaumont thought in a flash of imagination to rival Z's own, Mr Potts' part in the run had been by wheelchair?

Incredibly, they were computer freaks. One whole side of the south-facing room was filled by a two-tier bench. A multi-coloured screen displayed what appeared to be the ground plan of a country garden with areas of shrubbery, flower beds and lake. From a chattering printer alongside flowed a stream of fan-folded stationery.

'I think we're almost there,' the old man said smugly. 'I'll save it.' He bent over the keyboard and punched buttons. The screen blanked out.

Fascinated, Z asked, 'Are you planning a new garden?'

'Yes and no,' he said brightly. 'Sit down my dear. It's purely imaginary. Background, you see, for one of my blessed books. Half the fun of writing is the research, and with fiction there's no limit.'

'Not that he ever uses a tenth of what he mugs up, Miss Judd assured them. 'But he knows all the ins and outs of his characters' lives. They're stored here in the data bank, ready for use in a sequel.'

'I hadn't realized you wrote,' Z told him.

'Done it for ages,' he admitted almost apologetically. 'Nearly fifteen years now. Started when I was invalided out of banking. Got my spine shot in a hold-up. Bit dramatic, laid me up for a year or so. Not all bad, though: shook me into a new kind of life. Luckily people seem to like my stuff. Family sagas, y'know, with a touch of adventure. Probably not to your taste, my dear.'

'He's very popular,' Miss Judd said proudly. 'Of course there's not many know he's Claudia Fenwick. That's his dark secret.'

'I've read you,' Z said faintly. 'But the author's photo inside the dust jacket . . .' She stared at

Miss Judd. 'That must have been you, taken from behind.'

'Gazing out to sea at Lyme Regis,' said the old man. 'Mind, it doesn't say anywhere that it's a shot of Claudia Fenwick, any more than it says she's a man.'

'Black or white?' asked Miss Judd serenely, hefting the silver coffee pot. 'If that isn't too politically incorrect.'

Having transferred to his car the load of notepaper, loose sheets, continuous stationery and examples of the many fonts which Mr Potts' two printers were capable of producing, DS Beaumont moved on with Z to the final house in the Close. He rang and waited, rang again.

'Seems the Wichalls are out,' he decided. 'I thought Saturday lunchtime might find them in.'

'So shall we head for the Feathers and get a bite ourselves?'

'Good notion, but wrong place,' Beaumont corrected. 'Let's make it the less salubrious Barley Mow. I don't know about his father, but I fancy we'll find young Jasper performing there.'

Seventeen

The bar was filling with regular Saturday lunchtime drinkers, their competitive voices already rising to screech level against a background of thudding bass and yowling vocal.

'My shout,' Z called over her shoulder, leaving Beaumont to work his way towards the window and cast round for a table.

She came back minutes later with a pint of lager and a half of cider. 'I've ordered four-seasons pizzas,' she said. 'I hope that's all right. The alternative was toasted cheese sandwich.'

'Pizza's fine. We haven't scored with Jasper, though.'

'It's early yet. He may be rounding up the other three.'

Beaumont looked thoughtful. 'Wonder who he had lined up before the Dawson girl arrived.'

'Did there have to be anyone? Maybe in their case three wasn't a crowd.'

Prompt on their cue, the street door opened to admit the Field twins and young Wichall. They huddled a moment to pool their cash, then Colin approached the bar to order. Rachel disappeared towards the toilets. Jasper stood back from the crowd, sidling along the wall until he reached a vacant padded bench, where he stood guarding it in High Noon stance, bulky leather jacket topping wishbone legs, hands curving for the draw from nonexistent hip holsters.

'Not much in common there. Three loners pretending they're not. Thrown together by proximity and age.' Beaumont spoke sourly, from experience as a severely-tried parent.

Z considered this, sipping at her cider. 'You said yourself, "Jasper performing". So these two are his nuclear audience. But what do they get out of *him* — just amusement?'

'I wonder; maybe . . .' Beaumont frowned. 'As a woman, how do you feel about him?'

'Neutral. How should I? Hang on, do you mean — ?'

'He's wary of Rachel, who acts detached and disdainful. Closer to Colin, but something's grating in the relationship. Then with Gayle —'

'Leading her on?'

'I thought so at first. But having watched them together, I'd say it's something else. He doesn't attempt to attract her; rather the reverse. He goads her, mocks her as a female. Doesn't actually need her. Maybe resents Colin's increasing interest in the girl.'

Z stared across at Jasper. Homosexual? Why not?

As if he had picked up her silent vibes Jasper looked suddenly back. There was a flicker of uncertainty as he took in Beaumont's wooden lack of expression. Then his gaze shifted again to Z and his mouth twisted with sardonic amusement.

281

She had an instant sense of rebuff, embarrassed as if Jasper had picked up on her query of his sexual preference.

Rachel Field was threading back through the crush, her feet almost dancing, legs thin as pipe cleaners in their black stretch leggings. Her chunky top was black too, as was the velvet crush-brimmed hat low on her brow with its ridiculous pink rose. There was something neurotic, almost fanatical, about the pale, famished face beneath, disturbing by its very blankness and perfection. Z had guessed at anorexia; but when Colin brought her plate the girl seized it and wolfed the food down. So maybe her nervous energy burned it up fast. Or she was bulimic.

'At least that one's not on drugs,' Beaumont said drily.

'Are the other two?'

'I have a gut feeling there's some history there. Not that young Wichall needs much more stimulation than he gets from self-worship. But in his father's place I would worry.'

Z smiled at the bruised authority in her partner's voice. 'So what about Colin Field?' she tempted.

Beaumont disposed of the final forkful of pizza before he replied. 'I'm not too sure about him. Mebbe that's because he's not too sure about himself yet.'

Z considered the young man. A twin, with a complex attitude to his sister. Seeming to need her, yet also refuting the need. With artistic pretensions like hers, he'd settled for accountancy, the opposite. Spoilt with material possessions, estranged from his parents by years of boarding school, witness to their soured relationship and his shrewish mother's acceptance of his father's adultery, what were the principles guiding his life?

'Nineteen,' she reminded Beaumont. 'How well did you know yourself at that age?'

'If you're fishing for the story of my life you've a long line to cast.' Beaumont gave her an ironic smile which faded instantly as he went on, 'I'd say the Field parents don't do a lot to stabilize the family. She's a cold, moneyed bitch. He's behaving like a tomcat with a time bomb tied to its tail. And the whole act's decked out with a glossy magazine setting. What's anyone to make of it — let alone kids?'

'I think they're making a move.'

'Right. If you're ready to go, we'll catch them up. You make the approach.'

They waited until the trio were outside the door, then rose and followed. They hadn't far to walk, because the young people were waiting for them. 'That's a quid you owe me,' Jasper jeered.

'Nothing doing. I didn't take it on.' Colin looked annoyed. He was avoiding Beaumont's eyes.

'Hullo,' Z said generally. 'Isn't Gayle with you today?'

There was a marked silence. 'Studying,' Rachel offered at length. 'Or so she says.'

'Probably still rather shaken up,' Z suggested.

'That was a horrible experience she had Thursday night.'

Now all three were avoiding her eyes.

'Do you think,' Colin said hesitantly, 'it was the same man who strangled that woman? A serial killer who didn't quite make it?'

Z turned innocently to Beaumont. 'Do we?'

'More likely a copy cat.'

'But wasn't it the same MO?' The police term sounded foreign on the boy's lips. 'I mean, cutting her hair and that.'

'You seem well informed.' Beaumont sounded mildly amused.

'Well, we saw her. It looks a mess. There's a chunk chopped right out.' A note of indignation came through.

'Whoever did that could have known about the earlier case.'

'But nobody did,' said Jasper triumphantly, 'except the killer. That was the secret the police were sitting on. So all the newspapers said.'

'And you believe everything you read in the press?'

He hunched his shoulders and spread his palms. 'Who then?'

'You tell me. But there's something else I need to know first.' Beaumont put on his dumb cop face. 'What kind of word processor do you have at home? We're doing a survey, and your house is our last to visit.'

'In the middle of a murder hunt? Man, I don't believe this! Bureaucracy gone doolally! Why don't they slap it on the census form? Fuck-almighty, are the fuzz paid now for manufactur-ers' PR?'

'You do have one.'

'Who doesn't? My father brings work home, so we have an IBM-compatible.'

'Which we need to see.'

'Do you have a warrant?'

'Do you want me to register your insistence on one? You'll be the first.'

'Jes' joking.'

'So let's take a look now.'

Jasper shrugged again. 'Ok, Ok. Fall in behind and we'll parade there.'

'I've got a car,' Beaumont said shortly. 'We'll wait for you on the doorstep.'

Later at the Incident Caravan Beaumont pre-sented the newly acquired information to DI Jen-ner without comment. Also without the poem printout from Dr Goodwin's machine.

Z left them to sift through it together, disap-pearing with the excuse of writing up her notes on the Snelling visit. She was conscious of Jenner staring after her, on the point of demanding whether any scissors had been missing, but then changing his mind. There was no requirement to make any move about Harry Snelling before the Superintendent got back from Kidlington.

Z made for the private sitting-room at the Feathers, typed up her negative report, then sat staring into the coal fire, letting her mind drift on the theory of a manipulator leading them up a blind alley.

Its weak point was that nobody in their right mind killed and mutilated merely to run rings round the police. But if that was a no-go for the starting point, either there had been some trigger factor before the murder, or —

Yes, that was more likely: the killing of Sheena Chadwick could be a quite separate factor, but it had suggested what followed. And if the attack on Gayle Dawson had really been no more than an attempt — serious enough — to terrify her, then it narrowed the field in their hunt for the perpetrator.

Narrowed the *Field*, she repeated silently to herself. Like Colin and Rachel Field? Well, barring some private enemy from outside the village, who was more likely than one of Gayle's 'friends' in the Close? And given the choice of Rachel, Colin and Jasper, she knew who sprang most readily to mind.

'Jes' joking,' Jasper had said, after Beaumont warned him of the seriousness of demanding a warrant. He was Mardham's self-licensed clown, wasn't he? He had to be the joker she was looking for. But what reason had he to make such a violent attack on a girl who had apparently caused him no offence?

But hadn't she? While they'd sat in the car waiting for the three to catch them up, Beaumont had told her how Jasper had been fooling on that earlier occasion in the Barley Mow, horsing around in public, showing off at Gayle's expense. And she'd brushed him off, in front of the crowded bar room.

Not that he'd seriously been trying to charm her, if his leanings were not for women. Just putting himself across as irresistible. Well, that figured.

Gayle had felt insulted, sensing the mockery in it, and reacted with some spirit, did the unforgivable by making Jasper look small. If the young man couldn't laugh it off —

She shivered. Everyone was meant to take him as a joker. But it could be he was dead serious about one thing, and that was himself. Unstable?

The whole of Thursday night's attack on Gayle — the smashing of the overhead light, the letting down of the tyres, the glueing of the four dust caps on the bonnet, the removal of the valves, and then the actual assault on the girl, shearing her hair, shaking the car with her inside — that wasn't a normal prank. It was too prolonged, too deliberately malicious. No, it smacked of something far more serious.

Nobody had yet checked where Jasper was that night. Too much time had been spent on chasing Harry Snelling. And Gayle Dawson was quite certain now that the outline she'd glimpsed through the mirror, bouncing her car, wasn't Harry's. Yet he was the one who'd followed her home the previous week, possibly with no villainy in mind, but because she'd been a lone woman out after dark and he was afraid for her.

It was generally accepted now that Harry had been her original 'stalker'. Which could have suggested to a mean mind that a second attack — again on a Thursday night — would also be laid at his door. It took a twisted mentality to plan that someone so vulnerable should get the blame.

She returned to the table and Yeadings' typewriter. He had brought it in for the team's use, happier himself with the old search-and-peck technique for working out his moves. Its advantage was privacy. Any wild notions could be tried out this way without entering the computerized zone. Z had barely started to sort out her suppositions when the door opened and the Boss steamed in.

He wasn't in a mood for theorizing but for sustenance. He growled that he'd refused lunch with the brass at Kidlington mess to save time, then been hung up because the AC had been called away before they were through discussing the case. As a consequence he'd had to hang around, hungry and panting to get back to the action.

'Have you ordered anything?' Z demanded.

He hadn't. Moreover it smelled to him like steak and kidney pud. He'd promised Nan this morning that he'd stick to salad for lunch, but . . .

'But you can't refuse it, if it's placed before you.' She whisked out, bound for the pub's kitchen.

When she returned with a loaded tray Yeadings

had armed himself with a glass of lager from the bar and was beginning to look more human. 'What's been done about Harry Snelling?' he demanded.

'Nothing yet. He's still in the cells at Amersham. No scissors were missing from his home, and none have turned up elsewhere. I've just typed the report for DI Jenner. He's at the caravan with DS Beaumont, checking the samples of print and paper from the Close.'

'Leave the report here. I'd like you to get across and see to Snelling's release in person, give him a lift home and settle him in with his mother. I'll call Superintendent Batts to authorize it.'

She hesitated a moment. 'Anything new, sir?'

'For what it's worth, Wigan sent through that when Chadwick vamoosed so did his girlfriend Dolly Bell. Apparently they'd been in partnership as pub entertainers. Moonlighting. Which probably accounted for his bad timekeeping and absenteeism from work.'

'What did they do? As entertainers, I mean?'

'Country and Western. They probably needed the van to stow their gear. Their act should help London's Met to find them among the clubs and pubs.'

'A connection with Soho? And a fresh link with Sheena's death?' Z suggested.

'It's worth bearing in mind. But, although Chadwick might find himself uncomfortable between the two women, he'd not need to get rid of Sheena so dramatically. He'd been free of her for a matter of years, and he doesn't sound the sort to fret over the legal strings of marriage.'

'And he'd no connection with Mardham, that we know of.'

'Whereas Sheena had, if we can believe that scrap of paper from her waste bin. Why the blazes wasn't the rest of the letter in with it?'

'I wondered about that,' said Z. 'She could have torn it up small and thrown it all away, then had second thoughts, took the bits out of the bin but overlooked that one scrap. The others might have been flushed down the loo. Or — if ever we do find her handbag, I'd guess the rest could be in that.'

The Superintendent nodded slowly at her over his steak and kidney pudding. 'Could be.'

When his DS had gone and he had nobly refused the landlady's offer of a dessert, he wrapped up again and went out on foot to rejoin the other two at the caravan. 'So what have we?' he demanded on arrival.

Beaumont left it to Jenner to admit it was a nil score. 'I doubt anything here will be of use to forensic lab,' he confessed. 'Even to the naked eye there's no exact match with the print on the scrap of paper.'

'So do we assume it originated outside Orchard Close, and was simply part of a letter referring to the place? The venue for a rendezvous?'

'There would still have to be some connection

with Mardham,' Jenner objected. 'The address is specific.'

'Anything new from HQ?' Beaumont asked in the gloomy silence that followed.

'Had my knuckles rapped,' the Boss admitted, 'over the leak about the cut hair. I explained I might have been responsible myself.'

The two men stared at him.

'I'd mentioned it to Ms Morrison from Social Services. I hoped she'd give me her opinion, one way or the other, on Harry as a fetishist, and I relied on her discretion to let it go no further. Seems I could have been wrong.'

Over Jenner's inclined head Yeadings was aware that Beaumont's eyes had gone completely round, long-focused and unblinking. He recognized this as an established signal: the physical reverse of a wink, but certainly intended as a respectful substitute.

His eyebrows acknowledged receipt of the request for a one-to-one confab. Not that he should encourage his DS's short-circuiting the correct channels by cutting out a middle-ranking officer. However, as the AC had pointed out to him over the leak, there were moments when discretion was the better part of good policing.

'I don't have my car with me,' he said. 'If there's nothing more, I'd appreciate a lift, Sergeant.'

'Sir.'

'Right, and after that you can get all this written up,' Jenner granted, grimly reviewing the pile of papers on the table between them.

Beaumont shrugged on his bomber jacket and followed the Boss outside. He said nothing until they were both belted in the car. Then he handed over the poem printout, and explained how he'd come across the disk labelled 'Meredith'.

While he pulled out of the lay-by Yeadings read the few lines of verse. 'It's not signed,' Beaumont warned him. 'Anyone with access to the machine could have written it.'

Yeadings was looking sombre. 'I don't think so.' He sat slumped in his seat and waited before getting out again in the yard of the Feathers.

'Does it qualify?' Beaumont asked at last.

'As a suicide note? I'll have to mull it over. I think — probably — it's good enough for me. But officially it will rest with the coroner. It can be shown to him privately. He may decide it shouldn't be read out.'

'The inquest's on Monday.'

'Yes. Sometime before then Mrs Goodwin will have to be warned. I don't know whether it will help or hurt her to know what the poor devil was feeling. But somehow I don't think it will come as complete news.'

'Couldn't make head or tail of it myself,' the DS said almost defiantly as the passenger door slammed shut.

Yeadings watched him drive off. Beaumont denying he'd anything but cardboard for brains, because he'd a softer centre than he'd admit to. Well, everyone had to find their own way of coping with pain. As he would himself in his forthcoming interview with the widow.

Eighteen

Next morning Z was putting in some work on locals' visits to London. Following the Boss's information about the charity run she had listed everyone in the Mardham team led by Phyllida Field. Of Orchard Close residents the only other regulars were Eustace Potts' housekeeper at no. 5 and Meredith Goodwin, but Colin had twice been pressed into service when helpers' numbers were reduced by illness or absence on holiday. Middle-aged and elderly women were in the majority, although at least one man was included on each trip for security reasons.

Beyond the London Run, there were others who visited the capital for business or personal reasons. Rupert Crick followed an external degree course which took him to South Kensington every Wednesday. Meredith Goodwin's parasitic but domesticated brother occasionally 'mooched off there' (in his own words) to 'catch up with the intellectual world'. This he did mainly in cinemas and pubs in the West End. Jasper Wichall made sporadic visits to buy secondhand audio or video gear from shops in Tottenham Court Road or in the narrow streets behind Shaftesbury Avenue, and he was sometimes accompanied by Colin Field.

Since Rachel attended Dance Studio in Reading every weekday, monopolizing the twins' shared car, and Jasper had 'bent' his own, Colin and he were reduced to taking the train from Mardham Halt. The most recent occasion had been on Thursday, when Colin should have been attending college on his one day release from the accountancy firm in Amersham but had skived off to do some personal shopping, mainly clothes. Not that he'd bought much because Jasper had been picking up a pair of bulky speakers for his hi-fi and both were needed to transport them home.

'Did you come back by train together?' Z asked them.

'That time, yeah,' Jasper offered. 'Could really have done with our own wheels.'

'What time did you reach Mardham?'

'Must have been soon after four. There were school kids on our train. It helped old Col feel at home.' Jasper laughed, flinching theatrically from a blow that didn't come.

Colin was too subdued for such fooling, Z noticed. He'd been that way for some days now, ever since Dr Goodwin's death. It must have upset him more than she'd realized.

'So it was getting towards dusk when you left the train. Did you happen to see Gayle's yellow Triumph down in the station car park?'

'Nuh,' said Jasper at the same time as Colin said, 'Yes. I noticed because the lights were just coming on and hers was right under one, at the far end.'

So at that point the lamp hadn't been damaged. Interesting. She went on with her questions, hoping they'd overlook the detail's significance.

'Do you always return together?'

'Mostly.' That was Colin, tersely.

'Haveta keep an eye on the liddle fella, make sure he doesn't lose his purse again.' Jasper was keeping up the baiting.

'Did that happen once?' Z sympathized.

Colin had suddenly gone pale, his features taut. He mumbled incoherently.

'What did you say?'

'It was my *wallet*. A pickpocket.'

She stared at him. An awkward experience, but the boy was overreacting. He seemed to have difficulty in breathing. Was he asthmatic?

'Bad luck. When was this?'

'A few weeks back.'

'Three Saturdays back,' Jasper sang out. 'There he was, after our biz together, all for boldly going where no lone punter had ever gone before, and then coupla hours later he was back, yelling through to me on the platform that he hadn't a bean, not even his return ticket!'

'Lucky you were still around to help.'

But Colin was more than embarrassed by being made a fool of. He looked stricken. Teenagers! Z thought; and, not for the first time, thank God for growing up.

Her smile was meant to be reassuring. 'So where had the lone punter been bound for?'

For a moment she thought the boy was going

to slump in a dead faint, then he opened his eyes and said tightly, 'To get my camera fixed. It had shutter trouble.' He turned almost savagely on Jasper who had his mouth open to deliver the next taunt. 'Like you!'

Food for thought there? Z wondered, taking note. Possibly, but kids took themselves so seriously over matters which adults had learned to accept as the stuff of everyday living. Yet it was strange that all at once Colin seemed hypersensitive. He hadn't struck her that way on first meeting. Then, among his family, he'd been confident, even pert. He'd put on that drilled recruit act deliberately to disconcert her.

There must be a reason for his sudden alarm now. She'd hit a raw nerve with her question about that earlier visit to London. Jasper had suspected his friend of something underhand when he'd gone off on his own; and wasn't just ribbing him as kids often do, but spitefully taunting, with an intention to annoy. Perhaps, as Beaumont had perceived, not such close buddies after all.

'Right,' she said, closing her notebook and slipping its elastic band on the cover. 'I think that's the lot then.'

She mentioned her suspicions about Colin to Beaumont when they met for a Sunday pub lunch. There was more of a crowd in the Feathers than on the previous day at the Barley Mow, so despite the cold they'd taken their plates and glasses out into the garden at the rear.

'What d'you guess he was up to?' the other DS asked.

'Something he certainly regrets telling Jasper about. You're experienced with teenagers. What's your theory?'

'He was meeting a girl. Which could also account for Jasper's nose being out of joint.'

'Could be, I suppose. But who? Gayle? No, they hadn't even met then. Some girl he knew before.'

'Or else . . .' Beaumont had stopped eating, his cheeks bulging, eyes narrowed. He looked, Z thought, like a dozy hamster.

'Or else?' she prompted.

'Or he felt it was time he got some serious sex instruction.'

'You think he picked up a prostitute?'

'He'd been to Soho on his mother's London Run, hadn't he? He would hardly have had his eyes shut while the goodies were being handed out. He'd have picked up on the shady alleys and the lit upper windows even if the place's reputation hadn't reached him.

'If his only sex till then had been with other males, maybe he felt it was time to broaden his horizons, look out some experienced woman to wise him up. Just suppose — is it too fantastic? — suppose he'd happened on Sheena Chadwick!'

Z considered the notion. 'You're not suggesting she followed him to Mardham a fortnight after he'd had sex with her?'

'I don't know what I'm suggesting. We know she had an address from Orchard Close. It could have been no. 4, and she just might have got it off Colin. If there was a link — however tenuous — and she later turned up dead, practically on his back doorstep . . .'

'You haven't leapt as far as seeing him as the killer?'

'I'm simply trying to account for his overreaction to your questions.'

'If you insist he was linked with Sheena Chadwick, then either you must carry it through and connect him with the killing, or accept it was pure coincidence that she turned up dead in his home village. And I think we're agreed on the subject of coincidence: that ninety-nine per cent of the time it just doesn't happen.'

'Forget it. It was a wild idea. We know the lettering on the scrap of paper from Sheena's bin wasn't produced by the Fields' printer. So there can't be a connection.'

All the same, the image didn't go away, and next day, representing the police at the inquest on Dr Goodwin, Beaumont was alerted by the unexpected appearance of the Field boy at the back of the court, whitefaced and tense as he listened to the scant evidence made available. Afterwards, in the men's room Beaumont came upon him leaning sickly against a basin, shakily wiping off his face with a damp handkerchief.

Recognizing the detective he gave a weak smile.

'So there was a suicide note after all.'

'You heard what the coroner said. It's cleared up. Luckily no need for an adjournment. I didn't know you were interested in legal matters.'

'Oh. Yes; I mean — it sort of connects with accountancy sometimes.' Colin made an effort to tidy himself, brushed water off his lapels and straightened his tie.

The complete junior professional, Beaumont thought, pricing the smart business suit. Nothing like the jeans-and-trainers lad of the previous day: more like a clone of his father.

The thought gave rise to another, unexpectedly. Colin and Donald Field together. Colin's fear could have been on his father's account. He'd certainly have known about the man's affair with Meredith Goodwin. Could he have suspected his father of causing her husband's death? That could account for his presence here, and his obvious relief at the verdict.

He watched the young man depart straight-backed, and had doubts again. According to Z, Colin's fears had centred on some occurrence in London, not here. Which wouldn't concern his father.

Unless, of course, in London he'd happened to see his father. In Sheena Chadwick's company?

Superintendent Yeadings had been to see Meredith Goodwin the previous day. While Beaumont attended the inquest as senior officer present after the discovery of her husband's body, the Boss was now in session with DI Jenner and DS Zyczynski, to explain his move.

'The poem was a highly personal way of speaking to his wife,' he said. 'She told me he had once or twice done that sort of thing before, when he found it hard to express himself face to face. A very modest and private man, but also intensely emotional; he spoke through poetry. The first time was when he'd just proposed and she'd accepted him. Again when she'd lost their unborn child and found there could never be another. She kept those poems and treasured them. This one must be much more painful for her.'

The DI leaned over the transcript, frowning as he read silently:

> Such beauty, beloved,
> Such passion, cannot be contained;
> I would rather try
> To beat out a heath fire with a feather!
> And I so cold no longer dread
> The onset of my winter.
> Sterile, its shroud blots out
> The darkness and the doubting;
> Guilt that gathers with the gloom;
> Ghosts of angry words, the shouting
> Of passionate obscenities,
> Then tears . . . And now
> The necessary ruptures left behind.

'It's *her* beauty and passion?' Jenner said doubtfully. 'The middle bit's about his own death, but what does he mean at the end — necessary ruptures? Sounds medical to me.'

' ". . . And now/The necessary ruptures left behind," ' Yeadings quoted. 'Meredith Goodwin had no doubt about that. By now he meant after he'd gone. He understood her well. He knew she'd find it impossible to see or speak with Field again. He saw the break as inevitable, knowing finally she must move on to some better relationship.'

'I wish I'd known him,' Z said regretfully.

Jenner wasn't of the same mind. 'Maybe the doctor wasn't quite the saintly self-effacing character he tried to sound. This rupture could be the very result he'd set his sights on. A sado-masochist manipulator. Don't psychiatrists say there's a strong element of revenge in suicide? Certainly showmanship. And he didn't choose an easy way to go.'

Yeadings lifted his shoulders and let them drop. 'I can understand why he chose a rapid means, away from where his wife might come across his body. He could have thought the agony justified. This poem is the only indication we have of what was in his mind. And it was meant for Meredith, not us or the coroner. Maybe he did leave a letter too, and someone destroyed it.'

'Which could only be Meredith.'

'Or her brother.'

'I'll be having another word with the widow myself, but not just yet. She has a lot of heavy thinking to get through.'

He broke off to take a telephone call. 'That was Beaumont,' he explained, replacing the receiver after listening briefly. 'The inquest is closed, verdict suicide.'

His voice took on a brisker tone. 'Our interest in Dr Goodwin's death ends there. Which leaves us to aim for a rapid result on the murder of Sheena Chadwick and the attack on Gayle Dawson. Which may, or may not, have been the work of one person.'

Colin Field hadn't far to go between the Coroner's Court and his office. He arrived at morning tea-break to queries about how he'd got himself lost. The junior partner had phoned his home to see if he was ill, and was told that he'd left with his father for work as normal.

'I was suddenly sick, walking here from his chambers,' Colin claimed. 'Flaked out and came to at the hospital.' He still managed to look convincingly pale.

'Couldn't reach a phone to explain what had happened. I'd better give home a ring now.'

His call caught Phyllida as she was leaving for the hairdresser. She did sound a tad concerned; then asserted sharply it could be due to nothing she'd cooked. 'Everyone else seems perfectly all right.'

Good on them, he thought savagely, and went for a second mug of tea. The vomiting had left him dehydrated, with his throat strained and sore.

But it was over, the specific worry. Watching the police from the bridge as they'd gone about measuring the bank where Doc Goodwin had been floating, Gayle's mention of the large footprints found there had raised an unspeakable fear. After that shitty evening at the Goodwins' and Dad not coming back until late, who was he to think had stood there, making sure his mistress's husband went permanently under?

But the doc had killed himself and admitted it in a letter which the coroner had read and kept to himself. So there was going to be no open scandal. And the large footprints had been made by someone else: the flat-footed fuzz themselves, or the big dumbo Snelling when he came across the body.

No more fears over that matter. But nothing was going to wipe out the gut-grinding horror of the business with the whore. God, if only time could be turned back and it had never happened! He was safe so far, but how long before the police turned up what he'd done? The dark-haired woman sergeant had come dangerously close, probing about the lost wallet. Jasper was a vicious trouble-maker and he'd damn well keep clear of him in future.

Phyllida was waiting for her husband when he reached home. Donald Field knew he should have gone to a hotel, sent a message that he'd been called away. Away anywhere, the North Pole if necessary. Nothing could be colder than her eyes, the venomous way she faced him, ready to cut him down.

'So Stanley's death is officially suicide,' she said when he told her. 'And where does that leave you? I'll tell you.

'As the butt of all the dirty gossip, because now everyone's sympathy will be for him, the poor, downtrodden, unappreciated, cuckolded husband! Socially you and your tart are utterly out in the cold!

'Don't imagine you'll be let off the hook. This is a tight little community, and I for one have worked damn hard to earn a decent reputation in it, which I've no intention of giving up. And before you start thinking that we can slink off and start up again elsewhere, let me tell you now: you're staying put.'

'This isn't the time for —'

'For facing up? No, it never has been for you! Never will be. You're a craven coward, Donald. No good for anything but cheating on your acquaintances and manipulating words to suit your selfish ends. Well, understand this: there are others better at it than you, and I pay them well to look after my interests. Which do not include you!

'Don't imagine you've anything to gain by cutting free. I've enough on you to damn you utterly in your profession, even without those cheques you forged in my name. But it suits me to stay on in the comfortable home I've spent years and a fortune in building up. What's more you'll stay on as my nominal husband. And if Mardham sees me as the wounded party in your mucky little intrigue with the woman next door, I'll see to it that I'm not the one to suffer.'

As if from a great distance he watched her, swaying like a cobra, her unspeakably hateful face lunging at him as she stressed her loathing. He hardly heard the words which streamed interminably on and on; there was no need. They were a part of her and he knew it all.

She had meant only one thing to him ever: a means to success in his career. A career that once had mattered so much. But, like everything she came near, that had been soured and destroyed. No colleagues would ever respect a man whose wife could buy him in over their heads. Whatever success he might have achieved for himself was tarnished in advance.

She had been drinking before he came in. He should have bolstered himself equally. And yet there was a sort of perverted pleasure in standing there stone sober while she whipped herself from cold scorn into a purple fury, with her eyes bulging and the cords standing out in her abominable scraggy neck while the venomous mouth went on working, spewing out filth about Merry and himself.

Merry, Merry, he cried inside. If it weren't for this hellcat — God, I will kill her, squeeze the last of her life out, twist her false yellow hair round her windpipe and squeeze, go — on — squeezing.

Medusa, eyes bulging, purple tongue bursting from swollen lips.

Purple, purple, *purple!*

Nineteen

Superintendent Yeadings parked in the yard of the Feathers and, coat unbuttoned in response to the bright sunshine, set off briskly for the Mobile Incident Room. As he turned into the High Street the wind met him face on, but today it was no more than a teaser, bowling dry sycamore leaves along like children's hoops with an irregular faint ticking. The fruiterer, beaming on him as he set out the stall in front of his shop, was as shiny and rosy-cheeked as the polished apples piled in pyramids. There was a refreshing scent of green tomatoes and earthy carrots.

People nodded, passing on their way to work. Not accepting him as one of themselves, yet they seemed to find him tolerable; unlike some city streets where to spot a policeman was to mark up an enemy.

He lingered at the confectioner's bowed front window bright with glazed loaves, lemon puff pastry and sugar-sparkling doughnuts, strong-minded enough to enjoy them vicariously. From a grating by his feet rose the evocative, yeasty smell of fresh-baked bread. He felt wrapped around in cosiness. Village life, he thought, reassured; not yet too tainted with corruption.

But crime there was, seemingly as necessary to

human existence as eating and defecating; as universal as crawly creatures taking refuge under stones. And I make my comfortable living from others' misdoings, he reminded himself drily.

But perhaps his good humour on this morning after Harry Snelling's release owed less to the bright weather and surface innocence of Mardham than to the knowledge that injustice had been avoided for a man not well able to protect himself, despite the strength of his powerful body. Since Saturday even Jenner must be looking beyond Harry for the killer of Sheena Chadwick.

In the main section of the caravan he found the team assembled, the day's conference already under way.

'Sheena Chadwick,' Jenner announced as he wrote the name up again on the clean-washed blackboard. 'Back to Square One.'

He turned and challenged the others. 'Never mind how fantastic or libellous, let's have it. There's nobody outside these walls going to consider our private theories. Just the four of us. What does any of you make of the little we've got?' He tossed the chalk to Beaumont who rose and walked across while the DI resumed his seat.

'Aged forty-five. We've got that much from her last employers. Checkout assistant in a supermarket, and part-time barmaid. Married Leonard Chadwick, two years older, in 1976. The marriage survived until she left him in '94 for a Women's Refuge. A year ago she came south to London, worked as a waitress in the Victoria area, later as a barmaid at the Duke of Wellington. Took a room in Soho and turned her hand to "personal massage". A lone semi-amateur, apparently considered no great opposition to the organized sex industry. Drank moderately, smoked heavily. Suddenly a corpse at Mardham, with which no known ties, death occurring between 10 P.M. and 2 A.M. twelve days ago.'

'Right. Leonard Chadwick,' Yeadings cued in from his seat at the rear.

Beaumont wrote up the name, the man's age, address and previous occupation. 'Moonlighting around Lancashire pubs as a "Country and Western singer". Absconded with stolen van and current singing partner, Dolly Bell. In London the van passed via a street lot to Geordies running a fish scam at about the time of Sheena's murder. The Met is questioning the car trader about supplying false papers. The arresting sergeant is due to ring me at midday. Inquiries in London pubs and clubs have not yet turned up the missing couple.'

'Extend inquiries to the Home Counties,' Jenner snapped.

'It's in the Central Computer,' Yeadings assured him.

'We could get a positive at any time.'

'Mardham Connection,' Beaumont continued. 'D'you want to take over, Z?'

Zyczynski rose and complied, with a list of local

310

names. They all sat in silence studying it. 'Take your pick,' she invited. 'There's nothing material on anyone. Just wild guesses at motivation.'

'You haven't included Snelling,' Jenner complained.

'I thought he'd been eliminated.'

'Not conclusively.'

'Add him in, Z,' Yeadings said patiently.

Z included the name and waited for Jenner to make a case but he didn't, apparently satisfied that doubt had been spread.

'Let's try Colin Field for size,' Beaumont suggested, and proceeded to air his theory that the young man had been trawling Soho for a tom and happened on Sheena Chadwick.

'Or alternatively spotted his father with her,' Z put in, feeling the scenarios were getting madder by the minute.

'Donald Field's alibi is vouched for,' Yeadings objected. 'Any number of witnesses saw him at his Lodge at Amersham on the murder night until after twelve.'

'I suppose he could have killed the woman in Amersham and transported her back by car,' Beaumont said without much hope.

'Except that he had a passenger with him, whom he saw home and stayed chatting with until after 1.30.'

'Collusion?'

'I doubt it. The man he gave a lift to was Chief Inspector Bullen.'

'Ah.'

'Phyllida Field?' Jenner read off the next name, sounding almost shocked.

'The London Run organizer: distributes food and clothing at a point near where the dead woman lived. Whatever applies to her son applies also to Mrs Field. She might equally have glimpsed her husband in Soho leaving a pub with Sheena, an obvious tom, and have reacted viciously.'

'The strangler was righthanded,' Yeadings objected. 'I happened to notice when she was dealing with the secondhand clothing that Mrs Field's a southpaw.'

'Malcolm Barrow?'

'Alibi supplied by Dr and Mrs Goodwin for the night of Sheena's murder.'

'So we arrive at Jasper — sorry, *James* Wichall, who's also my fancy for Gayle Dawson's attacker,' Beaumont announced. 'Any disagreement with that?'

'He was back in Mardham on Thursday in good time to fix her car,' Z agreed. 'And although he denied noticing it parked there when he left the station, it's likely he did, because Colin — who was with him — admits he saw it.'

'The superglue trick sounds like Jasper,' Yeadings agreed. 'He'd have worn gloves. There were no clear dabs on the car's exterior apart from the garage man's, from checking the tyres on the previous day.'

'But why cut off a chunk of the girl's hair?' Jenner insisted. 'No, that aspect of the attack makes me certain it was the Chadwick woman's strangler going for another victim. At that time I'd swear there'd been no leak of the hair detail. We have a random serial killer here, possibly no one on our list at all, a total stranger.'

No one suggested Jasper as the Mardham strangler. It was too serious a crime for a lightweight like him.

The results left them flat. Well into the second week of the investigation, and nothing of any value had come to light. The longer they went on, the less likely was it that any clue remaining would survive. The solution, if ever one came, must depend on what was already to hand.

The phone rang and Jenner picked it up. 'DS Beaumont? Yes. A moment.'

The DS snatched a glance at his watch. It was ten minutes short of midday. 'Yes. Yes, that's OK. You have? Good. Who? Would you like to give me that again?'

He swivelled a note pad over and picked up a pen. As he wrote, Z read the words upside down and bit back a gasp of surprise. Beaumont thanked the caller and rang off.

'That was the Met,' he said, 'about the car dealer. They've checked a lot of unsorted bumf to do with his transactions. He's conveniently amnesiac about descriptions of purchasers, but during the sale of an old Ford transit van, colour blue and registration quoted, he noted down the buyer's driving licence particulars, which the Met thought would interest Thames Valley.'

'Get on with it, man,' said Jenner testily. 'Whose then?'

'James Wichall's,' said Beaumont serenely, 'of 6 Orchard Close, Mardham, Bucks.' He grinned at their thoughtful faces.

'Jasper's last car was in a pile-up,' Z reminded him. 'I ran a check. It happened over a month ago. A complete write-off.'

'So he looked for a substitute.'

'Did your informant mention any endorsement among the licence particulars noted down?'

'That's the sort of thing a suspect dealer could manage to overlook. But with a little persuasion from the right quarter he might recognize a photograph of young Wichall.'

'Get one and fax it to the Met,' Jenner ordered sharply. 'We also need to know the purchase date. I'll leave that with you. That's the second time this dealer's turned up. It has to be significant. If he bought one van from Chadwick and sold another to Wichall . . .'

'There's also the van seen by our drunk in the pub yard on the night of the murder,' Yeadings fed in blandly.

'Which we've proved couldn't have been Chadwick's, already gone to the fishy folk, but might certainly be Jasper's newly acquired Ford,' was Beaumont's guess. 'Two figures were seen to get out, one in leathers and wheeling a motorcycle. Does either Wichall or Colin Field have access to a bike?'

'Not known,' Z murmured as the others

blanked out. 'How are we going to approach Jasper Wichall?'

'There's enough to bring him in for questioning,' Jenner gave as his opinion. 'He's always been a marginal possibility. The hair fetishism is link enough between the two cases. There's no doubt in my mind he intended the Dawson girl to go the way of the other. As for Sheena Chadwick, he and his accomplice could have picked the woman up in London, driven her here in the van and killed her on the way. I want immediate publication of the Ford transit's description. He'd think it too valuable to destroy, so it'll be hidden locally. Somebody has to have seen it.'

He turned to the Boss, breathing fire and brimstone, and Z suddenly noticed his head cold had cleared. There was nothing like the thrill of the chase to heal the infirm.

'We bring him in for questioning?' Jenner demanded almost pugnaciously.

Yeadings conceded. 'Why not? But softly, softly. I'm with you on the two plus two. It's the five I'm less sure of. We don't want any costly mistakes.'

Nobody was in when Z and Beaumont called at No. 6 Orchard Close. Wichall senior would be at work in Amersham. Jasper, freelancing, could be anywhere. Patrol cars were already circulating with a description of the blue Ford van. Midday local television news would carry the same, together with a repeat of earlier footage of the murder scene at Mardham. The team were conscious of a new electric crackle in the ether.

Since the house appeared deserted, Beaumont took the opportunity to check the rear for buildings where a motorcycle might be concealed. The garage, glazed above bench level, offered no view of anything lower. There was also a small toolshed but this too was padlocked, and while Beaumont considered the wisdom of forcing an entry he was challenged from over the fence. Miss Judd, next-door's housekeeper, had him under observation.

'Oh, it's you, Sergeant,' she said, as he turned. 'I'm so sorry, but one does have to be so careful these days. Some very odd people about.'

'Are there, Miss Judd? Who, for instance?'

'I meant generally, you know. One reads about them.'

'I was hoping you'd seen something suspicious, an observant lady like you.'

'Actually no,' she regretted.

'You never by any chance saw the lad from this house with a motorbike?'

'No. I'm sure either Mr Potts or myself would have noticed if he'd had one. Such noisy things, aren't they? And smelly. There's just the one car there now, and Mr Wichall uses it for work. Young James does have a pushbike. He and Colin next-door used to go cycling quite often at one time.'

Beaumont thanked her, refused an offer of tea

and rejoined Z. They cruised back along the Close and in the garden of no. 4 caught a glimpse of Mrs Field getting into her Mercedes which backed out, passing them at speed before they made it out to Mill Lane.

'This is the point where the waiting gets painful,' Z muttered. 'Up till now we've had nothing to work on, but once there's a whiff of progress . . .'

'Bloody hell!' Beaumont exploded. 'What's that patrol car doing there?' He drew up opposite the uniformed driver who was winding down the window for a chatty word. Sandwiched between the two, Z followed the question and answer session after which Beaumont stamped on the clutch and threw the car back in gear, scowling thunderously.

'That pea-brained —'

'Jenner?'

'Ordered a surveillance on the Close in case Jasper made a run for it. Despite the fact there's no place to conceal a police car. If he gets any hint we're after him he'll be warned and could leg it.'

'Let's try the Barley Mow,' Z pacified. 'He may drop in. And we can catch the 12.50 P.M. regional news there.'

They hadn't long to wait. While Beaumont was still on his first pint the young man came in and sang out his order, gazed around, but seeing no intimates, waved a genial hand and bounced across to them. It was four minutes short of the local news time. He settled happily alongside, clearly reconciled to the company on offer.

The Mardham item came third, after a hotel fire in Croydon and a luggage handlers' strike at Heathrow airport.

'Police in Thames Valley are searching for a blue Ford transit van which may be connected with the recent murder at Mardham. Sheena Chadwick, of Dean Street, Soho . . .'

'That's us!' Jasper crowed with delight. 'Still in the news. Little old Mardham's keeping it up. And starring Thames Valley's finest!' He raised his glass tankard in salute and they lost the next words of the announcement.

'Shut it,' Beaumont ground out, disgusted that Jasper had displayed no sign of guilt. 'Sup up and then you can come and answer a few questions at Amersham nick. There's a thing or two you'll need to sort out if you want to get home tonight.'

A flicker of apprehension crossed Jasper's face. But nothing more, Z noted. For an instant she thought they might have the wrong man, or else his conceit was so insanely colossal he believed he could bluff his way out.

At the station he began by denying everything. He and Gayle Dawson were friends. Well, not close ones yet; he barely knew her, but she was a sweet doll, made up a group of buddies with himself and the Fields. What was this about hair? Sure, he knew the strangled woman had had some shagged off, but he'd heard that after he'd seen what a mess had been made of Gayle's. Not surprising that she'd gone and had it all trimmed even. Actually he thought it suited her short; more boyish.

He was waving his outspread hands like a frantic bat-man marshalling an erratic aircraft into its parking space. 'I mean, why'd I ever want to upset the doll? She likes me. I like her.'

Asked to empty his pockets, he resisted, then gave way. The duty officer listed the contents. 'No driving licence,' Beaumont observed. 'Let's see those keys. What are they for?'

Jasper counted them off and there seemed nothing untoward. No ignition keys or anything else to indicate he owned a car. He didn't bother to explain what had happened to the last one. Beaumont began to have doubts.

He handed him paper and a pen to list the clothes he had worn when he went to London on the Thursday of Gayle's attack. Z made a correction, remembering the black leather jacket that had topped the jeans and trainers. 'Yeah,' Jasper said. 'Guess you're right. I forgot.'

While they waited for them to be collected from his home, Jasper was offered the hospitality of a cell. Entering it he looked back, uncertain, like a child caught on forbidden ground. Z thought that the minute the door clanged on him he could well burst into tears.

Twenty

Before any microscopic examination could be made of the clothes brought in from Jasper's home, the contents of the pockets were listed. And seemed conclusive enough.

The two missing tyre valves from Gayle's yellow Triumph were found in the inner pocket of the leather jacket tangled with a single long blonde hair. They were placed in a transparent envelope which was labelled and initialled. The little tube of Fast Fret was sent to the path. lab for comparison with the trace sample taken from the bruised throat of Sheena Chadwick.

'Lubricant,' the scientific experts had declared, 'of a kind used by guitarists.' Immediate tests found no obvious difference in the samples, and further analysis was expected to make the identification positive.

Jasper, informed that evidence connected him with both crimes, was given a formal caution but had not yet been charged. His initial bravado had resolved into panic. He agreed now that he had 'horsed around a bit' with Gayle's car, and, yes, cut a bit off her hair, to take a rise out of her, but he'd nothing to do with the other thing, *nothing*. And he knew nothing about any Ford van.

Sure, he'd heard about the murdered woman's

hair, because he'd been on the phone extension while his father was talking with Ms Morrison. They often worked together and she naturally thought he'd be interested in the local murder.

His father demanded that the duty solicitor should be present during further interviews, and would be applying for Legal Aid on his son's behalf.

Before sewing the case up tight, DI Jenner intended to take full advantage of the time allowed for questioning, and on this Yeadings was in agreement. Beaumont and Z, taking turns at sitting in on the process, eventually found time to exchange impressions over a canteen coffee. Beaumont's regrets at dealing with a youngster who'd appeared not much wilder than his own son, were interrupted by a phone call and Z was left alone to ponder why she felt a sense of anti-climax.

The caller, Beaumont found, was a woman, none other than Rupert Crick's wife Madeleine. 'Thought you should know,' she said, 'somethun funny's turned up in Wychwood.'

'Which wood?' he couldn't resist demanding, but she was serious. 'The woods out over the railway lines.'

Where Harry had said there were badgers. 'What then?'

'The far end, down near the quarry, they bin blastun rock these last two weeks. Seems the water table's gone down. Any rate, there's less now in the old gravel pits, and somethun's showun above the surface.'

'What kind of something?'

'Metal, sort of darkish blue. Could be a car. And since the police are askun about a blue van, they thought . . .'

'They? Who, Mrs Crick?'

'Them folk you were askun me about. The ones who wouldn't talk to me but their wives might.'

Lord Almighty, his poachers! They'd come up with the goods. 'Mrs C, you're the business! I'll send PC Bond round for the details. Thanks a lot.'

With the best burst of adrenalin the case had given him, he set about calling in the cavalry, then with Z alongside he made up the vanguard.

His poachers had been right. There was anything between eight inches and a foot of van roof showing, tipped at a sharp angle, where it had been run in off the bank. Recent weather had destroyed any vital impressions on the grass and shale there, but once the van was salvaged there'd be no need for that sort of evidence. They'd have the tyres themselves.

And it was anybody's guess what they'd find inside the van. Such apparently total concealment could have left the killer overconfident. How could he have known that, within less than two weeks, work at the quarry would lead to exposure?

So much had happened in a few hours, that Z

felt days had gone by since she'd been sitting with Beaumont in the Barley Mow waiting for Jasper to walk in. Now they were all eager for the final evidence to be winched out of the gravel pits, and the case would be in the bag.

But it was a slow business. The right equipment had to be found, then manoeuvred to the place through tangled undergrowth and over lost tracks. The pits were just visible from the metalled road, and the van had taken a direct route there, but the bulkier salvage plant was heavy and the previous week's rains had left a slippery surface. It could be tomorrow midday before there was a chance for SOCO to get to grips with examining the van.

DI Jenner issued instructions that no whisper of events at the gravel pits should be allowed to reach young Jasper who was to be held overnight in the cells.

Z, conscious of others outside the immediate circumstances who were emotionally involved, delayed writing her report long enough to drive out to Polders in the hope that Gayle Dawson would be there. She, before anyone, had the right to know that Jasper had confessed to Thursday's attack on her, and that she need fear no repetition.

Mrs George was there alone, kneeling by a patch of earth near the front portico, busy with a trowel. 'Winter-flowering pansies,' she said brightly, looking up at Z hovering over her. 'A present from Gayle. Wasn't that sweet of her?

She took me to the garden centre in her car to choose them, before she went back to college. She's a very brave young woman, determined not to let that horrid business get her down.'

'I'm so glad.'

'And I'm so glad you came, my dear, because I don't think I can get up on my own.'

They had a little laugh together about the heaving that it took and then Z followed the elderly lady indoors where she made tea in the large kitchen overlooking the back garden.

'You must be feeling quite at home in the Close by now,' Mrs George suggested as she set out the tray.

'Yes, we have got rather involved. Life doesn't lack incident round here, does it?' And she broke the news of Jasper's arrest. 'That's what I came to tell Gayle. Perhaps you would pass it on. I thought she should know at once.'

The old lady seemed unperturbed that a neighbour should have proved to be the girl's attacker. 'Foolish young man. That was a vicious act. But you know, that wild sort often turn out quite well in the end. He feels a need to be someone special, and so far he hasn't found a way to do it usefully.'

Z wondered how true her prediction would prove if Jasper was sentenced to life for Sheena's murder. Not that it would necessarily come about. A conviction could well depend on what they found in the van.

She wandered towards the big Georgian window. 'What a wonderful view you have of the water meadows.'

'Yes, and bits of Buckman's Shoot between the trees. Sometimes there are flocks of plovers out there. You'd be surprised by some of the things I see from here. That's why I keep my field glasses handy. Why, only this morning . . .' and she confided the strange entertainment she had enjoyed while preparing lunch.

'I couldn't help laughing. The poor man was in such a plight, but quite ridiculous.'

Z smiled. 'You can see part of the Snellings' back garden too. Did you know that Harry claims to have a farm there?'

'Oh yes, he took me to see it. A snail farm. Rather ill-advised perhaps, and it augurs badly for my new pansies, but it makes him happy. I shouldn't think any of the other neighbours know.'

Since Mrs George was astonishing her with so much information on the Close, Z ventured to suppose that Mrs Goodwin would move away, after so much had happened.

'Oh no. Merry is made of sterner stuff than that. She belongs here and she intends to sit it out.'

'Have you spoken to her yet?'

'Indeed, yes. She's my god-daughter, you know. Her parents were our dearest friends when Adam was alive. We talk every evening. I don't know how I'd live without my telephone.'

Which shows how wrong you can be in your

first impressions, Z warned herself. I thought this old lady had switched off. Actually she must be at the very hub of village life.

Z was to find it fitting, looking back later at this conversation, that Mrs George should be the one to supply the final clue to pin down a murderer.

Despite torrential rain overnight, fine weather returned on Wednesday morning. Work began early on the salvaging of the van. By ten-thirty it was hauled out and sufficiently drained for the SOCO to get inside.

Beaumont's hopes were fulfilled: the killer had been so sure of concealing the van permanently, that he'd left evidence behind. Item: one woman's shoe, black, high-heeled. Item: one handbag, red plastic, lined black, containing a whole heap of material identifying it as Sheena Chadwick's. There were paying-in books for two savings accounts, credit cards, an empty purse for small change, items of make-up, an empty wallet and a number of torn scraps of paper including part of an envelope addressed to Colin Field and a letter concerning an overdue book on loan from a private library.

'So young Field was in this with Wichall?' Jenner demanded of the world at large. 'Bring him in,' he ordered Beaumont, in a desperate effort to gain time to think, rocked back on his heels by the shattering new events; because, besides audio gear and two guitars, the largest item the van had provided — now bagged and removed to the morgue for Dr Littlejohn's attention — was the body of an unknown, dark-haired woman.

Colin, he found, was already in the building, waiting outside an interview room while his father was in conference with Superintendent Yeadings. 'I can't come,' he said when Beaumont tried to march him off. 'It's serious. My mother's gone missing. She never came home last night.'

In view of recent violence in the area there was anxiety for her safety. Overlooking the normal twenty-four-hour period of notice, a search was to be organized at once.

Field had been ambivalent about his wife's intentions. At first he thought she'd gone of her own volition. 'She's been upset of late,' he admitted, 'particularly since the death of our good friend and neighbour Dr Goodwin. We were both very fond of him, and naturally distressed by the manner of his death. It's just possible that Phyllida, in depression, simply decided on an impulse to spend a few days away. She might even have wished to cause me some anxiety. She would sometimes accuse me of neglecting her, when I was particularly taken up with my work. It's often the case, I believe, with women who have no career of their own and are insufficiently occupied.'

He had rung all her acquaintances he knew of and had prepared a list of them, also of some he hadn't been able to reach. He hoped this would be of assistance to the police, because now he had to believe there was something sinister about the suddenness of her departure.

'Are you fully convinced this is a matter for the police, Mr Field?' Yeadings asked him.

The man gazed back from haggard eyes. 'In view of the recent attacks on women locally, we must face a possibility of something very serious. Foul play, Superintendent.' He bowed his head, overcome with emotion. 'She is a blonde, you see. I can't help — fearing the worst.'

'So you think she may have been killed?'

Yeadings stared at him for a long moment. 'For a hank of hair?' he demanded brutally.

While instructions were being given on following up Mrs Field's movements of the previous day, Field was invited to the second interview room to sit in on his son's questioning. He seemed unable to take in the circumstances of the inquiry. 'In collusion with James Wichall? In what, may I ask?'

'A serious assault, Mr Field.' Jenner had decided to snipe modestly before working up to the big guns.

Colin was indignant in denial. 'That was disgusting, what Jasper did to Gayle, I wouldn't have had anything to do with that! Of course I know about it. He couldn't pass up bragging, could he?'

'In fact he did it partly to spite you, as well as Gayle?' Beaumont suggested, interrupting. 'He was jealous, wasn't he? Because of your interest in her.'

'She's a really nice girl.'

Jenner's eyes gave a lizard flicker. 'Unlike Sheena Chadwick.'

For a moment it seemed Colin would choke. He had stopped breathing, his eyes starting from a face drained of all colour. Beaumont leaned forward, grasped his shoulders and gently shook him. Field started to protest, but the boy gave a short gasp and started to pant open-mouthed.

'He'll be all right,' the DS said. 'My son got taken like that once. No hurry, lad; there's plenty of time.'

'You — you know about that? That woman.'

'Some.'

'What woman?' Field snapped. 'Are you implying my son had some connection with — ?' but no one was listening.

'I'd no idea who she was until I read it in the papers. She never mentioned her name. It was pure chance. I was up in London with Jasper, over a fortnight back. He had other business, and I just — well, I wandered around a bit.'

'To find a woman, yes.' Beaumont made it sound an everyday thing, which for Colin it clearly wasn't. Field was listening intently now, breathing heavily, tightlipped.

'She was in a bar I went into. She was the one picked me up.' He was beginning to sound defiant.

'Took you back to her room?'

'Scruffy pink place. I — I did it all right, then dozed off afterwards, or maybe it was the drink. Anyway she must have gone through my pockets, nicked my wallet and left the loose change.

'I'd paid her up front, so I never missed it until I needed my ticket to get home. I could have gone back and had it out with her, but I thought — these women have minders. I could have got beaten up. I mean, she was a pro.'

'And you a rank amateur.'

The boy's head fell forward. 'Oh shit; never again,' he moaned, screwing his fists against the hard table.

'No need, I'm sure,' Beaumont allowed. 'Was that the last you saw of the woman?'

'Yes. I swear to God.'

'Then that's all for the present. Isn't it, sir?' he asked the uncertain Jenner, rising and pushing back his chair. 'Thanks for your help, Colin. We shall need your signed statement at a later time, but you can go now.'

They left, Field looking thoroughly unnerved at this revelation by his son coming on top of his wife's disappearance.

The team met up in Yeadings' borrowed office. 'So that explains how Sheena got the envelope with the Orchard Close address,' he agreed. 'The letter must have been in Colin's wallet. When Chadwick found it in her room he assumed Sheena had a known connection with the person it was sent to, a regular punter.

It offered him an alternative suspect after he'd killed her.'

'Why bring in *Chadwick?*' Jenner demanded, almost falsetto. 'It's those boys hired the Ford transit, using Wichall's licence.'

'From the very dealer Chadwick had sold the glazier's van to? Don't ask us to believe a coincidence like that! Chadwick was making an exchange. If he used James Wichall's licence for ID it was because he'd picked it up somewhere,' Beaumont asserted.

'Could it have been in Colin Field's wallet?' Z suggested.

'Why should it be?' Beaumont was being cautious.

'Colin looking after it for him? No, *using* it! I remember now seeing the twins' Mini parked at the house. It had detachable L plates. Rachel drives without them. Presumably she's passed her test . . .'

'But her brother hasn't!'

'And to use the car without an experienced driver alongside, he'd need more than a learner's provisional licence.'

'So, in case he gets checked any time by police, he carries Jasper's which just happens to have come free.'

'A well travelled licence in that case,' Yeadings grunted. 'From Jasper to Colin on loan; stolen by Sheena; picked up by Chadwick, and flashed at the dealer as ID when he bought the Ford transit in part exchange for the glazier's van.

Either he's got rid of it since or he's still using it.'

'Chadwick!' Jenner hissed, now reconciled to the sudden change of suspect. 'Quite a clever plan to dump her body in Mardham, thinking she'd an established link with someone there. It would be followed up, diverting suspicion from himself. But he read too much into that letter from the boy's wallet. Chadwick would be the one tore it up and stuffed it in Sheena's handbag, leaving one scrap behind in the waste bin. On purpose or by accident?'

Nobody troubled to answer. Beaumont was concerned with a possible charge of false arrest being brought by Colin's solicitor father. 'Maybe we should straighten it out with him while he's still a bit mystified. We'll need to have him in again and explain the whole business.'

'Ah,' said Yeadings, 'but Field senior's got some explaining of his own to do: concerning his wife's disappearance. While we wait for developments on the Chadwick front, perhaps we could turn our minds to that. Z tells me she saw Mrs Field leave the house in her Mercedes yesterday morning. You were there too, Beaumont.'

'That's correct, sir. She passed us as we left the Close. We can start from there, tracing her route.'

There was no name as yet for the new dark-haired corpse. Jenner was obliged to attend the post-mortem which Dr Littlejohn held later that afternoon. Hunched vulture-like in his rough-dried raincoat, he devoured each detail the pathologist confided to the microphone attached to his plastic apron.

The woman's age was between thirty-two and thirty-eight years. She appeared to have been in good general health. Immersion in stagnant water hadn't helped in estimating time of death, but it would be over one week and decidedly less than three weeks ago. Cause of death was a fracture to the skull, where the bone was unusually thin, and brain damage arising from a blow to the occiput. Wood splinters embedded in the scalp came either from a weapon or a rough object she struck against violently in falling backwards.

'Fell or was pushed?' Jenner breathed, as if to himself.

Littlejohn regarded him over his half-moon spectacles.

'Can't say, of course; wasn't there myself. But either way she did receive a mighty thwack. What you may find most helpful in identifying her,' he added casually, 'is an external detail. Doubtless you've already taken note of her nails.'

'Nails?'

'Fingernails. Right-hand, long. Left-hand, short. Both lots wearing slightly scratched red enamel. My guess would be — only I'm not a guessing man — that the departed lady played a string instrument with a fretted fingerboard.'

'Guitar!' Jenner muttered. If Chadwick had really been the purchaser of the transit, this had to be Dolly Bell the Country and Western singer, whose publicity shot with Chadwick they already held. In which case her partner in the act would have a lot of extra explaining to do. Once they found him.

Twenty-One

The search for a pair of Country and Western singers had been revised to cover a single male. Publicity fliers used in Lancashire and Cheshire to advertise the duo had Chadwick's photograph lifted for touching up with a variety of possible disguises, reprinted and circulated to all police forces.

Yeadings' Thames Valley team chafed at the period of waiting that must follow, but there were other cases requiring their immediate attention.

The Boss had personally taken on Jasper's release. All they had against him now was the attack on Gayle Dawson, and serious though that was, there appeared little need to continue holding him in the cells.

Gayle was dissuaded from dropping charges against him. The girl had been worried that a criminal record would ruin the young man's career chances. It took the combined persuasion of Z and Mrs George to convince her that just such a shock might be the challenge he needed to take life seriously.

'After the fright he's had, there's little chance he'll imagine himself a hero for having picked on a girl to mug,' the old lady maintained. 'There are those who will give him a good character reference, and Mr Yeadings says that there's a chance he'll be given the option of Community Service. Then if he's sensible enough to admit the disgrace when applying for a job, it may even be dismissed as juvenile high spirits.'

Z had been sent to take his final statement, which was frank and factual.

'I really am sorry,' he said after signing. 'I've been a prat. Right out of my depth. I used to think like that song: "If you must live for the moment, live till that moment is through." And after that it's a chuckaway world.

'I guess I'm slow on the uptake. It takes me ages to realize what I've got. And that's usually after I've screwed it. Perversely, I've always wanted things to last. And nothing does. *"Tout casse, tout lasse, tout passe,"* as they say.'

'Don't ask me to be sorry for you,' Z said crisply, taking the two pages of confession. As Mrs George had pointed out, he wanted to be a star, no matter as what. Maybe he'd shift himself now to find some better occasion. It had been heartless to scare Gayle by faking the killer's hair thing. And sneaky, using information picked up from his father's private phone calls. Jasper would need a sharp shock to shake all the kinks out of his system.

On Thursday they found Mrs Field.

News of the Ford transit's recovery from the gravel pits had brought out a crowd of sightseers. After the rutted mud-slimed banks and the fluttering police tapes marking off the no-entry zone had pandered to their morbidity, the sightseers began to scatter through the woods behind. It was the rosy-cheeked fruiterer and his wife, out together on the afternoon of their early-closing day, who came on the Mercedes half-hidden between a thick holly and the drooping lower branches of a beech tree. Curious, they had peered inside, and seen the body.

For the second day running there was a request for emergency police reinforcements. Only a killing could justify the further expense of such an exercise. Squads of uniformed men were deployed shoulder to shoulder beating through fifty acres of undergrowth for clues.

The news was broken to Field as he waited at home alone, the twins having been dismissed under protest to their aunt in Beaconsfield. Jenner arrived on his doorstep with a motherly WPC who hovered in the background until sent to make tea.

Field was shattered. 'I told Mr Yeadings I feared it might happen like this — but I can't believe it all the same. How do you suppose she got there? I mean, the killer must have been with her, forced her to drive —'

The DI made uncomfortable noises.

'You say your sergeants saw her leave here in the morning: was she alone? Anyone with her in the car? No? Oh my God, it's unbelievable. What is happening here; all these murders! The maniac's still among us. Did he — I mean, it wasn't a rape, was it? Did he cut her hair?'

'Nothing sexual, sir, as far as we could see. But yes, there was a length of hair missing.'

'So that's conclusive. It's the same man.'

'You'll appreciate, being a lawyer, Mr Field, that I am obliged to ask for your movements on the day your wife disappeared.'

Field stared icily back. 'I deeply resent the implication, Inspector, but I shall comply. My son will confirm we drove to Amersham as usual that morning, leaving here at about eight-thirty. My wife was then taking a bath, and my daughter had left about two minutes earlier. I went to my chambers and worked there until just after 1 P.M. when I was meeting a client for lunch at the Crown Hotel. We had a table booked, which I'm sure the manager will confirm. I paid by credit card.

'During the afternoon I had a full diary, starting at 3 P.M. I continued consultations until about 5.15 P.M. when I left for a 5.30 meeting in Wendover with a client concerning a new will he intended making. We must have spent some hour or so chatting over a drink, then I returned to Amersham to pick up my son, and so home.

'My wife being absent, we had a makeshift meal from the freezer which my daughter preferred not to share with us. She cooked something of her own. None of us went out again that night. By then I was getting really anxious about my wife and had rung up one or two acquaintances to find out if she'd been delayed with them. None of them had seen her all day. I was left to assume,

God forgive me, that she was deliberately playing on my anxiety.'

'Thank you, sir. If you would like assistance in preparing your statement —'

'I hardly think so, Inspector. Next you'll be asking if I should like a solicitor present.'

'I doubt it that will be necessary, Mr Field.' Stiffly self-conscious, Jenner summoned his WPC and withdrew.

The house seemed eerily still after they had gone. Field went upstairs to his bedroom and stood looking from the window to make sure there were no police cars parked on surveillance. There was no reason why there should be. He had told them everything they required. The two sergeants would confirm that Phyllida had driven herself from the house. What better witnesses than the police themselves? And his alibi was complete.

Should he perhaps have asked more about the killing? His account of his own movements had covered the whole day. He hadn't been told the estimated time of death. How close would they be able to tell it? Jenner hadn't even said when the post-mortem was to be held.

Maybe he should ring the coroner's officer and enquire. Or would that appear suspicious?

He turned up the thermostat on the central heating. The day had grown suddenly colder. He should have made himself something hot for breakfast. There was chicken and cold gravy he could warm up with some frozen vegetables, but he didn't feel like eating. Maybe a tin of soup, but it seemed too much bother to heat it up.

The nausea was coming back, and with it the clamping band round his head. He sank into an armchair and raised his face towards the ceiling. Spots of light danced up there, dropping like snow and piercing his eyes with shooting pain. His hands began to shake. The trembling had spread up his arms now.

The hideous thing was happening over again. He knew he was powerless to stop it, swept back in time.

The trembling had spread up his arms now. To still it he doubled over, hugging to him the sweat-shirt only half pulled on. He ached all through his body, his heart flurrying and leaping like a terrified wild rabbit he'd once clutched as a child, saved from a stoat. And it had died all the same, he remembered, its neck already bitten through to the bone by the predator's strong teeth.

Why think of that now? He needed to concentrate his mind, all his forces, to overcome this sudden feebleness. He hadn't reckoned on this. God, he couldn't be ill now.

It had gone so well up to this point, every meticulously planned detail perfect. And the worst was over. Hadn't cost him a doubt, because it had all been thought out so carefully before. Foolproof, and by God he was no fool. Organization his forte.

For a moment the ground he stared at swarmed

with little points of shifting colour then darkened back to dun. He looked upwards through the tracery of bare winter branches and the sky smudged into a yellow glare, the trees going transparent, invisible between. Then a viscous fluid drowned out even that. His eyelids were sticking together. He saw the back of them, a veined dark red with a wheeling white disc at the centre which slowly elongated, became itself an eye. Staring back.

There was a hip flask wrapped among his clothes. He tugged at the sleeves of the sweatshirt. One arm, then the other, went through. He tried to raise it to thrust his head in, and was petrified, found his elbows locked, refusing to budge, knew he couldn't pull the stifling folds over. They would choke him, strangle —

'Fool, fool!' he snarled. It was done, safely over. She was dead. He had only the final details now to get through.

Get through. But he couldn't. His arms, heavy as timbers, wouldn't lift. Refused to obey. But he *had* to. God-almighty, he'd achieved so much. He couldn't be halted now. Pull the damn thing over. He'd been dressing himself since he was two. His mother boasted about it. Such a capable little boy, so tidy. Such an eye for detail.

He found he was fighting for air in the thick folds of fabric as they tangled about his face. Someone was — no, his own hands, working on their own. Hideous, following their own impulse.

But now at least he was that much dressed in

his proper things. As far as the waist. Next he had to deal with the tights. Really he needn't have bothered. No one had seen them. One of his over-perfect details. But now he had to get rid of them. The feel of them disgusted him, the silky sleekness, as though they had a woman's legs inside. Hers. They'd have to stay on until he was safely home. He knew he couldn't — then watched in horror as the hands slid into the waist and tore downwards. He shot erect and the rape went on. Stripped off, the fine blond nylon lay shredded at his feet like a sloughed off snakeskin. He felt his bare legs vulnerable, quivering. He cast about him for the tracksuit trousers.

Careless! He'd let them spill out on the grass. They could get traces of green, leave some minute thread of their own to betray him. He'd known all the risks, taken every precaution, then suddenly things had started getting out of hand.

He stared at his hands and shuddered. Killer hands. Hands out of hand.

A few feet away, flattening the spongy grass he saw the hip flask and reached for it desperately. Empty. At some time he must have drained it. But he didn't remember. Something else out of control, acting on its own, mocking him and his meticulous planning.

Start again. Take stock and go on from that point. Everything had to be put back in the carrier bag. He stumbled forward, began to collect the detestable clothes he had torn off, stuffing them inside until the shiny white plastic with its grocer's logo bulged obscenely like a pregnant belly.

No room for the cream leather jacket; but he'd allowed for that. It was to go on the back seat, as though thrown off when the car started heating up. The tartan rug that had covered her on the floor was tidily folded in its usual position underneath. Brilliant touch. He'd thought of everything.

Everything. Except this awful weakness. The worst was over; he mustn't go to pieces now.

Shoes. Goddammit, where were his shoes? Under some bush where he'd tipped them out? No, the grass ahead was empty.

And he hadn't planned to put his shoes on yet, he reminded himself. Walk away in his sock soles, which he'd destroy later. The soft grass would quickly spring back. But shoes were a dead giveaway.

Carry the bike: that was the next essential. Get it now from the car boot. Hang the carrier bag from its handlebars. Gently he laid the folding cycle on its side on the grass.

He looked around. Where were those bloody shoes? Nothing but the spare tyre in here now, with the foot-pump, a tool-roll and the jack. He felt into the shadowed corners, in case, dark against dark, they'd escaped him. But the shoes weren't there. So not anywhere.

He slammed shut the boot lid and lay giddily back against it. Remember!

He saw himself at the open wardrobe in his

room, lifting out his trainers, deciding at the last minute on a slight change of plan. Easy to wash off, yes, but white. They'd show up, draw attention. Someone might see. Who? Well, someone. Anyone who was about.

He'd put them back and lifted out instead the brown Oxfords, removed and replaced the shoe trees which kept their shape, put the shoes —

Stop there. He'd put the shoes — in the carrier bag with the rest of his clothes, surely. But did he? They'd be here in that case. They'd have to be.

He remembered placing them on a bedroom chair, to pick up later. Then he'd closed the wardrobe doors and —

And remembered his wife's appointment book, fetched it to put in her handbag. *Left the shoes?* Could he have? Could he be such a fool?

Well, it wasn't the end of the world. He'd always meant to go the walking part in his sock soles, but strip them off when he used the bike, because they'd be wet and filthy by then. Only now he'd be pedalling barefoot.

He lifted the bike, held it high and began the trek back. Which was more difficult than he'd imagined. The ground underfoot was littered with sharp stones and twigs which pricked through the thick wool, and he was sometimes forced to make a détour to avoid exposed tree roots. Then, wary of the ground ahead he'd catch the bicycle frame in overhead branches.

He'd known the woods quite well as a child,

but since then they'd been neglected and over-grown. Farmers were forced to leave woodland intact, but they didn't waste money on tree surgery. Coming in, he'd followed faint tracks, made perhaps by animals or poachers; but to avoid damage from trees he'd had to drive circuitously to reach the dense centre. Now he wondered if he'd gone too far in, wasn't sure he was heading back in the right direction for the river.

His arms ached with the bike's weight and he lowered it, leaned over the saddle to recover his breath, and felt sudden nausea. The shaking began again. It struck him that he hadn't taken a final look round the clearing and inside the car, to make sure no evidence was left behind. With the realization came a flashing white pain behind his eyes and the familiar headache was gripping him again like a tightening band. Like strangling fingers.

He vomited, slipped to the ground helpless, still grasping the hard metal frame of the bike to him. For a hideous moment before he passed out it was his dead wife lying beside him in bed.

It was quite dark when Field came to himself again, in a chair in his bedroom, his limbs stiff and cold. He had no idea how long he might have slept, but it was the doorbell that had woken him. Now there was a prolonged knocking and someone calling his name.

He knew at once it had gone wrong, because this was the feeling he'd had about the future.

345

Afterwards — he'd thought; and there was a blank. This was that blank, happening now. A void, he'd supposed.

He went downstairs to let them in because doing anything seemed better than the void. It was the girl detective-sergeant and a constable in uniform. Not Bond, but an outsider. They wanted him to go with them to Amersham and answer more questions. That wasn't unexpected. But they had a warrant to search the house. Why? They wouldn't find anything here. There'd been no blood.

'Where is your friend?' he asked in the car. 'The other sergeant. You both saw, didn't you? You saw her drive away that morning.'

Z turned her head and looked out of the rear window. Anything to avoid those doglike eyes. The man was going to pieces. He would never stand up to Jenner's questioning.

Yes, she had seen the Mercedes drive out, and through the tinted windows what looked like a woman's shape. A woman with long blonde hair who was wearing a cream jacket.

But it had to have been Donald Field. How else could anyone explain what Mrs George had seen before midday in Buckman's Shoot, where just a corner of his car showed between the trees. She'd had to laugh, she said, as he struggled lifting a bike in, and then his carrier bag had burst open. She'd reached for her field glasses as he'd scooped up the things fallen out: women's clothing and what looked like a blonde

346

wig. She'd never imagined until then that her neighbour could be a transvestite.

Those clothes must still be somewhere in Field's house, among the soiled linen. Or there'd be ashes if he'd burnt them. Whichever, the searchers would find them, and traces of who had worn them.

'Where's the other sergeant?' Field insisted again, edgily.

Beaumont arrived back from Chelmsford with his prisoner an hour after Field's questioning began. 'We'll break off at this point,' Jenner said with false magnanimity. 'Doubtless you're ready for a cup of tea.'

Chadwick had been discovered in cheap lodgings in the Essex town, down on his luck because Dolly had been the magnetic part of the act. On his own he was just another would-be. All the kids nowadays seemed to play the guitar and they were into the heavy stuff.

Yeadings was sitting in on the taped interview. 'We've found Dolly,' he said quietly. 'In the van with some of Sheena's stuff.'

Chadwick nodded. 'I guessed you must've. She killed her. I tried to stop her. I musta lost my rag.'

Jenner was starting to demand who killed who when the Boss got in again before him. 'Let's start at the beginning, when you came down to London in the glazier's van you'd stolen.'

So, in a droning monotone, broken off only

when the man, overcome, covered his face to hide his tears, he told them how he'd gone to London to find Sheena. She seemed to be set up all right in that room of hers, on to quite a good thing. Even gave him some money to go away, and he'd admitted to her he'd got another bird himself. Only when he left she'd followed him back to the van, so the girls met. And he went off to get some beer and stuff.

Got back in time to overhear their barney. Hammer and tongs they were going at it, shouting. In the cramped space of the van Sheena made a wild lunge and knocked little Dolly down. She cracked her head first on the empty frame for the sheet glass, and then a second time as she hit the van's floor.

He'd pulled Sheena off as she was going in to kick her and he'd grabbed her by the neck. He felt really mad, and he shook her, gave her a good rattle. When he let go she slid down on top of Dolly, and fuckinhell didn't he find he'd got two stiffs there!

'And the hair?' Yeadings asked.

'That was later. I'd already found a 24-hour car lot and bought the Ford transit with a promise of part repayment if I brought the old van in. It was pitch dark up by a wall there. I was shit-scared someone would come but I got them moved — the girls — to the transit, wiped up a bit of Dolly's blood and handed the old van over. It was in better nick than the Ford but the dealer got stroppy, wanted to see my licence. In

348

case I'd sold him a dud, he said.

'Well, I'd picked some stuff up at Sheena's and there'd been this licence there that she'd nicked off a punter. No use to her. I showed him that.'

'And then you drove the transit to Mardham and dumped Sheena's body.'

'It seemed best. He'd written down the licence details, see? It had an address on. This bloke said, "Oh, I know that place. Nice little village near Amersham." So I thought, leave her there, that'll rattle the punter, give him something to explain away if the police trace him. And nobody'd look for me.

'So I followed the signposts and there was this river. I'd've dropped her in only I remembered how she'd hated water. Wouldn't go near the sea when I took her to Brighton. Always scared she'd get drowned. So I left her on the bank.'

'After tenderly bashing her face in,' Jenner reminded him coldly.

'So's you'd take longer to find out who she was. I couldn't look, just closed my eyes and took a swipe with the jack. I'd got thinking about our early days and that. Sheena was real lovely as a kid. Never was a girl could make me feel so good. So I cut off a bit of her hair. As a keepsake.'

'And so on and so forth,' Yeadings explained to Z and Beaumont later. 'A lot left out, and it may not have happened exactly the way he told it, but it fits the evidence we have.'

349

'So why dump the Ford in the gravel pit?' Z asked.

'Because as soon as he'd gone any distance he could hear the big end was going.'

'He'd bought a *bum* steer,' said Beaumont, brightening at the chance of another pun.

'He parked in Wychwood, Harry's badger place to the north of the village. He was still there next afternoon during the hue and cry over Sheena's murder. He was almost out of petrol but he had money, so he ditched the transit with all his wordly goods inside, came out by the railway bridge, walked along by the track to Mardham Halt and took a train to London.'

'So much for our showing the station staff his photo!'

'He said they were having a private conversation, two of them in the ticket office, and never even looked his way. Just took the money, hit the buttons and the ticket shot out.'

'I don't understand,' Z murmured, 'why he didn't dispose of both bodies together.'

Yeadings lifted his shoulders. 'I asked him that and he appeared quite shocked. He said, "They didn't get on together, did they?"'

'Well, that's the story he'll tell in court. Whether it's the truth or fiction remains to be seen. We don't know how long ago Dolly died. Her submersion has complicated that. Maybe she never fought with Sheena. Maybe Chadwick did strangle his wife and later Dolly panicked, so he had to kill her too in case she grassed on him. By then he was in such deep shit he decided to cut his losses, ditch the transit in the gravel pit and simply walk away.'

'That would explain the bodies in two different places.'

'It doesn't account for him cutting Sheena's hair.'

'No? It could have been a trophy; not a keep-sake.'

Beaumont had the petulant scowl of a school-boy. 'You know what? The lawyers are going to have a field day with this one. They'll get fat on arguing the case. And all off the taxpayers' back; yours and my money. While *we* get our overtime disallowed!'

Yeadings considered it time to rein them in. 'It remains for us to put our case together. Plenty of paperwork all round.'

Beaumont groaned. 'I haven't copied up my report on Goodwin yet. Then there's the attack on Gayle Dawson, the Field murder and this double killing. Talk about the peaceful country-side! I'll be glad to get back to inner city thud and blunder.'

'I've got something further on the Field case,' Z claimed. 'Apparently Mrs Field's bathroom door locks equally well from the outside. All her husband had to do that morning was leave the water running and tell the twins where she was supposed to be. Which fits in with Littlejohn's belief that she was strangled the previous night before being dumped in her own car.

'When I checked with Field's secretary I learnt it was her regular day off, so I went to see the temp who stands in for her. She's pregnant, and told me Field was working on case notes and didn't need to dictate. So he gave her the morning free to go across to Slough, shopping at Mothercare. Also gave her fifty pounds to buy something for the baby from him.'

'Well, now wasn't that generous.'

'But not enough to ensure her silence in a murder inquiry.'

'And Field was ten minutes late for his lunch appointment at the Crown in Amersham,' Beaumont contributed. 'The client was peeved enough to remember.'

'Only ten minutes?' Yeadings was mildly surprised. 'Pretty good going, considering what a busy morning he'd had. Now, before you all disperse,' he remembered, 'there's news of the pub-yard van and the man in leathers who wheeled a motorbike from it. A trail bike; and, as it happens, a false trail into the bargain. A minor villain from Pottersfield had "borrowed" the machine while its owner was having his appendix out.

'The bike's engine developed a fault, a passing Samaritan gave the lad a lift part-way home and he quietly wheeled it off undercover until it could be repaired.

'I had the full story as a send-off from my codger drinking friends.' He gazed at them benignly, the black brows raised as he commanded their full attention.

'There's no greater gossip, I find, than a man put out to grass.'

'Grass!' groaned Beaumont in disgust as the door closed behind the Boss. 'And they say I'm the one hung up on puns.'

We hope you have enjoyed this Large Print book. Other G.K. Hall & Co. or Chivers Press Large Print books are available at your library or directly from the publishers.

For more information about current and upcoming titles, please call or write, without obligation, to:

G.K. Hall & Co.
P.O. Box 159
Thorndike, Maine 04986 USA
Tel. (800) 223-2336

OR

Chivers Press Limited
Windsor Bridge Road
Bath BA2 3AX
England
Tel. (0225) 335336

All our Large Print titles are designed for easy reading, and all our books are made to last.